Trail
to
Medicine Mound

Other novels by Alfred Dennis

Chiricahua
Lone Eagle
Elkhorn Divide
Brant's Fort
Catamount
The Mustangers
Rover
Yuma
Yellowstone Brigade
Sandigras Canyon
Shawnee Trail
Fort Reno
Ride the Rough String

To see more books by Alfred Dennis visit
www.alfreddennis.com

Trail
to
Medicine Mound

by

Alfred Dennis

Walnut Creek Publishing
Tuskahoma, Oklahoma

Trail to Medicine Mound

This novel is a work of fiction. Names, characters, places, and incidents are
either the product of the author's imagination or are used fictitiously. Any
resemblance to actual events, locales, organizations, or persons, living or dead, is
entirely coincidental and beyond the intent of either the author or the publisher.

ISBN: 978-1-942869-12-2
First Edition, Paperback
Published 2015 by Walnut Creek Publishing
10 9 8 7 6 5 4 3 2 1
Library of Congress Control Number: 2015945788
1. Western 2. Action/Adventure

Books may be purchased in quantity and/or special sales by contacting the
publisher;
Walnut Creek Publishing
PO Box 820
Talihina, OK 74571
www.wc-books.com

"Trail to Medicine Mound front cover" is a derivative of "Wikimedia Commons
File: Wagons_History.jpg " by Karol Miles, licensed under CC BY 2.0,
combined with other photos in public domain.

This book is dedicated to my Uncle Hubert,
(Buck) Dennis, a little man with a big heart and
a great family man, loved by everyone.

Chapter 1

Campfires flicker in every direction as the remains of Robert E. Lee's Army of Northern Virginia settles down outside Appomattox in the final hours of the great Civil War between the States. Rumors abound all through the tattered regiments; will morning see the end of the great struggle between the North and south, will General Lee surrender? Soldiers huddle about the small fires staring dully into the flames all are hungry and ragged, but most are still full of fight. If their beloved General orders them forward come morning, it is their duty and they will stand to arms. Some smoke if they have the makings, but most pipes are as empty as their stomachs.

Four men sit around a small fire, sipping weak coffee and chewing on what stale hardtack they can find in their knapsacks. "You boys reckon the General will meet with Grant come morning?"

"Doubt it, George Raker." An older man speaks up. "I figure we'll fight our way through to the south and join up with General Johnston."

"We're whipped; most of us don't have anything but rocks to fight with." Another younger man shakes his head doubtfully as he glances around at the others. "Even rocks are becoming scarce in this man's army. No sir, we'll probably fight on alright, but I'm telling you it will be suicide."

"What do you think, Bowie Morgan?" George looked over at a tall young man sitting silently, listening to the others as usual. "Will Uncle Bobbie quit, tell us what do you think?"

The brown eyes flicker briefly as he shrugged his broad shoulders. "I couldn't say George, all I know is the General is a fighter, if he says fight, I'll fight."

"Suicide, I'm telling you; it'll be plain suicide." Ham shook his head in disgust. "They've got two hundred thousand or so against our twenty five thousand. That Private George Raker isn't what I call a fair fight, its pure suicide."

"They ain't got near that many, Hamilton Jenks." The old man spit in the fire.

"Look across at those campfires; they're all around us Talbert." The young man waved his hand. "And they my friend, are loaded for bear."

The old man shook his head. "I can see them fires plain enough. I can't even count you boys know that, but it takes ten yanks to whip a good southern boy."

"Maybe it did once, but without powder and lead, we're whipped and you boys know it." Ham shook his head slowly. "Shucks boys, they've got more cannons than we got soldiers."

Bowie Morgan looked out into the blackness taking notice of the many fires burning less than a mile from their lines. The smoldering dark eyes cannot count the endless blinking fires. He knows what Hamilton Jenks said is the truth, but he has his pride, the same as all men from the southern states. Still Ham is right; there are just too many Yankees. All the pride, courage, fighting spirit or whatever you want to call it won't change the fact they are outnumbered, outgunned, and beaten. Not by better men, but by more men, better supplied and that is the pure truth of the matter. An Army travels on its stomach and the men of the Southern Army have been starving for weeks. Come first light, the boys across there in blue will close in. Morgan knows it is over; he just wants them to change the subject. Talking about the situation won't change it one bit, and him being their Corporal isn't changing anything either.

Many times he has been offered promotions into the elite, so called "Officer's Ranks", but he had always refused. He is only a foot soldier, nothing more. Come sunup, if they order him forward to fight, that's what he will do. It's simple, a soldier just follows orders. To fight without powder and lead is pure folly and will probably get them all killed, but if ordered forward, then forward it will be.

"Well come tomorrow if Bobbie Lee surrenders, it's over and I'll be headed back to God's Country in Texas." George Raker leaned back against his pack and nodded. "I swear boy's, I'll never leave my ranch again."

"Where's your ranch George?" Talbert Yandell questioned the big man.

"Its located north and west of the small town of Medicine Mound, down on the Pease River." Raker looked off to the west with a knowing smile. "Its beautiful country down there with grass belly deep on a tall horse, and elbow room for all."

"You really got yourself a place down there?" Ham looked up curiously. "A place all your own?"

"I do, almost two thousand acres." Raker nodded. "I own more than six sections of land, plenty of water, grass, mesquite trees, post oak, plus our share of Comanche Indians and rattlesnakes."

"Man, ain't that something, you own your land." Ham sighed. "My Pa never owned land; never owned nothing we just sharecrop a few hardscrabble acres."

"You got a wife?" Talbert spoke up.

"Yep, I do." Raker looked over at the old man and grinned. "Prettiest woman in the country and boys, there's plenty of room for anyone wanting to ride to Texas with me."

"Not me." Ham rolled over to ease himself on the ground. "I'm headed back to Tennessee soon as they cut me loose."

"Why are you going back, you just said you didn't own anything back there?" Talbert questioned. "Let's go with George to Texas."

Ham shrugged. "Shucks Talbert, I don't rightly know, excepting its home, the only home I've ever known."

"What about you, Mister Bowie Morgan?" Talbert grinned. "You want to go to Texas?"

The four men are the last of the original men of C Company, which stood on General Stonewall Jackson's left flank at the Battle of Chancellorsville. Back when the Army of the Confederacy was in its full glory, marching forward tall and proud with its head held high, now it is an entirely different time.

Morgan nodded thoughtfully to the question as it is his nature to study any question concerning him. "I can't answer your question right now, old man." The brown eyes turned toward Talbert. "Reckon I'll just wait and see what tomorrow brings."

All eyes turn to the young man whom they have come to respect for his calmness under fire, his sharp mind, and leadership abilities. Always quiet and laid back, Bowie Morgan rarely voiced his opinion. However, the men have seen him in action against the enemy and with the best fighters from other company's or units. Most laugh, remembering the day one of the cavalrymen from General Pickett's Command started trouble in the mess line as they lined up to eat. Bowie Morgan is a tall man, well built, and powerful in his own right, but the troublemaker was huge, at least two hundred and fifty pounds of solid muscle.

The ranks of soldiers had quickly separated giving the two men room to fight. That morning Bowie had come to the aid of a smaller man who the giant held down on the ground with his huge boot on the poor man's chest. Some who were present that day and still alive after all the fighting remember and talk about how easily Morgan had dispatched the giant with one solid punch from his powerful right hand. The heavy blow landed hard right in the weak solar plexus of the giant and the fight was over. Every man clapped and applauded as the bigger man recovered his wind and finally regaining his feet had walked over to Bowie and shook hand.

Then there was the day outside Richmond when Tom Custer rode almost to the center of a large flat field separating the two armies. He carried a white flag of truce and yelled out his challenge to the southern boys. Mounting a horse Captain Lowe had ridden out to see what the cocky Custer wanted. The two armies were lined up in battle formation, for two days now they had been sitting and waiting orders to move forward. Tom Custer was known for his bravery even in the southern ranks and he was also known for his devil-may-care, cocky attitude and his love of a good fight. Lowe rode back to the lines, shaking his head as he dismounted.

"What did he want, Captain?" Colonel Henry looked at the officer curiously.

"Well sir, Captain Tom Custer has challenged us to a fight."

"A fight, what the devil does he think we've been doing for three years?" The Colonel puffed up. "Playing house?"

"No sir, not that kind of fighting. He's challenged our champion bare-knuckle fighter to meet their champion." Lowe shook his head. "He's put up enough cigars for every man in the regiment to have a smoke."

"You're joking."

"No sir, I don't think Tom Custer jokes." Lowe looked out to where the Yankee Officer sat his horse waiting. "He's a cool character, I'll give him that and he's bored."

"What does he expect from us if we lose?"

"He said he'll wager his cigars against twenty jugs of our fine corn liquor."

"What?" The Colonel cleared his throat embarrassed. "What corn liquor?"

"Ain't no sense denying it sir, he knows we got it." Lowe grinned. "Some of our boys have been trading corn to the yanks for coffee these last few weeks."

Looking about for the presence of any higher ranking officers, Henry stepped closer to Captain Lowe and whispered. "Did you see their champion?"

"No sir, I didn't." Lowe smiled. "Don't matter though we got us the toughest man in Bobbie Lee's Army right here."

"And just who would that be?"

"Him." The long thin finger of the Captain's hand pointed dead square at Bowie Morgan. "He can whip his weight in wildcats and outwrestle a full-grown grizzly bear at the same time."

"Are you talking about Davy Crockett or who?"

"I believe Mister Crockett is long dead, sir." Lowe grinned. "No sir, I'm talking about Bowie Morgan, standing right there."

"Is he that tough?"

"He's whipped everybody in our army that's ever tusseled with him." Lowe shrugged. "That's all I can tell you."

"That's a lot of liquor to lose Captain, and your man sure isn't very big." Colonel Henry eyed Bowie and shook his head. "He's tall, but not bulky."

"He's big enough." Lowe shook his head and smiled. "Trust me, Colonel Sir."

"Trust you, Captain?" The Colonel stared at Bowie. "If this doesn't end to our benefit I'll bust you back to private. How's that for trust?"

Lowe straightened his shoulders and smiled. "That'll be fine, sir."

Colonel Henry looked out across the broad field and grinned, a wicked gleam coming to his eye. Everybody in both armies knew Custer's arrogance; it sure would be something to give Tommy Custer his comeuppance, just once. At least it would give the Confederates bragging rights to something. The war sure wasn't going in their favor. "Alright Captain, make the arrangements." It had taken a lot of persuasion to get Bowie Morgan to agree to the fight. Regimental pride and the hurrahing he would get if he didn't uphold the pride of the unit finally made him change his mind and give in.

As the two armies stacked their weapons and closed together to watch the fight, the yelling and bantering was earsplitting until the Yank champion put in his appearance. Never before had the southern ranks shriveled up and turned completely quiet as they did when the giant appeared. You could hear a pin drop in the grass as the huge man walked shirtless into the empty spot left between the two armies for the combatants. Most heard stories of giants, but here stood one in the flesh. All seven feet and four hundred pounds of the man stood with his arms folded, grinning like a treed possum across at the Reb army who quickly turned solemn. It remembered Lowe of the Biblical story of David and Goliath.

"Dang Colonel, what is it?" Captain Lowe could only stammer as he looked at the giant. "I've never seen a man that big."

"It's a man of some kind, Captain Lowe." Henry swallowed hard. "Maybe three men rolled into one."

"Dat burn Yanks; you just can't trust them."

"I tried to warn you, Private." Henry eyed the monster standing before the Yankee lines. "Man, he's a big 'un for sure."

"Well sir, I'll have to admit I've earned a demotion this time."

Colonel Henry laughed. "Just funning with you Captain, who would have thought anything like that existed anywhere?"

Bowie Morgan stood off to the side staring at the big man as Lowe walked over to him. "Morgan, the Colonel said we'd just concede this one and give Custer the liquor."

"Where's your faith?" Bowie grinned. "He's just a man, ain't he?"

"I dunno about that Corporal, he's big enough for ten men." Lowe shook his head. "I'm afraid it's gonna take more than faith to keep you from getting killed, your head pulled off, or something even worse."

"We'll see sir." Was the only words spoken as the tall Corporal walked out to face the bigger man. "We'll see."

Lowe watched the back of the tall man and shook his head. "Bless you son and good luck to you, cause you're gonna need it."

Every man watching was expecting to see Bowie's head come rolling off as soon as the giant reached him, but in actuality it was the other way around. The Johnny Reb was unbelievably fast; two solid perfectly planted kicks to the big man's left knee brought the giant crashing to the ground as another hard kick to the big head laid the giant out cold. Custer stood on the sidelines, his mouth ajar as his champion was laid out stiffly on the grassy field in less time than it took a mule skinner to spit. Well who would have believed it? Both armies blue and grey, cheered as Captain Custer swallowed his pride, smiled his charming smile, walked over and shook the winner's hand, then raised Bowie's arm in victory. That was Bowie Morgan's last fight as no other fighter ever dared challenge him again.

The long barrel of the Sharps Rifle pushed slowly over the dead log pointing at the small fire where Bowie and the others are lying around the fire, talking about home, hashing out the war, and wondering what their future come morning will be. The night is black, too dark and shadowy to distinguish a face behind the barrel. If anyone is watching they can see the uniform is Confederate Gray there is no mistake about that, not even in the poor light. Suddenly the heavy boom of the rifle breaks the peacefulness of the night, causing men to grab their firearms and stand ready for what they think is a night attack by the Yankee Army. Turning from where he rolled behind a wooden crate, Bowie looked to where George Raker slowly turned over on his left side.

Looking across the short distance from their campfires to the log where the gunshot came from several men rushed forward only to find the area vacant. Standing Bowie walked over and looks around the log as several others rush forward with torches to examine the ground. Silhouettes of men flicker, and excited voices sound throughout the dark as soldiers search the area.

"There's nothing here." A voice sounds out of the dark. "Whoever fired that rifle is gone."

There had been no mistaking the sound of the heavy caliber rifle discharging. It was a Sharps and even a slight nick from such a rifle is serious, most times deadly. The heavy bored buffalo gun's used by snipers on both sides carries a forty-five caliber round, and they are deadly. Some soldiers swear, once they saw a sniper kill an enemy officer at almost a mile. Others tell they saw a bullet, fired from a Sharps kill two men and a horse with one shot. The rifle causes fear in both armies, every soldier knows the Sharps Rifle is a powerful, deadly killing machine, and they are afraid of the snipers that are so proficient with them.

Bowie turned back to the small fire to find Talbert kneeling over Raker. "How bad you hit George?"

"I don't know how bad it is?" Raker looked up at Talbert's face as the old man examined the wound. "Oh Lord, it burns like fire."

"Took you in the upper shoulder and tore a lot of hide in its passing." Talbert placed several layers of dirty cloth over the wound trying to stem the flow of blood. "The bullet went clean through you, George."

"Here, what's going on men?" A Major raced up out of breath. "Who's hurt?"

"A sniper got Private Raker, sir." Ham looked up at the officer.

"How bad is it soldier?"

"When you get hit by a ball from a Sharps sir, it's usually bad." Talbert looked up at the officer with contempt. "It can even be deadly sometimes."

"I know that soldier." The officer looked down his nose at the old man. "You men get him over to the field hospital, now."

"It seems kinda queer to me Major." Ham spoke up again as several men lifted the heavy weight of Raker.

"What seems queer to you, Jenks?"

"Well Sir, I don't figure it was a sniper. Poor old George ain't an officer, he was just sitting here talking with the rest of us in plain sight before the fire." Ham shook his head. "Why would they waste an easy shot like that on a simple private?"

"That's a good question soldier." Major Corbet shook his head slowly. "I don't have the answer for you. It was too dark to find tracks, but we'll take another look come morning."

"He'll be long gone come morning, sir, you can count on it." Ham shook his shaggy head. "Sure seems strange to me though."

"It is dang funny to me a yank would take a chance coming in this close at night." Talbert stared off into the dark. "Mighty peculiar."

"It wasn't a sniper Talbert; I'd bet on it." Bowie spoke quietly to the old man as they hurried to the hospital tent with Raker. "There's more to this than just a sniper doing his job."

"What do you mean? Are you saying it was one of our boys?"

"I would, providing I don't find anything different come morning." The tall man stooped slightly as they entered the tent and placed the wounded man on a bloody operating table. "I can't see a blue uniform roaming around inside our lines, shooting a man then walking out free as a bird."

"Maybe he was camouflaged, you know, with grass and everything."

"Nope, George was shot by one of ours, and it sure wasn't an accident." Bowie stood at the wounded man's head until an orderly ordered them all outside. "I'd bet on it."

"You men wait outside for your friend." The blood-covered aide moved to Raker's side as a man in a white blood-splattered apron entered the tent. "Please gentlemen, we're too crowded in here."

"Come on Talbert, we can't help any in here."

Two hours passed as Bowie, Talbert, and Ham sit around their small fire and watch the opening of the operating tent that suffices as a field hospital. Rising to their feet they surround Raker as he is carried from the tent on a camp cot and placed in line with several other injured men.

"You men give him water, keep him covered and warm." The same orderly that ordered them from the tent stared at the concerned faces. "Nothing to eat yet."

"How is he?" Bowie questioned.

"We'll know come morning, I reckon."

"That's it?" Ham slapped his campaign hat against his thimble leg. "That's all you know?"

"Morning boys, is all I know."

The three friends watch vigilantly throughout the long night, caring for their injured companion and talking. As the sun rises, they watch as General Lee passes along the dusty road by the hospital riding his horse Traveler toward the Appomattox Courthouse. Raker opened his pain racked eyes several times nodding thankfully as his friends give him water, then mop his forehead of fever sweat. Bowie sits beside Raker glancing toward the road from time to time, like everyone else he waits anxiously to find out what the result will be of the meeting between Lee and Grant.

"It's over, it's over." Solemn voices resound all through the ragged ranks as soldiers walk around in shock after the proud General and his grey horse passes by them, some in relief and some in disbelief. "The war is over."

Bowie Morgan looked down at the two Navy Colts strapped to his side, quickly digging a hole he hides them beneath his knapsack. He had taken the pistols from a dead cavalryman he had killed in the battle at Yellow Tavern. He doesn't intend to lose the well-balanced, hard shooting weapons to the first Yank that takes a shine to them. Rumor is already making the rounds the yanks will confiscate all weapons from the confederates after passing out food to the starving men.

The tall man knows his troubles are just beginning, George Raker's wound is serious and there are no horses to pull a wagon, even a small hack, and Texas is far away. He served with George Raker for three years each man had saved the other's life on several occasions, and he knows he cannot abandon his friend in his time of need. With the war fresh over times will be hard; there will be all kinds of men on the roads heading west, the pistols will be sorely needed.

Walking over to what passes for a recovery area for the wounded; Bowie knelt down beside the wounded man as the aide and doctor return to the tent after examining their patients. "How you doing, George?"

"I'm still kicking lad, but not too high." The pale face looked up from the woolen army blankets. "The doctor said he gave me something to kill the pain, I reckon he did."

"That's good George; you'll be fine."

"How about you, how are you making it?"

"I'm fine." Bowie nodded slowly. "Some Yankee Captain came by here and said they'd be passing out rations pretty quick."

"I ain't hungry, I doubt if I could eat anything if I was." Raker winced in pain. "This shoulder sure smarts some, I'm telling you."

"You've got to eat. You'll need your strength if you're gonna get back to Texas and that fine ranch you've been telling us about all these years."

The sweaty head rocks slowly back and forth. "Fat chance I'll get there now; not anytime soon anyway, not with this shoulder."

"I'll get you there, George. You can count on it."

"You'd do that for me, Bowie Morgan?" Raker looked up into the young face curiously. "I wouldn't hold it against you lad if you left me, you don't need the burden and worry of an invalid."

"Have you forgotten Chickahominy Creek already?" Bowie shook his head. "I believe you have."

"No I haven't, I remember carrying you out of there with that mini ball in your leg."

"That's better." The tall man nodded. "I believe you took a shot through your hand that day while saving my bacon."

"You'd do that for me?" Raker turned his head. "Take me home, it's unbelievable."

"Soon as we get this messy business ahead out of the way, we'll just head down to Texas."

"What business is that?" Raker looked up curiously as Yankee soldiers march their way. "Has General Lee surrendered?"

"The General just returned from Appomattox Courthouse, the wars over." Bowie shook his head sadly. "I spect they'll be having us surrender our arms, get our names and ranks, then have us swear a new allegiance to the North."

Raker nodded slowly. "Maybe my friend, you should leave me behind and get on with your life. I sure can't walk and I doubt there's a wagon or horse to be had anywhere in Virginia after this mess."

"I've thought of that, but we'll get you home, don't fret yourself."

"I would understand if you left me here." The wounded man tried to smile despite the pain. "I'll be fine, the army will just keep me in a hospital somewhere until I can fend for myself."

"We're going to Texas all of us, now lie back and try to rest." Bowie watched as several supply wagons roll down the dusty roads from the Yankee encampment. "Here comes the mess wagons, I'm gonna go get us a bite to eat."

Bowie was right, he had hardly finished feeding Raker when blue coated soldiers led by a well-dressed Yankee Officer, started up and down the lines of Confederates collecting weapons of any kind. Bowie watched intently as the Yanks pass rigidly ignoring the hatred pouring hotly from every southern eye. Every man hates, but he also knows to fight on is futile, the war is finished and over with they are beaten, helpless to stop the blue clad horde. To try would be as Ham predicted pure suicide.

The boots of the squad click to a stop alongside where Raker is lying on his hospital cot. "You men got any weapons on you?"

Bowie looked up at the officer and shook his head. "No."

"None?"

"I said, no."

"No sir, soldier."

"No sir Captain."

"That's better, you Rebs are beaten, now you need to learn to have respect for your betters."

George Raker turned his head painfully and watched the Bluecoats move on down the line. "You were right Bowie; they ain't even leaving us even a squirrel gun to hunt with."

"Didn't expect they would." Talbert spit. "That bunch of Yankee scum ain't fit to wipe our boots."

"That may be so Talbert." Ham tried to shut the old man up, or at least quiet him down some. "But, they sure whipped our tails."

Raker lifted his hand and took Bowie by the shoulder. "I'll never be able to thank you proper for tending to me and getting me home, if we're that lucky."

"You'll owe me nothing."

"I think I will, Bowie Morgan." The big hand grasped onto Bowie's shoulder harder. "When we get back to Texas, I'm partnering up with you and giving you half my ranch."

"What would I do with that much land George? I ain't no rancher or anything like that."

"When we get back to Texas, you'll change your mind," Raker grimaced in pain. "Believe me; you'll love Texas and the Circle R Ranch."

"Is that the name of your ranch?" Talbert looked over at the wounded man. "The Circle R?"

"Yes sir, it is the most beautiful cattle ranch on the Pease River." Raker closed his eyes. "You boys will love the land."

By nightfall, the Confederate soldiers that can still walk under their own power are already on their way home, dejectedly walking away from their former comrades and the army. No longer are they soldiers, now they are merely men looking to pick up where they left off, four long years past. Ham Jenks hesitates alongside the army cot, not wanting to leave his longtime friends. To him they have become like family. Finally, he can put it off no longer it is time for him to leave. Saying his goodbyes, he smiled down at Raker and wishes him well.

"You're in good hands, George." Ham looked over at Bowie and Talbert. "The best; good luck boys and live a long life."

"If you ever get to Texas, you come see us Ham Jenks." Raker nodded weakly from his cot.

"That's a promise George." The younger man glanced over at Talbert. "You planning on going west, Talbert?"

The old gray head bounced happily. "Thought I would Ham, ain't never been there before and my old pappy always said to look ahead."

"Well old man, you sure didn't look ahead this time did you?" Ham shook his head and smiled. "The war I mean."

"I did my duty as I seen it." Talbert looked up sadly. "It didn't turn out quite like I planned, but I did my part."

Looking off down the shadowy road where several Yankee Patrols are watching the scraggly but once proud Rebel Army limping away, Ham turned away. "Tennessee ain't but a hop and skip across those mountains boys, I best be lighting a shuck out of here."

"You take care of yourself Ham." Bowie nodded as the young man in the tattered uniform started away. "We'll be seeing you."

Comrades in arms who lived through a time of death and destruction have bonds that tie them together stronger than any chain or family ties. "Keep your eyes out boys; you may see me coming your way at any time."

"You'll always be welcome at our fire." Talbert waved, dabbing at a tear. "It's almost like losing family, watching that boy leaving."

"He's got a tough row to hoe." Bowie watched the scarecrow of a man fade away. "But at least he's alive to hoe it."

"Amen to that." Talbert touched his face trying to turn back the tears. "He talked a bunch, but he served his country from start to stop without one complaint."

"He did for a fact, Talbert."

Bowie moved back to where his knapsack and what is left of his war bag still lay where he had left it. Looking about slowly for any Yank soldiers, he quickly retrieved his pistols and pushed them deep in the pack. Texas is still a wild frontier, he had crossed into Texas once before the war when he was escaping the law in Louisiana, across the Red River the pistols will be needed. Walking back to the wounded Raker, he squatted down and motioned for Talbert to come closer.

"What are we gonna do Bowie?" Talbert scratched his gray head. "George can't ride a horse, and he sure can't walk."

Nodding, the tall man looked toward the Yankee camp that had begun to break up. "Those Yanks have plenty of wagons and horses."

"Are you crazy lad, how you gonna get a wagon away from them?"

"Why Talbert, I'm just gonna ask them for one real polite, that's how." Bowie nodded slowly.

"In a pig's eye you are." The old man wagged his head. "This I gotta see."

"Well you ain't gonna see anything." Bowie placed his large hand on Talbert's bony old shoulder. "Come dark, I'll be going after a wagon. You stay here, and have George bundled up and ready to go soon as I get back."

"Just like that, huh?"

"Just like that." Bowie glanced over at the field hospital. "I'll be right back."

Chapter 2

Walking to where doctors and nurses are busy working over the wounded soldiers, Bowie is surprised to find several newly arrived Yankee doctors helping the undermanned staff of the Confederacy. Slipping inside as if he is looking for someone, Bowie made his way closer to the lines of medical bottles and examined the labels closely. Knowing exactly what he is looking for he finds the same brown bottle, labeled Laudanum, that was given to him the two times he was wounded. The wound in Georges shoulder is severe, he will need a pain killer for several days until the wound starts to heal and the pain subsides. The rough bouncing of a wagon, providing he can get one, will cause the man severe discomfort. They will be traveling across the rough back roads of Virginia, trying to avoid the mounted patrols that will no doubt be watching every main road in and out of the state. Bowie doesn't have one bit of guilt about stealing the medicine or anything else he will need for Raker. The yanks have an abundance of ordnance and Raker needs the medicine, he must have it if he is to survive the long, bouncy ride and three bottles will not be missed.

"Can I help you find something Corporal?" A middle-aged nurse surprised the tall soldier.

"I'm just a plain civilian now ma'am." Bowie had already slipped the bottles into his pocket before she reached him. "I'm looking for Private Raker."

"I believe Private Raker is still where you left him lying a few minutes ago." The nurse nodded out the open tent flap and smiled. "Yes there he is, exactly where you left him young man."

"Yes ma'am." Bowie blushed he knows he has been caught in a lie. "Yes ma'am."

"Good day sir."

"Yes ma'am." Bowie turned red faced and exited the tent. "Good day."

The nurse watched him as he walked proudly from the tent, his shoulders square and his back straight. She smiled turning a blind eye to the theft; she had seen him take the Laudanum and knows why he needs it. The southern soldiers haven't been paid in months, a few bottles of pain killer for his wounded comrade is the least the army can provide.

Taking a seat on an empty wooden crate beside where Talbert is feeding the wounded man, Bowie accepted a piece of the offered Yankee hardtack. "You get what you went after Bowie, like Laudanum?"

"How'd you know what I was after old man?"

Talbert shook his head. "I may be old, gray headed, and a might feebleminded, but I sure ain't stupid."

"I'll be going after a wagon at dark, you be ready."

"Those Bluecoat sentries might object."

"I hope not too hard." Bowie shrugged. "If they do, it'll be their problem."

"Just remember lad, the war's over killing them Yanks would be considered murder now."

"I hear you, Talbert Yandell." Bowie looked over at Raker. "But, George needs a ride to get back to his ranch. He sure can't walk that far, and he's too heavy for an old coot like you to carry."

Two hours past sundown Bowie slipped unobserved into the gathered supply wagon yard and crouched out of sight in the dark shadows. Many of the supply wagons of Grants Northern Army had already departed headed north towards home thankfully leaving behind fewer sentries to guard the ones that are left. Slipping quietly up and down the picket lines in the moonlight the dark eyes of the young man seek out a team of mules the U.S. Army overlooked and neglected to mark with their regulation U.S. brand. Farther along he finds a small flat wagon with no markings on the canvas covering. Quickly looking in the back he can see it is full of wooden boxes, supplies of some kind. It's too dark; he can't make out the markings on the boxes inside the wagon. As the custom of the army, the harness for each team was laid out on the wagon tongues to dry, making it easier for the drivers to get the teams hooked quickly and in the dark if they are suddenly needed.

Untying the unbranded mules he had found, Bowie looked up and down the picket lines. As quietly as possible he led the team to where the old wagon sat at the far edge of the wagon yard. Hearing a slight noise as he dropped the trace chains across the mules, he quickly buckled the collars and hames' then slipped to the rear of the wagon. The noise had come from a slow moving sentry making his rounds along the line of wagons more engrossed in his unfinished smoke and probably thoughts of home than guarding the wagons. Pulling the long knife halfway from its leather sheath at his side Bowie tensed ready for the oncoming guard. He is taking the wagon it is a matter of life or death for a friend who has come to his rescue more than once. If this lone bluecoat's life is the price Bowie shrugged, so be it. Suddenly as he walked toward Bowie, the sentry for some reason turned and ambled away.

Quickly Bowie finished harnessing the team and led the mules and wagon away. Holding his breath he listened behind him knowing at any minute the alarm will sound and he may have to abandon the wagon and disappear into the night. The wagon is old, but the wooden hubs have been recently greased and tightened. Only the slight jingle of the trace chains or the squeak of the wagon sounded across the flat ground as it pulled clear of the wagon yard.

"You got it Bowie." Talbert came to his feet as the wagon pulled to a stop beside the makeshift hospital.

"Get in the back Talbert and make him a bed out of our blankets and knapsacks." Bowie retrieved his pistols and strapped them on. "Hurry!"

"I'm hurrying young'un, I'm hurrying."

The hospital nurse looked through the flaps of the tent watching as they lifted the wounded man into what appears to be a regular farm wagon. How the Corporal had gotten the wagon or where she doesn't know, but she does know he is good at requisitioning things he needs, first the Laudanum and now the wagon. Knowing he can't see her from inside the hospital tent she smiled and waved as the wagon disappeared into the dark of night. "Good luck, soldier."

Barely an hour had passed since the wagon pulled from her sight when a small cavalry patrol galloped into the hospital area and reined in their horses hard. Dismounting a Union Officer quickly approached the large tent as two other soldiers dismounted and examined the area where the wagon had left wheel tracks as it stopped to load the wounded man.

"Good evening Nurse."

"Good evening Captain."

"Ma'am, we're looking for a missing wagon reported stolen earlier this evening, we believe the one that we tracked here could possibly be it."

The nurse watched as the blue clad soldiers wave torches along the ground, trying their best to sort out the different tracks in the dark. "There was a wagon here this afternoon sir; it came to pick up a wounded confederate soldier."

"What kind of wagon, army supply maybe?"

"I'm afraid you're wrong Captain." The nurse smiled brightly. "Two darkies drove the only wagon I seen and it was so old, I didn't think it could possibly carry three men without breaking down."

The Captain frowned slightly. "You saw it yourself?

"Oh yes sir, it left here earlier today, sometime right after dinner."

A three stripe sergeant coming to attention beside the officer, agreed with the nurse. "That's what Reynolds and Nolen says, sir."

"What is that Sergeant?"

"They say a wagon pulled away from here earlier today."

"Are your sympathies Northern or Southern, ma'am?"

"Why Captain, can't you tell I'm from Philadelphia?" The nurse smiled sweetly. "I'm northern by birth, same as you sir."

Slapping his leg with a riding crop, the Captain studied the smiling nurse for several seconds then whirled and started barking orders. "Mount up."

Smiling she turned pertly and entered the makeshift hospital. "Trouble Miss Lee?"

"No Doctor, just scoring one for our side." The nurse laughed lightly. "Peers to me those Yank soldiers don't track much better than they fight."

Early morning found Bowie pulling the wagon inside an aged structure of a barn. The day is still young, but figuring patrols will be on the roads searching out renegade Confederates he decides to travel late at night when the Bluecoats should be sleeping comfortably in their bedrolls.

"How are you doing George?" Bowie looked over the wagon's tailgate.

"I'm still with you and kicking."

"Good." Bowie looked to where Talbert leaned against the wagon's side boards. "Talbert, stick your nose into those boxes and see if there's anything edible back here."

"Edible?" Talbert held up a handful of crackers and laughed. "What do you think me and George have been eating on since we left the hospital and Appomattox behind?"

Grinning, Bowie held out his hand. "Pass some out here."

"That ain't all young feller, we got enough grub to get us clear to California with plenty of coffee too boot."

"Well that's good, except we ain't going quite that far."

"Where are we Bowie?" Flat on his back Raker couldn't see over the side of the wagon.

"Heading west is all I know George." Bowie looked out the broken down door of the old barn. "I'm not too familiar with this country."

"That's close enough, west is the direction we need to be heading."

"You hurting, you need a little Laudanum?"

"I hear the stuff is habit forming." Raker shook his head.

"Just take a little, enough to ease the pain for a few days then we'll throw the rest away,"

"You're a persuasive young man; okay maybe I'll have one small taste."

Bowie smiled and handed Talbert the brown bottle. "Just a little for him now."

Patrols passed from time to time during the day, but the men were lucky none bother to even slow as they ride by the weathered barn. A week later and many miles to the west, the wagon is making good time as it rumbles noisily along the rugged mountain ranges of Kentucky, hopefully far away from any ranging Yankee patrols. Back in the deep mountains most folks are loyal to the south and almost every one of the families has lost relatives to the north, some don't even know the war is over. They will attack anything in Yankee blue entering their mountains, unless it is a large, heavily armed cavalry patrol.

Bowie considers trading a few supplies for some store-bought civilian clothes, but now that they are out of Virginia the Confederate Gray might just help them on their journey west. Studying on the situation, he decides to swap for regular clothes and keep them in the back of the wagon, just in case they are needed. He knows most westerners, unless it is the Kansas Militia or Red Legs, are all of southern sympathies and will be loyal to ex-confederates.

"How are you doing back there George?"

"Better, the shoulder is sore as the dickens, but it's really itching. That means it's mending, doesn't it?"

"It should be mending Bowie; he's gone through a box of crackers and enough hardtack to fix anything." Talbert laughed.

"Whoa." The deep voice whispered softly to the mules as the wagon comes to a stop overlooking a small river crossing. Bowie has no idea what river it is or even where they are, but the team of mules needs rest and feed and this out of the way crossing is perfect. "We'll let George rest here for the night and you can boil us some of your good coffee Talbert."

"Sounds real good to me." The old soldier stood up stiffly in the wagon box. "This old wagon ain't exactly the most comfortable transportation for an elderly gentleman."

"Beats walking don't it old man?" Raker laughed softly, then flinched from the pain it caused him. "Dat burn, I'm sorer than I thought."

"It's the wagon George, the wagon." Talbert shook his head. "I'm used to walking, shucks we walked all the way from Richmond, then to Gettysburg, down the Shenandoah Valley, then back to Richmond. I wasn't near as sore then as I am right now."

"Well Talbert, I reckon Bowie would allow you to walk beside the wagon all the way to Texas if that's what you want."

"Funny George." Talbert slipped from the wagon and looked at Raker. "You want me and Bowie to take you out of this contraption?"

"No, I'll just stay here for a spell. A cup of coffee would sure hit the spot though."

"Coming right up." Talbert looked about. "Let me throw a fire together and I'll fix you a pot."

While the old man tossed wood together for a fire, Bowie unhitched the team and led the tired mules down to the water. Several large brook trout moving lazily along the bottom in the shallow water caught his eye as the team drank greedily. His mouth watered, he hasn't tasted fish in several months, but to catch the trout he needs a hook and line.

"What you studying on so hard Bowie?" Talbert knelt filling up their battered old coffeepot.

"Trout." The tall man pointed down at the water. "They sure would taste good."

"That they would, you catch some and I'll cook them."

"No string, no hook, and no bait." Bowie shrugged his shoulders. "And old-timer, that means no fish for supper."

"You ain't done much fishing, have you sonny?" Talbert shook his head. "Boy, ain't you ever heard of a fish trap?"

"I have, but there's nothing around here to fix one."

"Here, you fix the coffee and I'll make us a trap." Talbert handed over the coffee pot and pulled his large knife. "And we'll have fish for supper."

Bowie leaned contentedly back against a log sipping on hot coffee and studying the small river. Talbert had been true to his word as the reed trap had produced several frying size fish. Across the fire Raker sat propped up against several blankets, eating his part of the fish. Bones are piled high in the small fire as each man eats his fill.

Patting his flat stomach happily Bowie suddenly stiffened then sat up straight. From somewhere above them, up along the ridge they came down earlier in the day he heard the unmistakable sound of horse hooves as they clatter across the rocky trail. Rolling to his feet Bowie put his fingers to his lips then disappeared into the heavy foliage, silent as a ghost. Only a few minutes pass before three riders riding abreast and spread out come ride into sight. Moving slowly down the mountain trail toward the small fire the men are wary, their hard eyes watchful, missing nothing. The smoke from the blaze Talbert has burning is plain to see as it drifts lazily into the tall trees. Pulling up ten feet from the fire the rough looking men wait motionless, stonily staring over at Talbert and Raker where they sit alongside the wagon. Long rifles rest across their saddle swells pointing casually into the woods, but there is no doubt they can be brought into play fast if needed.

"Your fish smells good pilgrim." The roughest looking of the men stared down on them from his horse. "You got any to spare for three hungry travelers?"

"It was as good as it smelled." Talbert nodded slowly. "Sorry, you boys got here too late to help us eat it."

"Your uniforms show you to be Confederate."

"We were Confederates alright, I s'pect you boys fought with the south?"

The question is ignored as the men study the camp. "He hurt?"

"Got himself shot at Appomattox."

"Do say." The bearded man spit. "Now, ain't that too bad?"

"You fellers live here in these parts?"

"Nope."

"Y'all?"

Talbert shook his head. "No sir, we're headed home to Texas."

"Do say?" The big man smiled a toothless grin. "You hear that Jasper, they're from Texas?"

"I heard him Doke." The smallest and filthiest of the men nodded. "That's a far piece from here, you boys got any money?"

"Can't see that's any of your business Mister." Raker looked up from his blankets. "None at all."

"Well now, the dead has come back to life." Doke cast his eyes down at the wounded man.

"I'm alive alright." Raker tried to rise then fell back as Doke pulled his pistol. "You men are Kansas Red Legs, ain't you?"

"Smart man, yeah that's what we are alright."

"Are we near the Kansas border?" Talbert stalled, trying to defuse the situation as he stared at the deadly pistol. "We've never been in these parts before."

"Nope, you're camped along the Missouri border."

"Well then, we'll be pulling out come sunup."

"You think so pilgrim?" Dokes voice hardened and his eyes narrowed. "I doubt you'll be going anywhere come daylight."

"What you fellers planning to do?" Raker looked up at the mounted men. "We ain't done you any harm."

"Why nothing much pilgrim, we're just aiming on putting you out of your misery is all." Jasper smiled a toothless grin. "Then we're gonna take your money and everything else you got."

Bowie moved into sight from his place behind the shrubbery with both pistols cocked and ready. "You boys do a lot of talking; now open the dance with your big mouths."

Doke's eyes widen as the heavy Navy Colt slug lifted him bodily from the saddle. Jasper cried out as he takes the second slug through the heart. The third and last of the men raised his hands into the air begging. "Please, mister, this weren't my idea."

"That's a weak argument for a man that was just now planning to murder two men in cold blood. Reap what you sow, Red Leg." The Colt roared, throwing the man backward from his horse. "Pretty weak."

Talbert's eyes blink several times as he stared down at the three men. "You killed them all."

"I did that alright, they were fixing to do the same for you and George." Bowie looked over at the ashen face of the old man. "Talbert you've seen many a dead man in the last four years, this shouldn't shock you."

"I reckon so, but this wasn't war, you just shot them down cold."

"It's worse than war Talbert; these men were the scum of the earth." Raker spoke up. "They were lower than scum, they were scavengers. That means they were killers, pillagers, rapists, and who knows what else."

"Talbert shake out of it and unsaddle their horses." Bowie had already noticed the U.S. Brands on the mounts. "Pile everything near the fire and we'll burn what we can."

"The men too?"

"No not the men, we'll drag them downriver and hide them out of sight." Bowie started going through the pockets and coats of the dead men. Never in the worst days of the war had he smelled men as rank as these three. Placing two pouches holding folded bills and silver inside his coat pocket, Bowie stood up and looked to where Talbert worked piling saddles, blankets, and bedrolls near the fire.

Turning the three horses loose, Talbert stampeded them into the mountains, hoping they would travel far from the campsite. Anyone finding them would just think they had gotten loose from the army and corral them for their own use. The McClellan Army Saddles were the standard cavalry issue of the army, they wouldn't completely burn but Bowie wanted nothing in the wagon to tie them in with the army, just in case they happened to run into a union army patrol.

"You ready George?" Bowie looked at the wounded man lying in the back of the wagon. "Can you ride a few more miles tonight? We need to get clear of this place."

"I can travel alright." Raker nodded. "Just in case we didn't say so, thank you for saving our bacon back there."

"Yeah, thank you lad, I reckon me and George would have been done for if you hadn't of put out their lights."

Chapter 3

Wichita, Kansas in the summer of eighteen sixty five is just a wide spot on the prairie. It has been raining on the Kansas Prairie for two weeks and the roads are sopping wet. Deep cut wagon ruts and muddy ground exists because of the hundreds of horses passing through the only town where supplies and liquor can be found this far west on the endless plains.

The worn out mules plod tiredly pulling the old wagon down the muddy path that passes for the main street of the young town. The team of mules is exhausted after being on the trail for several weeks, pulling the wagon and men with little feed and less rest. Bowie has to admit, the mules are honest most of the long eared critters would have already sulled up and balked, lying down in their traces from such a long hard pull.

"What town this be?" Talbert couldn't read the small sign as they entered town.

"Wichita, Kansas."

"Is she friendly to Rebs?"

"It will be soon as we get a bath, some clean clothes, and begin to look respectable." Bowie studied the street. "Folks have a little more respect for people who look respectable."

Raker nodded from his place in the wagon. "Yeah, I reckon we look a sight alright."

"Yeah, and smell a sight too." Talbert studied the people as they passed. "Pretty good size place."

Raker wasn't lying; all three of them were shaggy, lice ridden, and looking far worse than any of the stray dogs roaming the town. Covered with long hair, full length dirty beards, filthy, ragged Confederate uniforms, none of them had bathed in weeks, they probably could be smelled farther than they could be seen. Bowie pulled the team to a stop in front of the first livery stable they came to.

"Towns cost money young'un." Talbert scratched at his chin whiskers. "Lots of money."

Bowie nodded as he wrapped the lines around the brake handle. "We've got plenty for our needs."

Raker looked up curiously at the young man in the driver's seat above him. "Where did us poor rebel soldiers get money Bowie?"

"We got some back yonder a piece George. I found some Yankee money and coins on our Red Leg friends when I went through their pockets." Bowie stepped down from the wagon seat. "Ain't a whole lot, but it'll see us to Texas and then some I reckon."

"Well, in that case I for one am ready for a bath." Talbert dropped down from the wagon. "Let's get to her."

Bowie is surprised he didn't figure the old man would take a bath without force, at least an argument. Looking to where Raker is trying to rise from the wagon bed, he made out like he was in shock. "You hear that George, he's gonna take a bath."

The big rancher laughed lightly. "Last time he had one, the boys of C Company had to use lye soap, a GI brush and help him with it."

"Yeah, took almost the entire company to get the job done, didn't it?"

The memory of the bath caused Talbert to turn beet red, it had been an embarrassment to him. "Those boys almost took my hide off with that brush."

"As I recollect Talbert, they did at that." Bowie smiled slightly.

"Ya'll quit fussing and smell that air." Raker sniffed the wind. "We're getting close boys; I can smell Texas on the wind."

"It's just you that's smelling George Raker, or maybe this horse stable." Talbert eased his old bones straight. "Man, something is ripe."

"Nope it's Texas I'm telling you, smell that sweet air."

"You feel like getting out of there George, I'll give you a hand."

The big man smiled. "Thanks to you and Talbert, and that bottle of Laudanum, I believe I'll be able to make it by myself."

"Well, slide out of there and I'll get the wagon taken care of." Bowie looked over at the barn and corrals. "Now I'll help you if you need help."

"Thank you kindly Bowie, but it's time I start doing for myself." Raker eased a leg over the side and using only his right arm lowered himself to the ground. "Now, you boys just stand back and let me walk by myself."

"I believe you'll make it just fine." Bowie showed a small smile then watched the hostler approach. "I'll talk with this gentleman and get the team taken care of."

"You do that."

"Can I help you fellers?" The skinny stableman studied the three skeletons closely, trying to stem the stench from his nose as he approached where they stood. "Gentleman."

"Yes sir you can, take care of our team and keep a watch on the wagon for us mister. It'll be worth an extra dollar." Bowie looked the stable man square in the eyes. "Take real good care of it."

"I run an honest place here mister; I don't have to be paid to watch my customer's property."

"Well now, that's good to know." Bowie handed the man a crumpled up Federal Note. "Feed and hay them, and if you've got the time, grease the wheels on the wagon."

"I'll get right on it." The man looked at the twenty dollar note hungrily. "You'll have change coming mister; I'll get it to you when you return."

"We'll be wanting us a bath and some clean clothes." Bowie nodded. "Where can we find the local barber?"

A bony finger pointed across the street. "Right over there is the bathhouse and barber."

"And clothes?"

"Next door to the barber shop is a mercantile."

"We've got clothes in the wagon Bowie," Talbert spoke up. "You ain't forgetting them are you?"

"Nope, the ones we traded from that farmer are almost as old as our uniforms, we need some new ones."

Talbert's eyebrows raised. "It must be nice to be rich, mighty nice."
"Come on, old man shake a leg."

Two hours of soaking in copper tubs, a haircut and shave, then a splash of lilac on their smooth faces, and the clean clothes the barber sent for had made new men out of the three. Stepping into the street Bowie pointed across at a local eatery. "You boys hungry?"

"Man, I feel alive." Talbert grinned as he looked at himself in the long mirror outside the barbershop. "Really alive."

"Me too." Raker eased cautiously down into the road from the boardwalk. "For the first time in four years, I feel clean."

Buckling on his pistols Bowie nodded his agreement, then followed them from the barbershop. He knew what Raker meant, never in his life had he ever felt so dirty and filthy. For the past four years, he had lived with the lice and fleas moving about under his uniform, he sure wasn't alone; the whole Southern Army shared the nuisances. If the pests could have carried a rifle, the Yanks would have been whipped for sure.

"We'll grab us a bite, then we'll see the sawbones."

"What do we need a doctor for?" Talbert looked over curiously at the tall young man. "Are you thinking they might poison us with their food?"

"I want a doctor to look at George's shoulder before we pull out for Texas."

Talbert eyed the approaching waitress worriedly as they took seats at one of the tables. "We still got money, Bowie?"

Nodding at the girl, Bowie smiled slightly. "Yes Talbert, now order."

"Order what?"

"Ma'am." Raker looked up at the pretty girl. "Just bring us the house special, three times."

"Yes sir, and to drink?" The girl looked across at Bowie coyly.

"Coffee will do nicely."

The girl glanced down at the heavy Colts buckled around Bowie's waist and shook her head. "Something wrong, miss?"

"Yes sir, I should warn you our local law doesn't allow the carrying of guns inside the town boundaries." She looked around the eatery. "I wouldn't want a nice young man like you to get in trouble on his first visit to Wichita."

"Well now, I wasn't aware of that law, never ever heard of anything like that before." Bowie nodded. "Thank you for the information."

"Our town marshal is a cruel mean man mister, if he sees those guns on you, there will be trouble."

"Well now, we wouldn't want that, what do you suggest I do with them miss?"

The girl glanced at the front door. "If I were you, I'd check them over at the counter; the marshal will be coming in for his dinner any minute."

Being new arrivals and in a Kansas border town, the last thing Bowie wanted was to have a run in with the local law, which always could outman and outgun their opponent, almost the same as the Yankee Army. Nodding, Bowie stood up and walked to the long counter and removed the Colts. He had just turned back for the table when he noticed a swarthy man with the marshal's badge standing in the open doorway. The hardest blue eyes he has ever looked into, stared coldly at him from under a wide brimmed flat hat. Not a word comes from the man as he sits down at a corner table, just the cold hard stare.

Bowie shrugged and returned to his seat where all three men start eating hungrily as soon as their food is placed before them. Few words were spoken as the men quickly finished their meals, then Bowie retrieved his pistols carrying them from the eatery across his shoulder.

"You're a smart young man." The gruff voice stops them as they reach the doorway. "Next time you boys cross the line, leave the weapons wherever your bailiwick is."

"Yes sir Marshal, with a man like you protecting us we don't need a weapon of any kind." Bowie smirked at the man's insolence. "Do we?"

Red flushed up Bowie's neck as he walked away from the eatery and the rough, hard spoken town marshal. For the past four years, it seems as if everyone from army officers and now the local law has been giving him orders. The dark eyes smoldered as he turned and walked away with Raker and Talbert following.

"He's a rough'un I'd say." Talbert took one last look at the marshal as they walk toward a sign that reads Louis Johnson M.D.

"Looks the part alright," Raker agreed. "I'm fine Bowie; you don't need to waste any more money on a doctor."

"It won't hurt none to have him check you out, George." Bowie pushed through the door. "We're going into Texas and you said that area is remote, real doctors may be real hard to find way off down there."

"Alright Bowie." Raker shrugged. "You're calling the shots."

Removing his shirt, the big man sat down on the doctor's examination table as the old sawbones peered over his spectacles and examined the healing wound. "Looks to me like you men did a fine job taking care of your friend here."

"The shoulder okay, Doc?" Talbert stared over the short doctor's shoulder at the nasty looking scar tissue covering the wound.

"Its fine, but it will probably take a little time to work the stiffness out." The doctor pushed his glasses up on his forehead. "Just stretch it son and keep it working within limits, you'll be fit as a fiddle in a few weeks."

"How much we owe you Doc?"

"Two bits will do it just fine."

The livery owner had just finished greasing the wagon axles when the three arrive back at the stable. Looking up at the fresh groomed men, the hostler smiled and shook his head in surprise. "You fellers sure don't look the same as when I laid eyes on you last."

"Well, it's us alright." Raker sat down against the stable wall, exhausted.

"I got your wagon all fixed up; even patched that rear axle some."

"Will it make Texas?" Bowie bent over and looked at the patchwork the man did on the axle. "Our friend says the roads down there ain't real smooth, says most ain't even good goat trails."

"Should, it's your mules that might not get you there." The stable man looked to where the jaded bay mules are hungrily devouring hay. "They've lost a lot of weight and to tell you the truth, they just don't have much more travel in them without rest and good feed."

"They're good mules."

"Yes sir they are good mules, just wore out good mules." The thin man's head bobs up and down in agreement. "We could do some trading; I've got a mighty good team of horses out back."

"We're kinda short on money." Raker spoke up.

"I'll trade with you for fifty to boot, my team have new shoes all around."

Bowie looked suspiciously at the skinny man. "What's wrong with them?"

"Nothing, not nary a thing." The stableman looked over at the mules. "When I get your mules cleaned up and fattened they'll sell high, higher than my horses. It seems most folks around here prefer a mule over a horse."

"Tell you what I'll do."

"And what will that be?"

"I'm in need of a saddle horse and a saddle." Bowie looked over at the corral. "I'll be wanting a real good animal, how about us doing some horse trading."

The stableman studied the gun belts hanging from Bowie's shoulder. "You boys have a run in with Marshal Hebbit?"

"No sir, only a few words passed between us." Bowie answered the nervous hostler. "Why?"

"He came down here and questioned me about you soldiers, looked your wagon over, then left." The skinny man shrugged. "Hebbit scares me with his hard eyes and cold stare."

"Hebbit." Raker rubbed his jaw. "Is he Abner Hebbit, the 'Killing Marshal' from St. Jo, Missouri?"

"That'd be him alright; he's been here three months and already killed four men." The thin man looked over his shoulder nervously. "He kills like a mad dog."

"What did he kill them for?" Talbert was curious.

"Nothing really, only one of the four deserved killing, he was trying to rob the store where your clothes came from. The others, well they were just drinking and having a good time over at the saloon when they wound up deceased."

"He killed them for downing a couple?"

"It wasn't just the whiskey; they just didn't jump fast enough when he hollered." The liveryman shook his head. "And one was making time with the good marshal's woman."

"He shot a man down for talking to a saloon woman?" Talbert looked toward the saloon. "You're joking ain't you?"

Raker looked across at the man. "You mean your town council lets that sort of thing go on around here?"

"Boys, I sure ain't joking one bit." The hostler shook his head. "As far as the council goes they're scared themselves, so they don't dare say much about anything."

"Scared of Hebbit, are they?" Raker eyed the hostler. "Well sir, I don't blame them much, he looks like a hard man."

"Let's do some trading." The liveryman knew he had talked too much. "The saddle horses are in here."

The morning sun found Bowie, Raker, and Talbert in good spirits. New clothes, well fed, and refreshed from a good night's sleep in a real bed they were ready to start out for Texas. The fresh horses stood hitched to the old wagon and pointing southwest for the Oklahoma Territory. Bowie sits astride a well-made chestnut gelding saddled with a double rigged, a fork saddle made by Dan Brown out of Wichita. The saddle has seen lots of use, but it is a bonafide Brown one of the best made saddles on the frontier.

For a solid week now Talbert has driven the team following the rough road on a southerly course toward the Nations. The new team is fresh, full of energy and a good traveling pair of horses. The stableman said they were full brothers; both were dark red duns and around twelve hundred pounds each. Raker still shakes his head as he rests in the rear of the wagon skeptical about their good fortune on the horse trade, he is nervous, something about the trade just isn't on the up and up.

"I'm telling you Bowie, if we get out of Kansas with these horses without getting ourselves hung for horse theft, we best count our blessings." Raker looked up at Talbert's back. "There's something mighty shady about trading two wore out mules for three sound horses and a fine saddle."

"You thinking they're stolen ain't you George?" Bowie laughed; it sure felt good to be horseback again, and out of the bumpy wagon. "I'm telling you boys I traded for them fair and square."

"I bet they're hotter than a July sun in Texas." The big man wasn't convinced. "A man that knows horses ain't about to swap the way that feller did, no sir."

"What do you think, Talbert?"

"I'm up here on this seat riding not walking, and that's all I care about."

"They catch us with stolen horse's old man; you'll be swinging from a tree with nothing under you to ride."

"They're clean George." Bowie held up a bill of sale. "The stableman gave us this as a reminder."

"Well, why didn't you say so?" The look on Raker's face is pure relief. "That makes me feel some better."

"I forgot to say anything." Bowie shook his head; neither George nor Talbert saw him pay the skinny stableman a hundred dollars in boot on the horse trade. "Now relax and enjoy the ride."

"You know it's kinda dangerous crossing the Nations with just three men." Raker looked anxiously off to the south. "A lot of dangerous men from both armies have moved into the Nations not to count the Indians that roam that forsaken country."

"What's next?" Talbert spit. "You boys are just full of good news, ain't you?"

"We're headed for Texas boys, we're well armed, have plenty of provisions, and we're in a hurry." Bowie looked over at the wagon. "And straight across the Nations is the fastest way they say to get there."

"True enough, Bowie Morgan." Raker relaxed and smiled. "I am in a hurry too, so drive on Mister Yandell."

Nothing marked the border crossing of Kansas and the Territory of Oklahoma except one small stake and Raker couldn't swear if the marker is actually the state boundary. He doesn't recall any boundary markers when they rode up from Texas to join the Confederate Forces. All the Texans had been anxious and in a hurry to get into the fighting so they were riding hard and fast to Virginia not looking for signs. The men had been led and financed by Captain Harrison, a local rancher who owned the Diamond H Ranch outside Medicine Mound. The other men who had followed Harrison from Texas were all dead now or lying in hospitals throughout the south.

A week out of Wichita they had passed few travelers and the ones they had seen gave them only a friendly wave, nothing more. Travelers in this untamed country had learned to give strangers a wide birth if they wanted to stay alive. The Nations after the war is wide open, a wild and unsettled land abounding with all sorts, safety meant staying alert and watchful.

"That's Hide Benson's place up ahead." Raker looked from the wagon bed. "I remember the place from when we stopped for supply's on our way east, seems like a century ago."

"Well, we ain't needing any supplies George." Bowie took in the rough-sided store and corrals. "You wanna stop or keep moving?"

"I think we ought to stop and rest up for the night, we just might pick up some useful information before we move deeper into the Territory."

"Okay, you're the boss."

"Benson is a squaw man, but he runs a well-supplied trading post and being married to an Indian woman he'll know about any trouble we could run into crossing the Territory." Raker watched from the wagon as it rolled closer to the buildings. "He's a friendly sort, but he rolls with the flow as they say. I wouldn't trust him no farther than I could throw him and believe me that wouldn't be far."

Hide Benson all four hundred pounds of him stepped out from under the brush arbor and into the store's sun-bleached yard as the wagon came to a stop beside the store. Round as a barrel, the rotund store owner smiled and walked to where the three are dismounting.

"Howdy boys welcome to Benson's, the last trading post and last white settlement you'll see before you reach the Red." The fat man grinned broadly as he surveyed the wagon and men. "Providing you reach it that is."

"Any reason we shouldn't?" Bowie's voice shot back hard.

The fat trader looked over at the tall man holding the reins of a chestnut horse. "No offense young man, but its two hundred miles give or take to the Red depending on which trail you take, and the Territory is alive with every kind of hard case, Indian or white known to man. Some running from the law and other's running for it."

"We appreciate that, Mister Benson." Raker smiled as he eased down tenderly from the wagon. "You got any objections with us staying the night?"

"Not one you're mighty welcome, maybe we can talk some and trade some news. You boys are fresh from the war, I reckon." Benson nodded, noticing Raker apparently had been injured. "It would be good to get the straight of that story for once."

"How's that?" Talbert stared at the fat man. "Ain't you been getting the truth about the Confederacy winning the war?"

"I'm fat not stupid mister." Benson laughed. "Ya'll make camp and come in, I'll have the woman fix you some dinner and the first drink is on me."

"After all that fighting and winning, I could use a drink." Talbert laughed. "Yes sir, sounds real good to me, we'll just take you up on that, Mister Benson."

Benson smiled and wagged his finger. "That's funny old man; the Confederacy won the war."

"Yeah, ain't it though." Talbert reached for the traces to unhitch the team. "I almost laughed myself to death when I heard."

The log ceiling inside Bensons is low, almost low enough to brush Bowie's hat as he crossed to the table where the Indian woman had set their plates. Coal oil lamps giving off their shadowy light hang from the round poles sufficing for rafters holding up the almost flat ceiling. Benson is true to his word as three glasses of brown liquid is set beside tin plates. Bowie pushed his glass toward Talbert, then pulled the plate to him. Squirrel, rabbit, fried potatoes, poke salad, and wild onions fill the plate along with a huge round pan of cornbread.

Bowie watched the tall Indian woman out of the corner of his eye as she moved about the dim lit room. The woman is tall, slender, and actually quite pretty. She and Benson are completely opposites in size, weight, and height.

Raker smiled at Bowie. "I reckon you never had much doings with Indians?"

"No sir, we have Indians in Louisiana, but they stay mostly far back in the Bayous away from white men."

"There's a shortage of women out here so white men sometimes marry up with Indian women."

"Sounds like a good arrangement, and convenient to all concerned."

"It is a good business arrangement for a trader like Benson." Raker winced as moved his shoulder. "Indian women like it because it raises their status among their own people, to marry a white man."

Talbert raised his glass of homemade corn liquor. "I didn't know you were from Louisiana."

"I was born in the Bayous."

"How did you wind up in the war?" Talbert sipped his drink slowly. "That is, if you don't mind me asking?"

"No, I don't reckon it matters much now." Bowie bit into the back leg of a rabbit. "I had a difference of opinion with a rich Creole over his daughter and was challenged to a duel."

"And the Creole lost, huh?"

"Reckon he did, I'm here."

"Was she pretty Bowie?"

"She was a lady." Bowie studied his plate. "Yes, she was very pretty."

"If you killed her father, I reckon that romance ended." Raker glanced across the table.

"Her father was an old man; it was her brother that challenged me. I had no choice but to defend myself." Bowie picked up his coffee cup. "But yes, it did end the relationship."

"Why, what was wrong with you speaking with the young lady?" Benson had been listening but doesn't understand the aristocrats of Louisiana or their strict rules of protocol.

"She was rich, with a long line of aristocrats in her lineage, while I was a poor boy from the backwoods and bayous."

"And that's bad?"

"In Louisiana yes sir, it is very bad." Bowie nodded. "It's an affront to their honor and being chivalrous people they won't stand to be dishonored."

Raker looked across the table. "Was it a fair fight?"

"John Pierre Lanbeaux was twenty six years old; he had already killed seven men in duels."

"Peers to me that Mister Landeaux liked to fight." Talbert took a hard swallow.

"Lanbeaux was an egotistical aristocrat, a very proud young man, and his word was law on his pappy's plantation." Bowie nodded as he remembered. "The least infraction or wrong word, and he would challenge the offender to a duel."

"The code, I've heard about it even up here." Benson put in. "Bad business, especially if you come out on the losing end."

"Exactly, and Mister Lanbeaux said I broke the code and insulted his sister." Bowie wanted to change the subject. "Let's eat and get some rest."

Benson suddenly recognized Raker. "I remember you now; you stopped here with several young men on your way to the war."

"You've got a good memory."

"You've aged some, but a man your size is hard to forget."

Raker nodded as Benson stood to pour another round of drinks. Sitting back down, he caused the rickety wooden seat to squeak and moan under his weight. "You ain't related to old Jim Bowie of Alamo fame, are you young man?"

Bowie stared curiously at the fat store owner. "Matter of fact Mister Benson, my mother was Jim Bowie's first cousin, that's how I came by my first name."

"It's a small world young man." Benson smiled. "My father died at the Alamo alongside Jim Bowie. Both were great patriots and great Americans, same as you men are."

"Well thank you sir." Bowie nodded. "Our compliments to your wife, tell her thanks, that was a wonderful meal."

"I'll second that." Raker rubbed his stomach. "I'm full as a tick."

"Case you're wondering she's full-blood Cheyenne, one of Black Kettle's daughters." Benson had caught Bowie looking at the woman. "She cost me six horses, but she's worth ten times that much when her people come here to trade."

"Who's Black Kettle?" Talbert slurred his words a bit. "This sure is good drinking mash."

Benson's homemade brew is known far and wide for its potency and two snuff glasses already has Talbert kind of addled. "Black Kettle sir is the Chief of the Southern Cheyenne, known as the People.

Talbert burps happily. "Okay."

"Tell me, whom did you boy's serve with in the late war."

Raker looked across the table then lowered his eyes. The late war Benson refers to is a sore subject, one they would like to forget. "Stonewall Jackson's Brigade."

"Jackson, we've heard stories of that general all the way down here in the Nations." Benson nodded. "Some say if he hadn't been killed, the south would have won the war."

"Perhaps sir, but I doubt it."

The sound of horses reining up in front of the store brings one of Benson's Indian workers slipping silently through the doorway and motioning outside. All eyes in the room turn as the front door bursts open letting two men enter the long room. Bowie's hand automatically goes to his pistol, pulling the tie down loose from his right hand Colt.

Hardly a second had passed when the swarthy faced Marshal Abner Hebbit followed closely behind his deputies. Staring out from under his dark felt hat and down at the three men, his eyes linger several seconds taking an especially hard look at Bowie. "Well well gentlemen, we meet again."

Raker nodded slowly. "Marshal."

"Have you come in for supper, Marshal Hebbit?"

"You go tend to your chores Mister Benson, and we'll tend to ours." Hebbit stood spraddle legged less than ten feet from the table. "Be sure to do your chores outside and take your time."

"Yes sir, Marshal." Benson hurriedly motioned his people outside. "I'll just go feed my horses; you and your deputies help yourselves to whatever you need."

Bowie's dark eyes stared up from the table looking across at the hard face of the marshal. The cold hard eyes of the lawman never waver from the men as he moved closer to the table. "You boys were in an awful hurry to leave Wichita a few days back."

"Is there something wrong with us doing that Marshal?" Raker pushed back his coffee. "Last I heard, it's a free country and we're in a hurry to get home."

"Your hands move the slightest and you're a dead man pilgrim." Hebbit smiled coldly at Bowie. "Get both of your hands on the table where I can see them."

Slowly Bowie placed his hands on the edge of the square table, for now Hebbit had them cold. The marshal and his two men are standing ready and prepared to draw while he is sitting down in an awkward position. Every man at the table can see the lawman is just itching to strike, almost as cold hearted and deadly as a Texas rattler.

"What's the problem here Marshal?" Raker shrugged. "We're just three ex- soldiers heading home."

"Well gentlemen, I'll tell you the problem." Hebbit spoke slowly enjoying his power; he knows he and his deputies have the upper hand. "I got a report that three bodies were found just across the line in Missouri. The bodies were three prominent Kansas citizens carrying quite a bit of cash and then you fellers show up in Wichita, ex-soldiers who should be broke, and guess what?"

"What?" Talbert takes the bait.

"You three go to blowing money like it grows on trees." Hebbit frowned. "Now wouldn't that strike you as a little peculiar if you were me?"

"I reckon it would some." Raker agreed. "But, you're barking up the wrong tree here."

"What about you tall man, wouldn't it strike you funny too?" Hebbit looked at Bowie.

"Not me Marshal." Bowie's expression never changed. "I'm a right peaceable citizen; nothing strikes me funny I like to mind my own business."

"I wouldn't think a peaceable man would serve in any man's army?" Hebbit opened and closed his fist. "Most peaceable men are yeller."

"He served Marshal, and he sure ain't yeller." Talbert growled.

"Stay out of this Talbert."

"So the old man's name is Talbert." Hebbit turned his full attention on Bowie. "Tell me, what's yours boy?"

"Bowie Morgan."

"Any chance you're from Louisiana, down around Baton Rouge maybe?"

"Maybe."

"I've got me a little circular here on you." Hebbit produced a yellow wanted flyer from his pocket and tossed it on the table. "Say's on it you killed a senator's son down in Louisiana over one of them Southern Belles."

"Does it say he challenged me, Marshal?" Bowie tensed. "Does it say the fight was a duel and witnessed by several well-to-do, upstanding men?"

"Now, I wouldn't know all about that." Hebbit shrugged. "But, it says you killed him dead and there's a five-thousand dollar reward on your head."

"Five thousand dollars!" Talbert swallowed hard. "That's a lot of money I bet."

"It is a lot of money old man, seems the dead man was the son of a local plantation owner who was also a State Senator and County Judge with many social connections and power."

"Is he right about this story Bowie?" Raker shook his head acting like Bowie had never told them of the duel.

"Some of it, but he's got the telling of it mostly wrong." Bowie goes along with Raker, stalling for time. "Dead wrong."

Hebbit looked down at the paper. "Says here you're from a family named Trouilliard down in Sera Leone, wherever that is, and that you're a very dangerous man with any weapon, even your hands."

"Marshal ain't you a little out of your jurisdiction." Raker started to rise. "This isn't Wichita, Kansas."

"Shut up and sit down big man," Hebbit spit out the words. "Now, I'm taking Mister Trouilliard in, the rest of you can go about your business, just see to it that you stay out of my way."

"I asked you a question Marshal." Raker persisted.

"I am as you put it a little out of my jurisdiction, but who's to tell it, you big man?"

"Maybe." Raker eased back in his chair.

"This paper if you care to read it, gives me or anyone who apprehends this bad man the authority to bring in one Bowie Morgan, no matter where he's taken." Hebbit offered the paper to Raker, then looked at Talbert. "You move another inch old man, and you're a dead man."

Raker pointed out the date on the circular. "Marshal you realize this paper is five years old, by now that old judge could be dead and the money gone, due to the war."

"Yea I thought of that, but there's still the killing of those three men back in Missouri." Hebbit glared down at the men. "And the money."

"That's two states away and far out of your jurisdiction for sure." Raker shook his head. "What proof have you got that he killed those men?"

"That wagon out there for one thing, and possibly other proof." Hebbit nodded out the door. "And the five hundred dollars you paid for that team of horses hitched to it."

"The wagon?" Bowie blinked. "Five hundred dollars, why you're crazy Hebbit."

"Yep, when old Hank fixed your back axle he didn't tell you it had been leaving a particular drag mark on the ground just like the one described in this here telegram." Hebbit tossed another smaller piece of paper on the table and started to pull his pistol. "Maybe I am crazy, but I'm through talking boy. Stand up, you're under arrest or so help me I'll kill you where you sit."

Raker caught only a blur from his eyes as he rolled away from the table taking Talbert with him. The heavy explosion of gunfire erupts, making dust and small particles of dirt drift down from the low rafters of the building, settling upon the prone body of Abner Hebbit. Bowie quickly covered the other two men as they stared down in disbelief at their marshal. Hebbit's reputation with a pistol and his sudden move were so quick, they hadn't figured he would need their help.

"Don't kill us mister, please." The fatter of the two deputies pleads, his hands extended in the air over his head. "He made us ride with him, we've got small children."

"Alright, drop your pistols and ride and just maybe you'll live to a ripe old age." Bowie waved the Colt. "Talbert, go out and relieve them of any saddle guns they might be carrying, get the marshal's rifle and horse then look through their saddlebags for shells."

"I'm a going." The old man headed for the door.

"When you boys get back to Wichita, you better tell this as it happened." Bowie looked down where Hebbit lay staring up at the ceiling. "The good marshal was out of his jurisdiction and wanted to kill me. Those papers that got him killed were tore up two years ago when Judge Landeaux committed suicide because of losing his beloved plantation."

"We will mister, we'll tell it exactly like it happened." The fat deputy stood sweating like a pig. "We sure didn't want to come down here after you boys."

"Killed by a kid, a snot-nosed kid." Hebbit mumbled his last words.

"He was man enough." Raker raised his glass and took a long pull on it as Benson and the Indian woman slip timidly into the smoke-filled room. "Have yourself a good trip to hell, Marshal."

The old wagon with Talbert driving pulled away from Bensons almost at sun up right after breakfast. Passing where two old Indians are busy digging a grave Talbert grinned then waves. The long, dusty road before them weaves its way across the Indian Territory like a snake twisting and turning heading due south into the Nations, far away from all the comforts and safety of civilization. Bowie takes one last look at Benson and his woman, then turned his face toward Texas.

"Well there's one thing for sure, Marshal Hebbit knew a good horse." Raker patted the neck of the sorrel he now sat on. "They'll probably be after us now for horse stealing."

"How you feeling George?" Bowie turned towards the man riding beside him.

"You can't imagine how good it feels, for a horseman like myself to be riding again." Raker grinned. "Two months ago, I would never have believed I'd still be alive, much less riding again."

"Yes, I can imagine how you feel." The young face never broke a smile, he only nods. "And I doubt the law will follow us clear across the Nations for one horse."

"Well, from now on we best be on our toes like Trader Benson said, this is a wild and dangerous country."

Talbert laughed from the wagon seat. "Shucks boys we have no worries, with all these rifles and pistols we've been collecting since leaving Virginia, we're better armed than the whole Confederate Army was."

"That we are." Bowie agreed. "And if we stay alert and on our toes, it'll take an army to get them away from us."

Still in sight of Bensons, but heading south toward home, the three men were pre-occupied with their journey none looked back long enough to notice the lone rider sitting his horse alongside the store. A filthy Confederate uniform and a year's growth of beard covered the slender frame and the narrow hawk-like face that matched his body. The man absently eased the weight of the heavy forty-five caliber Sharps rifle lying across his saddle swells into a more comfortable position. Staring hard at Raker and the wagon he raised his hand and pointed at the big rancher as if he is firing a gun.

"You were a lucky man, Private George Raker." The voice spoke softly with a slow Texas drawl. "Very lucky, but this old rifle still has another bullet in it with your name on it."

Hide Benson standing close enough to hear the man's cold words paled slightly. "Light down soldier, I'll have my woman fix you a bite to eat."

Brace Caldwell stared down at the fat man; to engrossed in watching Raker he hadn't realized the man was there. "You do that, mister."

Chapter 4

The Red River with its muddy water and sandy banks flowed slowly past where the old wagon rested before a well-beaten buffalo crossing. For ages this very trail had been used by thousands of buffalo as a crossing into Texas from the wild Indian lands of Oklahoma. Talbert held the team back and watched as Bowie and Raker made the first crossing, testing the river's depth and checking for quicksand. Finding the water shallow enough to cross safely without getting their supplies wet, the old man clucked to the team and drove them slowly into the slow current.

Reining his horse around Bowie rode back to the wagon as it neared midstream. "Old man do you want to cross, make camp, and fix supper, or sit here on your coon-dog and let them wheels soak for a couple hours?"

"Two hours, that's a long time to just sit." Talbert grinned stroking his whiskered chin thoughtfully. "You talked me into it, I'll soak the wheels."

"I figured that you old cuss, drive the team out into deeper water then hold the team and let them wheels soak." Bowie shook his finger at Talbert. "Move'em up from time to time and keep the wheels under water."

"I know how to soak a wheel, Mister Morgan." Talbert growled. "I've done it a few times in my day."

"That's good to know from now on you're our elected wheel soaker."

"Good, that settles that." The old man stuck out his tongue as Bowie turned back for the west bank and rode onto dry ground. "Very funny."

"Lie back, take a nap, smoke, whatever, but you soak them wheels until we tell you different or else." Raker hollered across.

"Or else what?"

"Or else Talbert Yandell, we'll wind up soaking you."

"You wouldn't dare."

"Wouldn't bet on it, were I you."

Except for the occasional crossing of a deep creek or river, the wagon wheels fitted with oak spokes and iron rims hadn't been soaked since their quick exit from Virginia. Every spoke in the wheels have dried out and shrunken, most are almost loose enough to fall out; they squeak and rattle with every rotation of the wheels. Out here in the territories and across the Red in the middle of nowhere, a spare wheel would be impossible to find or repair. Bowie is surprised that the old wagon has made the long journey across four states without a mishap so far.

"Well boys, we're in Texas now." Raker leaned back against a wagon wheel and smiled. "Just smell it."

Talbert sniffed the air shaking his head. "Air smells the same to me over here as it did over there, George."

"No it doesn't, and you dang well know it." Raker spit. "We're almost home, Talbert."

"Which direction from here George?" Bowie studied the timber along the river.

"We'll turn west for five days then pick up the Pease River, follow it a day or two then we're at the Divide, and a skip and a holler from the ranch and Norma."

"What exactly is the Divide?" Talbert is curious Raker has never called it a town or a mountain, just the Divide.

"Well old man, it's a town on this side of the Pease River called Medicine Mound. The land is divided by a small mountain range running the length of the plateau where the town begins. That's how the road and mountain trail gets its name." Raker stretched his long arms. "Yes sir, Medicine Mound the prettiest little town in Texas."

"Sure is a wild, uninhabited land out here." Bowie hadn't seen a live person since leaving Benson's Post. "We've hardly seen more than a jackrabbit since we left Kansas."

"Maybe we haven't seen them, but I'll guarantee you, there have been eyes on us for quite some time."

"Friendly or hostile?"

"Well let me put it this way boys, we need to be on the alert for anything that walks, crawls, or slithers." Raker had taken to carrying Hebbits sidearm along with his repeating Henry rifle. "The Comanche could hit us at any moment, this is their land and they think any white man trespassing on it is free for the taking."

"Pretty rough bunch, huh?" Talbert lit up his old pipe.

"They don't come any rougher, and we've got what they want." Raker surveyed the open flats. "Believe me they'll kill to get them."

"What's that, George?"

"Guns and horses." Raker pointed at the four horses. "Horses are their livelihood. The more a Comanche has, the more prestige he has and believe me, Comanche warriors don't mind dying trying to steal them."

"I ain't walking another step, so they'll have to fight me for that team." Talbert growled. "Tooth and nail."

"Don't think they won't old man." Raker grinned. "Then there is the Kiowa, they are the real sweethearts out here."

"They bad ones too?"

"Bad enough old man, I believe in some ways they're actually meaner than the Comanche, just not as many of them."

"Great."

Raker's prediction of the Comanche was right. Two days from the Red, as they rolled across the grass covered flat lands the wild mounted warriors of Texas suddenly appeared, riding in from the west. Sitting their horses without moving a muscle or making any threatening gestures the warriors waited quietly several hundred yards out from the wagon. The three whites studied the line of Comanche Warriors, but so far not a move had been made towards the wagon. The red men just sat their little mustangs and watched the whites the same as the curious prairie dogs living in their burrows across the sandy plains had watched them pass their little towns.

"What are they waiting for?" Talbert stared across at the mounted warriors. "Reminds me of Richmond when the Yanks stood and stared back at us across that field for the whole day."

"You're right George; they are a rough looking bunch." Bowie squinted. "They look wild and proud to me."

"You called it, they are proud, they're wild and they love to fight."

"Well then, why don't they come on?" Talbert eyed the waiting warriors nervously. "Let's get this dance started."

"They're just sizing us up, they want to see how you feller's nerves hold up." Raker studied the warriors. "Don't fret yourself; they'll be here soon enough."

"What nerves." Talbert spit. "Mine are frazzled already."

"Just sit still, but be ready to move the wagon into those trees if they charge."

"I count twenty of them." Bowie quickly checked the loads in his weapons. "Some look awfully young, just boys."

"That makes them even more dangerous." Raker shook his head. "If they got their younger boys with them, they're probably on a hunting trip."

"Why does that make them more dangerous?" Talbert squints. "Peers to me they wouldn't want to put their kids in danger."

"They're proud people, they don't want to show fear in front of their younger warriors. To turn away from just three whites would show they are afraid to attack us."

"So you figure they'll charge us?"

"I'll guarantee it, just as sure as you're sitting there Talbert." Raker looked over at the stand of oaks. "When I tell you, whip them horses hard over to those oaks and tie them up tight, real tight."

"Don't figure it at all, we ain't bothering them any." Talbert gripped the lines ready. "Live and let live, that's my motto."

"Out here they're lord and master of this land, have been for time unknown and they consider us trespassers on their hunting grounds."

"And they want our horses?" Talbert adds.

"Exactly, now old man, whip them horses and let's get under those trees."

The Comanche warriors watched as the wagon suddenly raced over to the small stand of trees and stops. Brandishing their long spears the warriors taunt the white men as they dismount and tie their horses securely behind the wagon. The younger boys race their small ponies back and forth in front of the line, imitating their elders.

"What are they yelling about?" Talbert sighted his Henry across the wagon bed. "I don't see anything to holler about."

"They're building up their courage to charge." Raker answered without taking his eyes from the Comanche. "They like a good fight, but they still respect our rifles, don't think for a minute they don't."

"You think they will?" Talbert watched the antics of the warriors. "Charge I mean."

"They will, you can count on it now listen to me." Raker studied the Comanche line as the warrior's move their horses into a straight line. "Unless I'm wrong, the first charge will just be a mock charge to test us, fire over their heads and don't hit one of them."

"Why?" Bowie looked curiously at the big rancher. "I thought they want to fight?"

"If we let them have this charge, they can show off their bravery then maybe they'll just ride on." Raker answered without taking his eyes from the warriors. "If we kill one of them, they'll have to fight their pride will be at stake."

"Ok George, you know them better than we do." Bowie laid his rifle over the wagon beside Talbert. "Leastways, I hope so."

"Here they come boys, rapid fire, but remember over their heads."

The Henry repeaters belch round after round over the heads of the charging warriors as the small pony's race across the flats toward the wagon. The Comanche's split their racing column passing on each side of the wagon and yelling their war cries as they race by. The booming sound of the high-powered rifles going off across the flats sounds like claps of rolling thunder, even worse. The whites admire the horsemanship the warriors display as they pass underneath their running horse's bellies, firing arrows as they sweep by. Protected by the oak sideboards of the wagon, the arrows either stick into the hard boards or fly harmlessly over the defenders heads. Out of range of the rifles the warriors pull in their blowing horses and turn to face the whites waving their weapons in defiance. A lone warrior in splendid attire, riding a long-legged dun gelding, rode out in front of the others and raised his arm for several seconds, then turned and rode away.

"What was that all about?" Talbert spit a stream of tobacco. "He was a splendid looking cuss."

Raker lowered his rifle and raised his own hand. "I believe that was old Black Hoof himself."

"What was he doing?"

"The old devil knows the accuracy of our rifles." Raker watched the retreating backs of the warriors. "I figure he was thanking us for firing high, he knows what we were doing."

"Are they that civilized?" Talbert reloaded his rifle. "I mean polite."

"Just because they wear breechcloths don't make them stupid." The big man untied his horse. "They respect bravery and honor in an enemy same as we do."

"We're wasting daylight." Bowie returned his rifle to its saddle boot. "If they're finished playing around, let's ride."

"They're finished for now." Raker looked again at the departing backs of the Comanche. "Never forget, the Comanche don't play around."

Raker was right in his estimation of the distance they would be traveling after leaving the Red. Watching anxiously ahead he grinned as he starts to locate and pinpoint landmarks he remembers. The land is mostly flat but gullies cut the sandy land in places where buffalo have worn them down as they moved down the steep bluffs to water. Small tree groves dot the trail in places, but for the most part the prairie all looks much the same, flat and grassy. Passing through a deep line of timber the rancher reined in and studied the small river before him.

"That's the Pease River ahead boys, we're almost home." Raker pointed excitedly to a tall rock outcropping in the far distance. "That's the beginning of my range below it; I planted my first marker right at the base of that rock so I would never forget."

"That would be a good landmark, even in a snowstorm." Bowie took in the far off rock cliff.

"It has been, twice it saved my bacon in a blizzard."

"How'd that rock do that George?" Talbert questioned.

"Pointed me toward home, otherwise I would have kept riding straight out onto the flatlands and froze to death." Raker looked over at the old man. "That's a good thing to remember Talbert, in case you ever lose your way out here."

"Not me hoss." Talbert spit and shook his head. "Cooks don't go out riding in a blizzard; we're too smart for that."

"Now, that sounds real sensible to me." Bowie grinned over at Raker. "Real sensible."

From what he can see around him; Bowie knows why Raker feels the way he does about this land of Texas. The sweet smell of the cool evening air is clean and fresh as the slight breeze brushes itself smoothly across his face. The post oak, blackjack, live oak, and mesquite growing among the tall grass and wild flowers are beautiful even in the dim light. Pushing hard they cross the Pease early the next day; the little river and the grassy land are beautiful exactly as Raker had described it. Flowing water ripples clear and cool across a rocky bottom in places and sandy in others. Trees and flowers of all descriptions grow along the riverbanks, giving off their aromatic fragrances. Bowie inhaled deeply and nodded, yep George hadn't exaggerated this land was a spectacular place, beautiful.

Hours later only the flickering light from the coal oil lanterns hanging from each side of the wagon break the pitch-black dark. The remnant of a pole gate suddenly emerges from the night as the wagon pulled to a stop before it. Sitting the tired sorrel Raker looked down in shock at the battered poles and the leaning gate posts all that remain of what once was a stout gate. Staring down at the shattered and thrown back gate, he can tell by the disrepair it hasn't been used for a very long time. The cedar poles lay broken and strewn about and the road leading through has grown up with grass and shrubs. Tracks of cattle and a saddle horse or two can be seen passing back and forth through the gate, but nary a wagon track show's in the sandy soil. Kicking his gelding Raker moved on toward the west at a slow trot dreading what he might find at the ranch house sitting in a grove of tall oaks less than a mile ahead.

The silent, darkened ranch house of the Circle R sits back under several huge oaks, giving the silent homestead an eerie, almost ghostly feel about it in the dark. There is no light from the windows, no smell of wood smoke in the air, nothing nary a sound as they stop under the huge oaks to stare at the dark silent building. As the wagon comes to a halt beside them in the grown-up, littered yard, Raker dismounted slowly pulling his pistol as he stepped onto the porch. Striking a sulphur, the rancher looks through the wide open door, squinting into the dimness of the empty room.

"Bring a lantern, Talbert." Raker looked around in shock as Bowie followed him through the house. "The place is vacant, they're all gone, my wife, the Mexican workers, everyone is gone, the house has been vacant for a long time."

"You were gone almost five years George." Bowie took the coal oil lantern from Talbert and started looking around inside. "Anything could have happened."

Nodding his head, Raker stared solemnly at the empty cabinets and turned over tables. "I'll check the barn."

Raking his fingers across a dusty table Talbert seemed sad. "This place hasn't been lived in for a long time."

"Yeah I know, a real long time."

"What do you figure happened here?"

"It's hard to say Talbert, sickness, Comanche's, anything can happen out here."

Bowie turned toward the door; he'd been watching Raker's face as they neared the Circle R Ranch and now as they examine the house. He felt the big man's elation at coming home, and now the happiness had turned to disappointment. "How far is this town of Medicine Mound?"

"Three hours ride upriver." Raker stopped in the doorway to answer the question. "Not far, why?"

"Nothing just thought we'd ride in come morning to find out about your missus is all." The tall man took another look about the room. "Someone there might know her whereabouts."

"That's thoughtful of you Bowie, thank you." Raker started on through the door. "I'll put up the horses, if I've still got a barn out there."

"Wait, I'll go with you." Bowie turned towards the old man. "Talbert will you bring in our bedrolls and knapsacks, then start some grub. We'll help you clean up this place as soon as we tend to the stock."

The old man looked doubtfully at the cook stove then shrugged. "I ain't never been much good with one of them things."

Turning Raker pointed toward a pile of dried kindling and small logs lying in a battered wood box. "Just get a hot fire going, we'll help you cook, soon as we get back."

The silhouette of a large, well-constructed barn showed itself in the lantern light as the two men approached the building. Raker nodded deep in thought as he entered the structure. He found everything is in good repair, looking almost the same as when he rode out for the war, except for a little cow manure. Even one dusty set of chain harness hangs untouched from a wooden peg, exactly where he hung them when he left. The two corral gates stand wide open swinging in the slight breeze, but they are in good shape as well.

"I'll go get the horses, but I reckon we better leave the wagon close to the house so we can keep an eye on our supplies." Bowie turned for the house, leaving the big man behind to look around the barn that he had been so proud of.

Raker nodded absently, his mind racing, full of bad thoughts as he stood in the doorway of the darkened barn. Where is she? What has become of her? Pouring oats into the long feed trough sitting in the center of the corral he fidgets nervously.

"You didn't leave her way out here alone did you?" Bowie watches the sad face in the lantern's light as he returns with the horses. "I know you better than that."

Shaking his head, the large man looked towards the house. "No of course not, but she wouldn't leave her home. Several Mexican families that worked for me agreed to stay behind and help her work the ranch."

"Those trappers we talked to back on the Red said the Comanche depredations became worse since the military pulled the troops out of North Texas back in sixty one."

"I know Bowie that's what haunts me, but there is no evidence of any wrongdoing around the place." Raker shook his head. "If it were Comanche or Kiowa, they'd have burned the place down, that's their nature."

"Let's go eat, tomorrow we'll ride into Medicine Mound and find out what happened to your missus."

Turning toward the house, both men jump as the loud report of a pistol goes off inside the building. Racing forward as the second and third shots sound, Bowie and Raker draw their weapons and bust through the door as Talbert yells from his perch atop a chair.

The big horse pistol the old man holds is shaking and waving around as he trembles, causing the chair to shake in danger of collapsing. Bowie looks about for the cause of the trouble, shaking his head dumbfounded, but for the life of him he can see nothing.

"Talbert you dang fool, what are you shooting at?" Raker looked around the room confused. He too is at a loss as to what is scaring the old man. "What?"

Only muttering gibberish comes from the old lips as Talbert points the shaking pistol toward the woodpile. Finally, the word rattler squeaks from between his lips. Shaking his head in disgust, Raker walked over to the stove where the wood box sits. He could see Talbert hadn't missed, the old soldier had managed to hit the box dead square in the front, two out of three shots. Lifting the wooden door with his boot Raker shook his head and laughed as he pulled out a large black snake almost six feet long.

"Well, you missed him Talbert." Raker held up the snake. "I'll say one thing though; you probably done scared him out of a year's growth."

The old man stands bug-eyed his knees shaking as he watched Raker carry the snake outside. "I hate snakes of any kind."

Laughing Raker pulled Talbert down from the chair. "With shooting like that, I see why we lost the war."

"He surprised me you ninny, he had his ugly little face looking at me from out of that box, then he stuck his tongue out at me." Talbert's hands are still shaking as he wiped the sweat from his face. "I hate them things, they give me the willies."

"Talbert, I swear you near scared me out of a year's growth." Bowie set the lantern down. "I ought to shoot you myself."

"Shoot me if you want." The older man looked nervously around the room. "You think I weren't scared."

"Let's get something to eat." Raker pushed Talbert back. "Get out of the way."

"I won't sleep a wink tonight, no sir." Talbert stood eyeing the wood box. "You know they say; where you see one snake there'll always be another."

"Well old son, you can go sleep in the wagon, but you know snakes can crawl up anything." Bowie winked at Raker. "And they love a good warm bedroll to snuggle up in."

Only the faded blue eyes of the old soldier move as he looks hard at Bowie. "That ain't funny, you young whipper snapper."

"Sorry Talbert." Bowie shrugged innocently. "Just trying to save you from those nasty little snakes is all."

"Alright, you saved me."

"I always heard when you talk about snakes, one will show up." Raker added; in the excitement he had forgotten his worries about Norma.

Raker had made a mental note of the scattered Longhorns they passed as their horses trot along what was once a well-worn wagon road traversing the land between the local ranches and farms, then leading on toward the little cluster of buildings called Medicine Mound. Every animal carries the Lazy Bar brand, a mark he doesn't remember being in these parts before the war. When he left for the war there were many brands running on the rich deep grasses between the Pease and Wichita Rivers. Now all he can see is one lone brand, a brand he doesn't recognize. Not wanting to take the time to investigate several of the vacant homesteads they pass, Raker rode on without stopping. There is no use wasting time, every turn off from the main trail is grown up with weeds, unused, they probably are deserted the same as his.

"Only one thing could have cleared this country of people," Raker mumbled, thinking no one heard him.

"What would that be?" Bowie had heard the worried remark.

"Indians!" The big man cussed. "The Comanche and Kiowa probably raided through here while I was gone, and killed or ran off the local settlers."

"You couldn't have done anything George." Bowie looked over at the big man. "Even if you had been here."

"I shouldn't have left her alone." Raker argued. "My responsibility was here, taking care of her."

Reining in at the edge of the small town the two men eyed the layout for several minutes, then kicked their horses forward, down the dusty road. This morning only the two of them had ridden into town, after the snake scare and very little sleep during the night, Talbert insisted on staying behind to guard the wagon and clean a little on the dusty house. Studying the few stores along the main drag, Raker nodded at the few people that are out early, but no one seems to recognize the big man as he passes by.

"The town sure ain't grown any since I left."

"Something has, there's a brand-new building over there." Bowie pointed at a freshly built board structure with the Lazy Bar brand burned deep into the sign hanging across the doorway. "That sign is brand new, it sure ain't been hanging up there for too long."

"Says whoever runs the place is a land and cattle buyer." Raker studied the sign curiously. "With what, I would think after the war, money would be mighty short in these parts."

"Must not be that short." Bowie looked the sign over closely. "Lazy Bar, isn't that the brand on all the cows we rode past this morning?"

The big felt hat Raker wore bobbed slowly as he studied the sign himself. "Yep."

Dismounting in front of the only general store in town, Raker and Bowie slowly survey the wakening town then step across the board porch and push open the door. A small mouse of a woman busy folding material behind the long counter fails to hear the bell or notice them as they enter. Turning sharply as Raker called her name, the woman dropped the cloth she is holding and covered her mouth.

"George Raker!" The name came out in a startled gasp as she took a step backward. "It can't be you, you're dead."

"No Mrs. Scott I'm alive, why wouldn't I be?" Raker tried to advance on the woman only to have her step back. "What's wrong with you woman, you've known me for years."

Nodding, the woman's eyes turn to where Bowie stood beside the long counter. "Yes, I have known you for years George, but you're supposed to be dead."

"Dead?" The rancher blinked. "Last time I checked Mrs. Scott, most dead men don't walk around talking or riding horses."

"Is this some kind of joke or prank George Raker? If it is, it sure ain't funny." The little woman retreated quickly to the end of the counter and called through a blanket-covered door. "Mister Scott, come out here."

Standing near the door Bowie watched intently, his eyes traveling from the woman to Raker, then over to another man as he enters the room.

"My heavens, George Raker." The man stopped dead in his tracks trying to adjust his wire-rimmed glasses.

"It's me Tom Scott, now don't you start that silliness about me being dead." Raker approached the small man and pushed out his huge hand.

"George it is you, bless the saints." The little man took the big hand. "We were told you died three or four years ago."

"Well, as you can see, I'm alive and kicking." Raker turned serious. "Who told you folks I was dead?"

"A Reb soldier came home from the war all shot up, he was on his way west." Scott shrugged. "Said most all of you that rode east with Ben Harrison were dead and gone under."

"He's pretty near right about that." Raker agreed. "The ones that ain't dead are lying back east in a hospital somewhere."

"Captain Harrison?"

"Killed at the Second Battle of Bull Run."

"Kit Woods?"

"He was killed two days later, only a stone's throw from the same place." Bowie answered. "Sniper got him."

Shaking his head as he pulled off his glasses and dabs his eyes, the store man sniffs. "They were all good men all good neighbors, we heard of their deaths, just didn't want to believe it is all."

"My wife, my place, what happened out there, where's Norma?" Almost too scared to broach the subject he fears the worst. "Was it Indians?"

"You've got to understand." The storekeeper looked over to where the small woman diverted her eyes. "She thought you were dead George, dead."

"Where is she, Tom?"

"When you left we had a new rancher settle in here."

"Go on."

"He came in from South Texas, with plenty of money and cattle." Tom Scott shook his head sadly. "We had neither; it was rough, lean times during the war. This new fellers name is Caldwell, he seemed nice enough at first and he brought cash money with him, something we hadn't seen in many a year. After he got himself settled on what used to be the Diamond H, Captain Harrison's Ranch, he renamed his layout the Lazy Bar and started bringing in hard cases for ranch hands. Next thing we know, he started producing liens he bought up from banks on several local farms and ranches. He became ruthless foreclosing on the occupants, mostly widows and children, he took over everything. His once friendly riders turned mean and started roughing up the outlying farmers that were left, and one way or the other forced most of them from their lands. Caldwell isn't nice any longer; he's grown meaner as he's grown richer and more powerful."

"Just like that?"

"Oh, he's a friendly sorta type when he wants to be, but make no mistake he runs a rough crew out there." Scott dropped his head sadly. "The only land he couldn't buy was places like yours, ones with the taxes paid up and no liens against it. Plus, your land was listed with only your name on the deed, here in the store."

"My wife Tom?" The big man stepped closer to the store man. "Quit stalling, where is Norma?"

"About a year after we got word you were well, when we got word you were deceased, Norma married Bacon Caldwell."

"The same rancher you've been talking about?" Raker leaned back hard against the long counter. "My Norma married to another man, no it can't be."

"We're sorry George, but she is."

Maggie Scott stared up at the big man as he swiped his face in shock, then looked over at her husband. "She had a young baby girl to see after George, she thought you were dead."

"A girl, what are you saying?"

"You had no way of knowing she was in the family way when you rode out, it wasn't your fault."

"The baby's mine, you mean I've got a daughter?" Raker blinked in dismay. "And I've lost her too."

"Norma is married to Bacon Caldwell, married in church." The small woman scolded. "She's his wife now, all legal and the Christian thing to do."

"I'm still alive Mrs. Scott, doesn't that count for something?"

"She had you declared dead, there's even a head marker alongside the church that says it." Mrs. Scott persisted. "Ain't that enough for you?"

"No, not by a long shot it ain't." Raker glared at the woman. "I'm still alive and she's still my wife."

Retreating behind the counter the woman seems to pale as she looks at the crazed face. "She's married George Raker; you've come back too late to help her."

The big face turned red as Raker looked wildly around the store. "Where is she, Tom?"

"Now George." The storekeeper started to argue, but the look of cold death from the big man stopped him. "She's out at the Lazy Bar outfit."

Wiping his face the rancher started for the door, then hesitated. "Where is Miguel Ortiz and his family?"

"They're out east of town living in a small sod and frame house, with several other Mex families."

Turning Raker walked from the store and stopped beside his horse. "I'll be riding out to the Lazy Bar, why don't you ride back to the ranch and keep Talbert safe from the snakes."

"No, I'll just trail along with you." Bowie mounted. "Talbert can fight his own snakes while we fight yours."

"Suit yourself." The big man looked back at the store. "You stay clear if trouble starts, this is my fight."

Chapter 5

The sweat stained and dust-covered gelding walked slowly from the side alley that sided the mercantile store as Raker and Bowie reached the edge of town headed west. Ragged Confederate Grey covers the thin, mud-splattered frame sitting atop the gelding. The rider's eyes stare hard from an unshaven face, watching closely as the two unsuspecting men ride away. The thin hands of the bearded, filthy rider stroke the walnut stock of the Sharps rifle lying across his saddle. Kicking the tired gelding into a high lope the thin man skirts the west road leading from Medicine Mound passing far out of sight of the two riders. The rider is Brace Caldwell, brother of Bacon Caldwell. The thin lips smile cruelly as he heads for the Lazy Bar Ranch; his brothers spread. Riding fast he quickly outdistances the two men leaving them far behind. The face seems scarred, not so much from wounds, but the look on his face is hard, cruel, and full of hate, making it appear that way. Spurring the tired gelding cruelly the slender man rides with the fluid motion of a cowboy or a cavalry soldier, the big sharps resting snugly across the swells of his saddle.

Taking a shortcut across the grassland, away from the main road leading to the ranch, Brace keeps his travel worn horse in a hard lope. Cutting the road at the outskirts of the big ranch house and barns, Brace reins in hard as several mounted men intercept him as he comes into sight. Placing his hands in plain view until the men ride close enough to recognize him, Brace rolls himself a smoke and strikes a sulphur.

Strangers are not welcome or wanted on the Lazy Bar; a huge sign says it plain enough and it means exactly that. His brother's so called ranch hands, actually hired killers, have strict orders to shoot on sight anyone trespassing on the Lazy Bar. Brace knows they are a rough bunch; he sure isn't giving them any reason to shoot before they recognize him.

"Howdy boys."

A tall horseman slightly slumped through the soldiers, looks curiously at the newcomer then grinned. "Brace Caldwell, is that you under all that hair and dirt?"

"It's me alright, Frank Fisher."

"In a Confederate uniform too, we didn't know you were the patriotic kind." Another cowboy laughed. "Where you been keeping yourself?"

"Why boys, I've been back in Virginny fighting the war." Caldwell pulled on his smoke. "You know, doing my patriotic duty."

"The boss was about to give up on you Brace." Another laughed. "How long you been gone?"

"I reckon more than two years, but it seems like ten."

"You see any fighting back east?"

"Boys I'd like to sit and jaw with you, but my brother Bacon is expecting me, so I better get." Brace started to kick his horse then stops. "I slipped past a couple fellers riding this way several miles back, they might be coming here in the next hour or so, y'all stay on your toes."

"Are we to stop them?"

"I don't know what Bacon wants to do." Caldwell looked down his back trail. "Frank you come with me, the rest of you lay low and watch the trail until he gets back."

"What if they get here before Frank gets back?"

"I reckon if that happens, just shoot'em for trespassers." Brace suddenly dismounted and motioned at one of the riders. "My animal is done in, let me have yourn."

"I'll be back soon as I can." Fisher hollered as he followed Brace toward the ranch at a hard run.

Norma Raker now Norma Caldwell, watched from behind the house where she has been hanging out clothes as the two men ride into the ranch and slide to a stop near the corrals. Even at this distance in the afternoon sun, she recognizes Frank Fisher by the slouchy way he sits his horse. The other man dressed in a gray uniform she can't make out, but she remembered the soldier who stopped by the Circle R to tell her about George's death wore the same color uniform. Shrugging, she turned her eyes to the small girl playing on the back porch and forgets the two men as she refocuses on her washing. She figured the uniformed one was probably just another drifter looking for work or riding the grub line. Well he was in for a disappointment, Bacon wasn't the kind to pass out free meals to just anybody riding through, most outsiders knew it and stayed clear of the Lazy Bar.

"Ride over to the house and get my brother Frank." Brace noticed the woman in the backyard. "I wouldn't want my sister-in-law to see me looking this way, now would I?"

"I'll get him." Fisher spurred his horse across the wide yard stopping in front of the big house.

Brace looked around in surprise as he pulled the saddle from the sweaty horse, turning him in the large corral with several others. Looking about the ranch's huge new barn and corrals he nodded and whispered to himself. "Well, Brother Bacon, you have been busy while I've been away."

Bacon Caldwell is a big man, larger even than George Raker in size. And for a solidly built man, he moves with the surprisingly easy stride of a cat with the same way of watching everything around him from the corners of his eyes. Embracing his brother as he entered the barn's bunkhouse, the big brother pushed Brace back and smiled.

"Boy you're a sight for sore eyes and ripe to the nose to boot," Bacon laughed. "We done gave you up for buzzard meat."

"Sorry Brother, I just ain't had much time for the nicer things in life, like a bath or shave." Brace nodded. "I was almost a goner several times back east."

"I imagine you were busy, right in the middle of all that blood and guts." Bacon stepped back. "You did have us worried though."

"Well, I'm back now."

"And it's good to have you back, I've missed you."

Brace turned his attention on Fisher. "Wait outside for a minute Frank."

"Sure thing." The tall stoop shouldered man retreated. "I'll be right outside."

Bacon looked at his brother curiously, then walked to where a coffeepot simmered atop a potbellied stove in the bunkhouse part of the barn. "Cup of coffee Brace?"

"Sure, it's been a long ride from Virginia, I just can't seem to get enough coffee anymore." Brace looked about the huge building. "Don't reckon I've ever seen a bunkhouse inside a horse barn before."

"We could be caught in the middle of a range war any day now." Bacon filled the cups. "Thought this set up would keep the boys closer to their horses, ready to ride at the drop of a hat."

"Is it that bad already?"

Bacon shook his head. "Not yet, right now I've got the bluff or the deadwood on everyone around Medicine Mound, but it could easily come to that, just thought I'd be ready."

"I like it." Brace took in the heavy enforced walls. "Almost like a fort, ain't it?"

"It was Fisher's idea, the thicker walls and extra firepower." Bacon nodded towards a gun rack hanging on the back wall. "Best rifles money can buy and ammunition aplenty."

"Good idea."

"You've lost some weight." Bacon handed over the coffee. "How did it go?"

"I didn't get Raker, I did put a bullet in him, but somehow he survived."

"What about the others, Harrison and the rest?" Bacon frowned thoughtfully. "Did you get them?"

"I wrote you a letter, and as you should already know, Harrison and Brockton are long dead." Brace looked about the barn and grinned at Bacon. "Most of the others are dead or in hospitals somewhere back east."

"What happened with Raker?"

"Like I said Brother, I got lead in him. That big man must be tougher than hickory to survive the Sharps, but that's exactly what he did."

"Where is he now?" Bacon sipped the coffee absently. "Do you know?"

"I know, because I've been following them for a month." Brace tasted the coffee. "They're on the road just three miles east of here, last time I seen them."

"They, is someone with Raker?" Bacon tensed, he can hardly believe his ears that Raker is here alive, in Medicine Mound, and at this very moment on the Lazy Bar itself. "Are you positive?"

"I'm sure brother; I just followed him and another gent out of Medicine Mound a couple hours ago." Brace grinned evilly. "I trailed them all the way from Virginia, across Missouri where they killed three men, across Oklahoma Territory where the young one killed a Kansas Lawdog. Yep, I'm sure where they are, where they are heading, and it's this way brother, straight at you."

"Sounds like a rough bunch, killing so many that is." Bacon lifted his cup.

"They're tough as hard oak; don't underestimate them in the least." Brace looked over at Bacon. "That marshal the younger one killed, he was Abner Hebbit."

"Abner Hebbit, the crazy killer marshal from Missouri?"

"That's him alright or was him." Brace stared out the doorway. "The fat squaw man that runs the trading post said the tall one outdrew Hebbit straight up and shot him dead."

"And he's headed out here right now to help Raker get back his wife?" Bacon wiped his face. "Is that what you're saying?"

"That's probably why they're headed this way, Raker was in town talking to that big mouth storekeeper Scott, then both of them got on their horses and rode this way." Brace frowned. "One thing was certain; he sure didn't look any too happy when he left the store."

"Maybe he wasn't headed here." Bacon mumbled. "Could be, he went to find that greaser, Miguel Ortiz."

"You should have run that Mexican off, same as the rest." Brace cussed. "No, he's headed here I followed them from town, I figure he's more interested in coming to see your wife than a Mexican."

"You really think Raker will come riding in here big as day?" Bacon looked out the window worried. "The odds are stacked against him."

"I do, and if you had seen the look on his face as he left town, you'd know it too Brother." Brace pushed back his grey campaign cap. "He could be coming out here to kill you, Bacon. We ain't got much time to discuss the matter, you best be sending Fisher back out there and have the boys stop them."

Bacon looked off to where the woman and small girl are hanging out clothes. "I sure can't have him riding in here, Norma thinks he's dead."

"You want him just run off or dead?" The smaller man's hands seem to itch, aching with anticipation of picking up the Sharps and using it on Raker.

"If she finds out the soldier who spread the word about him being killed, is a liar…"

"Don't worry none about that Bacon, that soldier boy is long dead. She'll never know that you paid him to spread the rumor when he passed through." Brace grinned. "You can bank on that."

"Good."

"Did you get Raker's place signed over yet?"

"No, Raker was smart on that part, he paid up his taxes before he left Medicine Mound and he owned that place lock, stock, and barrel. Norma's name wasn't anywhere on the deed."

"How did that come about if they were married?" Brace shook his head in disgust. "He didn't trust her or what?"

"It was nothing like that." Bacon took a long pull on his coffee. "He came here and bought the land before they were married, then the war came along before they thought to get the deed changed."

"So, she doesn't own it clear and can't sell it until there is a court hearing to settle the estate, is that it?" Brace scowled. "Kinda puts a fly in the ointment."

"Exactly." Bacon nodded. "A big fly in the ointment named Raker."

"Why didn't you get the deed legalities settled already?" Brace had never known his brother to delay taking possession of anything he could own immediately. "What have you been waiting on?"

"I have been busy settling other range disputes and the Judge wanted us both in his office to sign the papers." Bacon shrugged. "I'm telling you Brace I'm glad your back, I need you."

"So that's why you brought in all these other gun hands, huh?" Brace looked about at the blanket covered beds in the bunkhouse. "You're figuring on having trouble with the local homesteaders?"

"They're good cowhands too." Bacon added. "To answer your question yes, I've had to use them occasionally to settle some disputes."

"You being her husband." Brace turned from the window. "Once the papers are signed that would put you as the owner, wouldn't it?"

"Yes, as her loving husband the Circle R would be mine." Bacon cussed. "But not now."

"No you're right, Mister Raker has come back home alive and neither you nor your new wife have claim to the place."

"Not unless he comes up dead real quick, we don't."

"That should be easy to arrange."

"Dead, he would be easier to manage." Bacon glanced to where the Sharps rested against the wall. "A lot easier."

"Most dead men are, easier to handle that is." Brace laughed.

"How'd you miss him with that buffalo gun I gave you?" Bacon looked baffled, his eyes darting again to where the Sharps stood. "How?"

"Bad light, hundreds of soldiers around." Brace shrugged. "It doesn't matter; I missed him once I won't again."

"We'll kill him alright, but we'll have to make sure it looks like it was Indians or rustlers, then we can get our hands on his place without any questions."

"Even if you don't get the Circle R away from Mister Raker, you've been making progress." Brace looked about the barn. "I reckon you've bought up a lot of land around here and you got a new wife and kid."

"I have thousands of acres." Bacon frowned. "For barely a cent on the dollar from the deceased men's wives, it seems dead men don't need land and the grieving wives can't run a ranch or farm one by themselves."

"I wish we had gotten Raker's place, I wanted to lay out my traps on that land. I like the place, the huge oaks, the coolness of the sweet air that blows through them in the hot afternoon. Yes sir, since I first rode over there after Raker pulled out for the war, I wanted to live there." Brace shrugged. "But now we better hurry up and send Fisher, what do you want to do about Raker and the gunfighter with him?"

"We can't kill him here on the Lazy Bar; it would cause a lot of suspicion." Bacon slapped his hands together. "Have Fisher and the boys turn him back, just don't let him ride in here, I sure don't want Norma to see him."

"What difference does it make where it happens or who kills him?" Brace threw up his hands in disgust. "Ain't no law but you out here, big brother."

"Norma's gonna find out he's back sooner or later." Bacon argued. "I don't want her or the girl thinking I was responsible for his death."

"You're right about that Brother; she's gonna find out he's alive eventually." Brace set his coffee cup back on the stove. "Even isolated way out here, she's bound to find out."

"She will, but I'll tell her in my own good time." Bacon stepped to the door. "After you send Fisher clean up, then come to the house for dinner."

"Ok big brother, I'll get Fisher on the road and stop your visitors." Brace turned and walked outside speaking a few words with the Lazy Bar gunfighter. Watching as the man mounted and spurred his horse into a hard run Brace looked across the wide space between the house and barn where the woman and girl are just stepping back inside the house. Something sure isn't right here, Brace knows his brother normally prefers everything nice and tidy, this is unlike him.

Ten miles from town as they near what used to be Harrison's Diamond H Ranch which is now renamed the Lazy Bar; Bowie spots several riders waiting alongside a large sign. Watching closely as the waiting riders kick their horses and advance to meet them, both Bowie and Raker rein in. "Well, I do believe this is the Lazy Bar crew coming to greet us and you heard what that store man said about them."

"I remember alright." Raker undone his holster tie down. "Be ready, they look like a tough bunch to me."

"Mister Scott was right; they are a scrappy looking outfit." Bowie undoes his own tie down and loosening the thirty eight. "Those boys are downright waspy looking, I'd say."

Frank Fisher with four riders backing him rein in across the sandy road leading to the ranch house, showing Bowie and Raker plainly they aren't going one step further towards the Lazy Bar. "You boys lost?"

Looking across at the hard cases before him; Raker knew Bowie was right none of these men are typical cowmen. True cowboys don't wear low-slung tied down pistols and some of these so called cowboys even have two pistols. Handpicked for their guns and fighting ability there is no doubt these are tough men that would do as their boss tells them no matter what it is.

"Nope, we ain't lost mister."

"You must be lost; this road only leads to the Lazy Bar." Fisher shifted in his saddle. "Now we both know you don't have any business there, so you be nice little boys and turn them horses around."

"This used to be the Diamond H, belonging to Ben Harrison before the war." Raker looked straight into Fisher's eyes.

"It's the Lazy Bar now, pilgrim." Fisher turned his horse slightly, putting his pistol on the near side of Raker. "Trespassers ain't welcome around here, nor wanted."

"Well, if this is the Lazy Bar as you say then we're at the right place, I reckon. We've come to see Bacon Caldwell." Raker smiled over at Fisher. "And pilgrim, out here we're neighbors not trespassers."

"He ain't here right now." Fisher sneered, showing his contempt for the two men. "He's gone to visit a sick neighbor."

"What about Mrs. Caldwell, is she home?" Raker raised slightly in his saddle. "Or has she gone to visit a sick neighbor too?"

"Reckon she's gone too." Fisher smiled smugly. "Matter of fact, she's gone to visit a sick uncle of hers."

"I didn't know she had an uncle."

"Yeah, she's got several uncles." Fisher turned cold. "I figure you'd know more about that than I would."

"I'm afraid I didn't catch your name."

"Frank Fisher."

"Well now Mister Frank Fisher, is anybody home?"

No reply is forthcoming, not a sound. The five Lazy Bar riders sit across the road their hands resting lightly on their pistol butts as Fisher's voice turns hard. "Turn back boys, right now."

Bowie tensed watching Fisher as the man's eyes narrow; Raker can sense the same thing. "We're riding mister, but we'll meet again."

"That wouldn't be smart." Fisher's cold stare bores into the big man. "Not smart at all."

"Well mister." Raker spit onto the road. "Far back as I can remember, nobody ever called me smart."

Riding slowly back towards Medicine Mound Bowie stiffened, then nodded over to where three other mounted men sit their horses under a live oak. "They were laying for us George." Bowie eyed the riders. "They were just waiting over there for us to start something."

"Why didn't they take us then?" Raker eyed the riders. "They had the deadwood on us and there sure ain't any law out here to go crying too."

Bowie shrugged. "I don't know why they didn't start shooting; I reckon we were lucky this time."

"In the future, we won't be as careless." Raker walked his gelding slowly, his body staying in motion with the easy gait of the horse as he rolled himself a smoke. "We can't afford to be."

"It'll be healthier if we weren't." Bowie watched as the other Lazy Bar riders turned back to the west. "What do you have in mind?"

"I'm planning on getting my wife and daughter back, that's all." The Circle R owner pulled hard on the smoke. "We know what we're up against out here now, that'll keep us on our toes."

"What if she doesn't want to come back to you?" Bowie had to ask. "What then?"

Raker ignored the question, just looked over at the tall man. "I don't know what I got you into Bowie, but I wouldn't blame you and Talbert if you mount up and light a shuck out of here."

"And let you have all the fun by yourself?" Bowie laughed. "Why, we wouldn't think of such a thing besides, Talbert would miss his snake friend."

"My wife is back there somewhere." Raker turned in the saddle and looked back down the road behind them. "I don't know the right of it, but I want to talk with her and let her explain, but mainly I got to see her just once before I get myself killed."

"Well old friend, I can't speak for Talbert, but I reckon I'll stick a while yet." Bowie nodded remembering the girl back in Louisiana. She wasn't his wife and he didn't love her, but he understands caring for a woman. "Knowing Talbert, I reckon he'll stick around providing that snake hasn't run him off already."

"She's married Bowie." Raker shook his head dumbfounded. "I can't believe it."

"It wasn't her fault George." Bowie can feel the pain in the big man's words and tries his best to ease him. "She was told you were dead, she didn't know any different and she had the little girl to think of."

"She married so fast though." Raker seemed to slump in his saddle. "She didn't wait until my bones were even cold in the ground."

"How was she to know you were alive?" Bowie argued. "Wait and hear her side of it, give her a chance to explain."

Bowie is young and he has never been in love, nor does he have much experience with women. He can't possibly understand the thoughts, rage or jealousy a man feels after losing a woman he thinks so much of to another man. The wealthy and rich blooded girl in Louisiana wasn't anything personal; he really didn't even know her. Bowie was visiting a well-to-do friend in New Orleans and accompanied him to a social given by the aristocratic Landeaux Family. Introducing himself to the pretty girl he had no idea who she was as they danced and laughed throughout the evening. Her father Judge Landeaux had watched his daughter and the young commoner from the bayous as they enjoyed themselves then walked out on the patio together, all alone. Enraged, he sent his proud aristocratic son to tell the lower class young man to leave his home immediately or suffer the consequences.

The times before the great Civil War in Louisiana, were a time of deep family pride. The unyielding pride of hot bloods like young Landeaux caused many a duel to be fought and was the cause of many a young man's death. Duels of honor and to the death are a badge of honor in Louisiana, especially New Orleans, where wealthy landowners of higher society lord it over the lower class. No man could hold his head up with pride and respect if he refuses a duel in a society where any insult usually results in a fight to the death. Hearing the harsh words of his proud father, the younger Landeaux eagerly went about finding Bowie, not to tell him to stay away from his sister or to leave the premises as his father ordered. Landeaux practiced since childhood to be an expert in the use of the sword and pistol, and he had become proficient with both. Thinking he had no peers when it came to dueling had made the proud young Landeaux eager and willing to face anyone willing to fight.

The words of the older Landeaux, were all the excuse the younger

Landeaux needed to send him hurrying to find Bowie. Not to have him leave the Landeaux home, but to challenge the low class backwoodsman to a duel on the pretense his sister had been insulted by a commoner from the bayous. It was his excuse, all the reason the hotheaded young Landeaux needed to challenge the young Bowie Morgan and to kill again. His blood raced with the thought of challenging Bowie to a duel, all on the pretense of protecting his sister's good name and honor. In the younger Landeaux's mind, the slightest of insults against any member of his family would not be tolerated. In his way of thinking, any insult even of the slightest nature needed to be dealt with harshly to erase any stain or blight attached to his family honor.

Bowie remembered the slap of the glove across his face, as the hot-blooded Creole challenged him to a duel in front of several guests and the young woman, who Bowie learned later, was Landeaux's sister. Early the following morning brought about the subsequent meeting of the challenger and the challenged under the great lofty sycamore trees lining the river bottom. Several high profile men, judges, lawyers, even senators tried to talk the two young men out of fighting the duel, but to no avail. Every man present knew Landeaux's reputation and prowess with weapons, and they had little doubt of the outcome of the coming duel. Receiving their instructions, the two young men stood back to back, then walked off fifteen paces and turned.

"Fire!" The word barked out sharply across the clearing from the impartial judge followed by the roar of one pistol, then the second shot sounded as black smoke belched out between the two combatants.

Bowie felt the bite of the pistol ball in his shoulder then watched as the young Landeaux looked across at him, bewildered and stunned, then slumped slowly to the mossy ground. Landeaux made a fatal mistake hurrying his shot, confident of his expertise with the dueling pistol. Shaking his head in shock Bowie watched as the attending doctor bent over the downed man, then as the word dead was spoken he thought of the beautiful woman who was the unknowing cause of the duel. Looking across at the dark scowling faces he hastily walked to his horse and without looking back, departed the dueling field and the state of Louisiana forever.

"She's married Bowie; my daughter carries another man's name."

Raker hissed loud enough to pull Bowie's attention back from the unpleasant memories of his past. "What side of it should I wait for her to see?"

Bowie can feel the bitterness and hatred already starting to boil and fester as the loss of his wife comes over the normally good-natured George Raker. He doesn't know what or how to say the right words to help cure the heartache, which suddenly changes his friend, the man that befriended him through so much bloodshed and danger. Raker is normally a jovial man, but the arrival at his ranch finding his wife missing and now learning of her marriage to another man leaves the rancher empty, filled with jealous rage. Bowie is still young he doesn't understand yet, but love for a woman is a strange thing, at times beautiful, at times strained, but a feeling that can change quickly when love turns to hate.

"We'll ride over to see Miguel and his family before we ride back to the ranch." Raker reined the gelding down to a walk. "Maybe he'll move back onto the Circle R and help out until we can get the ranch back on its feet."

Bowie feels some relief as the big man changes the subject and calms down as they come closer to town. "Sounds like a good idea. You've mentioned him before; he used to ride for you didn't he?"

"He did, it seems like an eternity ago." The big rancher wiped his face with a trembling hand. "You'll have to overlook me Bowie, now I know what a nightmare feels like and believe me, this is a nightmare."

Less than a mile out of Medicine Mound the few Mexican families who had settled this far north in Texas, now have been pushed into their smaller sod and rough board homes by Caldwell. Bowie watches as the playing children and working women suddenly grow quiet and gather together as the two white men approach. Reining in at one of the houses Raker called out a greeting in Spanish to the women and asked for Miguel Ortiz. None will answer, only shrugging their shoulders as they look down at the ground.

"Señor Raker?" The voice comes from the doorway off to their left where a slender built woman stands with her brown hand shielding her eyes, blocking out the sun. "Is it really you, señor?"

"Yes, it is me Señora Ortiz." Both men watch as the small woman walks toward them.

"This cannot be; you are dead."

"I'm not dead, Maria." Raker dismounted looking into her shocked face. "You can pinch me if you want to."

"Oh señor!" Much to the amazement of the other women and older children she threw herself into his arms hugging him tightly then stepped back in embarrassment. "Señor, does Señora Norma know you are alive? We were all told you were dead, that is why we left the rancho."

"No, I expect she doesn't know or care."

"Maybe señor she doesn't know, but she cares and you know she does." Maria stared up at Raker. "When the soldier came with the news of your death, she cried for many days and would not eat until we begged her."

"Then tell me Maria, if Norma loved me so much, why did she marry her new husband so quickly?"

"For the same reason she had to eat, it was so the baby could survive." The little Mexican woman shook her head. "You were dead and the señora was alone. We had to survive drought, Comanche's, Mexican Banditos, and rustlers. Señora Norma wanted your child to live. Never would she have married this bad gringo if she knew you still lived, never."

"Does she know this man is evil, señora?"

"Can a woman live with a man three years and not know such a thing?" Maria's black eyes bored into his. "She is a strong woman, a proud woman; her child is all she lives for since hearing of your death."

Visibly shaken at the woman's words, Raker shook his head and looked around at the few houses. "I've come to talk with Miguel, where is he?"

"He works the fields with the other men, the gringo Caldwell only gave us the poorest land here to farm. The men have to work hard to make this land feed all of us." Maria pointed to the east. "He is there, out past the trees."

"You have no cattle, hogs, nothing?"

"We had many animals, but Caldwell's men came here during the night. They shot all of our animals, cows, hogs, chickens; even our dogs then they rode away laughing."

"All of your animals?" Raker couldn't believe his ears. "Why señora, why would he do that?"

"Señor Caldwell left us nothing; he wants us to go from this place." Maria looked into his eyes pleading. "He tries to starve us out, we need help Señor Raker."

"Why haven't you left here and gone back where you came from?" Bowie asked from where he sat. "No insult ma'am, I'm just curious."

"To leave is impossible, if we travel to the south alone and unarmed, the wild ones, the Comanche and Kiowa would slaughter us." Maria gazed up at the mounted man. "No señor, that we cannot do."

"I see I'm sorry I asked."

"You see, but do you understand." A slender, dark haired woman walked from behind one of the houses and stood next to Maria. "Medicine Mound is Maria's home along with the others, the same as it is mine."

"Jackie Harrison, is that you all grown up?" Raker walked to where the young woman stood. "I can't believe my eyes."

"It's me alright, Mister Raker." No smile comes from the young woman as the rancher embraced her. "And I am all grown up as you put it."

"Girl, it's me George Raker, why the frown for me?" Raker looked down into the beautiful face. "Me and you used to be friends."

"Friends?" The girl looked over at Bowie. "What are friends, Mister Raker?"

"Before the war girl when your pa was alive, you spent many a night with me and the missus." Raker shook his head. "What has happened to you Jackie, you've grown hard."

"Hard Mister Raker, my father is dead; we lost our home and the ranch, now we are paupers." Jackie stepped back away from the big man. "My mother and I have to work at the Mercantile; we even take in washing to make ends meet. Trust me that'll make a person hard."

"And you blame me?"

"I blame both you and my father for going off to that terrible war, and leaving us alone and defenseless." The girl looked over at Bowie. "So men like Caldwell could come in and run us from our homes."

"I'm sorry Jackie, where are you and Mrs. Harrison staying?"

"Behind the Mercantile Store; Mister Scott lets us use his extra room for helping him and the misses out in the store from time to time."

"How is your mother, girl?"

"She's in poor health since the news of my dad came." The woman looked over again at Bowie. "She's grown old before her time."

Bowie is curious. "Who brought that news ma'am?"

The brown eyes flash like fire across at him. "That's none of your business stranger, but just to answer your question it was the same man that brought word of Mister Raker's death."

Raker turned to where Bowie was dismounting. "I'm sorry ladies, meet Bowie Morgan from Louisiana."

No words come from the pretty girl as she turned away ignoring Bowie. Walking proudly back to the building she had appeared from, she disappeared without a backward glance.

"Friendly young lady, ain't she?"

"Please forgive her señors; she does not mean to be rude, but with the loss of her father then the ranch, she has been so sad. Now I am afraid she has turned very bitter." Maria shook her head sadly. "For one so young she has been loaded with many difficulties and hardships taking care of her frail mother."

"I'm sorry Maria; it seems to be hard times for all of us."

"She is a strong young woman, she will survive."

"Tell Miguel to come to the ranch if he wants his old job back." Raker hugged the woman softly and mounted his horse. "Just as soon as he rides in."

"I will tell him when he returns." Maria looked up at the big man. "I think maybe he will ride over to see you, mañana."

"We'll be there." Raker looked down at the woman. "Start packing señora; tell Jackie the ranch needs a good cook if she and her mother would like a job. They'll be welcome and just maybe I can make up for some of the mess I've caused."

"I think Miguel will come to work for you señor, and perhaps some of the others." Maria shrugged. "But she will not come, it would not be proper for a young, unmarried lady to come to work for just men, and she is very proud."

"But, I have known her all her life."

"She will not come, but I will tell her." Maria shook her head. "Times are rough for her, but she still has her pride."

"It is not a handout Maria; she will earn what she makes." Raker stared at the woman. "And you will be there to chaperone her along with her mother."

"I will talk with her."

"You do that, it'll get better, I promise."

Walking back to the small house, Maria stepped through the doorway and discovered Jackie staring in deep thought as Raker and Bowie rode away. "The young gringo, he is a very handsome man and so tall."

"Yes he is, but he is a gunman, Maria."

"Maybe so Jackie, but I can feel he is a good man." The little Mexican woman smiled. "Perhaps we need a gunman like him who is not afraid of Señor Caldwell."

"His kind can only bring grief, guns killed my father."

"Guns are only as bad as the man using them." Maria argued. "This tall one is a good man; I can feel it in him."

"He is a gunman Maria, a cold man and I can feel that in my heart too."

"Perhaps, but the heart is not ruled by reason Jackie, but by love."

"Maria!" Jackie gasped. "I'm not in love with that man, I just met him today."

"Si señorita, but the eyes tell everything, and time is of no meaning when a woman sees a man she is attracted to."

"You're loco." Jackie raced from the room red faced. "I don't even know his name, and I sure don't want him."

"I do not think so, little one," Maria laughed merrily. "I think you have looked at this one."

Chapter 6

Dismounting in front of the barn, Bowie stripped his saddle from the tired gelding and turned the animal into the corral where the work horses stood hipshot in the far corner. Talbert who had been watching them as they rode up walked out to the barn relieved to see the two men home safe. After greeting the old-timer, Bowie tossed his saddle over a saddle rack then surveyed the flat, sandy yard and surrounding pasture before turning his eyes toward the house. The huge oaks covering most of the ranch yard in cool shade are picturesque, standing like giants compared with the smaller oaks and blackjacks. Raker had described the ranch perfectly. It is a beautiful place, a place a man would be happy to live out his days. Bowie turned to where George Raker is unsaddling, and thinks if only the big man's wife was here everything would be peaceful.

"You've been busy, Talbert." Bowie turned his attention on the well raked yard. "I've got to hand it to you old man; you've worked hard cleaning up the ranch today."

"Busy as a ten tailed cat in a room full of rocking chairs." Talbert threw out his chest proud of his work, then glanced sideways at Raker curiously.

Bowie shook his head at the old man, stopping any forthcoming questions. "What you got on the stove, black snake?"

"Funny youngster, funny, nope cornbread, poke salad, and some mighty tasty beans are waiting on you boys."

Raker looked back at the two, then pointed at a gate. "There's a small horse trap with plenty of grass behind the barn, tomorrow we'll turn our horses out there. That way, they'll be close in case we need them during the night."

"Sounds good, it'll sure save Talbert having to hunt them." Bowie laughed.

"Not me, I don't need a horse to ride."

"Just open that back gate that way they can get all the grass and water they can hold." Raker pointed at a smaller gate behind the barn. "Like you said, it'll sure beat walking them up."

Talbert walked behind with Bowie watching Raker as the rancher started back to the house, his shoulders slightly slumped. "Didn't find her, huh?"

"We found her alright, would have been better for him if we hadn't."

"What are you saying Bowie; she dead or something?"

"I guess George will tell you in due time, it's not for me to say."

"While you boys were gone a couple riders sat out there and watched the place for a while." Talbert motioned toward a growth of trees alongside the road. "Rough looking pair I'm telling you, they weren't just plain cowboys."

"Lazy Bar outfit I reckon, we ran into some of them hard cases ourselves today."

"George didn't lie to us it is a beautiful home place, but without his woman I figure it means nothing to him now."

"It means something alright." Bowie stared towards the house. "What it means Talbert, is now we have a private war all our own, if I'm not mistaken."

"War, I don't understand, what do you mean?" Talbert scratched his shaggy grey head. "I thought the war was over, who are we fighting now?"

"Give it some time, old man. You'll find out pretty quick if I don't miss my guess."

Arriving at the house, Bowie and Talbert found Raker already sitting on the front porch, staring off at the far pastures almost in a trance. In the fading light the big man's face is a mask, hard to read but plainly full of hate. Absently, Raker pulled out a sack of tobacco and rolls himself a smoke.

"You want a cup of coffee before you eat supper George?" Talbert asked from the doorway of the house.

"Sure Talbert, thank you."

"I'll bring you a cup too, Bowie."

Watching Talbert as he entered the house, Raker looked over at Bowie. "I expect my cattle are all gone, but come tomorrow anything I find running on my range; I'm gonna slap a Circle R Brand on."

"That could cause trouble George, real trouble." Bowie shrugged. "We ain't rustlers and there's the law."

"I want trouble Bowie, killing trouble." Raker swore, then pulled on the cigarette hard. "I had a wife, a hundred head of mama cows with calves and bulls when I left here. Now I've got no wife, daughter, nothing. Speaking of the law, out here there is no law, except the law you make yourself."

"You mean kinda like dog eat dog?"

"That's exactly what I mean, and starting tomorrow this dog is gonna do the eating."

"Okay by me, you're the boss."

"I told you once today, you and Talbert can ride out anytime you want to, this ain't your fight." Raker stared out into the darkening evening. "I'll send you what money I owe you soon as I get it."

"I believe we've already had this conversation once today, we'll stick."

"I know we have and I appreciate your help, all of it."

"That's what friends are for."

"You didn't take notice as we rode from town, but we passed several head of my cattle with their brands changed to the Lazy Bar."

"You sure they were your cows, Longhorns all look alike to me."

"If you were raised out here, worked and sweated for every cow, you'd know them, I'll guarantee it."

"I reckon you're right."

"I know I'm right."

"You reckon your wife told him to change the brands?"

"Maybe she did if so, I reckon it was her right, but now Norma is no longer my wife." Raker flipped his burned down smoke away and accepted the steaming cup from Talbert. "I aim to have my cattle back, whatever the cost."

"You boys come get it or I'll feed it to the snake."

Daylight came early, finding the three friends already at the long table finishing their hot black coffee. After warning Talbert to stay alert, Bowie and Raker walked out to the barn and inspected the shape of the corrals. After patching up a few holes in the fence and the pole run that was used as a squeeze chute, the men saddle up and start for the back side of the rolling ranch. Several head of longhorns, branded with the Lazy Bar, shy off then turn and stampede into the heavy mesquite with their tails in the air as they pass. Ignoring the cattle and letting them go, the men head for the back side of the large ranch before swinging back and starting their drive toward the home corrals. Raker is quiet, only speaking as he points out several older cows he recognizes as his own and hollering for Bowie to push them in with the bunch they have been driving.

"You watch those longhorns." The big Rancher pointed at a sharp horned cow. "They'll tear the guts clean out of a horse then take in after you."

"I'm watching them; they look kinda ornery to me."

"Amazing ain't it Bowie, how simple a Circle R brand can be made into a Lazy Bar." Raker shook his head. "I've already counted ten head of my cows with changed brands since we've been out this morning."

Bowie only nods, unfamiliar with western ranching and cattle markings, he is still able to pick out the same badly altered brands on several cows as they push the small groups of cattle together. Raker's face hardened as he studied the altered brands on some of the same cows he drove in from south Texas just a few years back.

"I have seen several with changed brands myself, now that you point it out." Bowie pointed at a large, rangy, slab-sided brindle cow with huge horns. "Like her."

"I take it you're not too familiar with brands?"

"No sir, in Louisiana we never owned cattle." Bowie slapped at a horsefly. "We weren't that privileged, cattle were for the rich land-owners."

Raker looked over confused at the tall man beside him. "I thought Jim Bowie was rich and all that, I thought...."

"You thought my family was rich?" Bowie laughed. "Not hardly, my mother raised three children alone on a hardscrabble piece of land that barely fed us."

"What happened to your father?"

"I don't rightly know. When I grew older, my uncle explained to me that he left Louisiana when I was about four years old, just a few jumps ahead of the local law."

"Why was the law after him?"

"Killed a man was the story." Bowie shrugged. "That's all I know."

"You've never seen him again in all these years?"

"No." Bowie pointed out a red cow, changing the subject. "There's another one, I believe."

Raker reined in and studied the cow. "She is another one like the brindle back there. She was one of the first, Norma and I drove them here from south Texas going on eight years ago."

Noticing the sloppy burn marks over the old brand, Bowie frowned. "Even I can see how someone botched up changing her brand."

The first day's drive netted thirty-two longhorn cows and one bull enclosed inside the horse trap behind the barn. Closing the pole gate Raker has Bowie wait outside while he slowly pushes the wild cattle on into the pole corral that links with the barn. "That'll hold them, not a half bad gather for one day."

Some of the cows milling about the corral have unbranded calves following at their sides while others are dry. The bull Raker doesn't recognize other than he carries a Lazy Bar Brand. "Get a fire going Talbert; the Circle R is back in the cattle business."

The smell of burning hair and hide drift across the barnyard as the longhorns bawl and fight the chutes as the hot running iron is touched to their thick hides. Whirling as they are released from the confining, narrow chute, the maddened cattle come charging around the heavy corral wild eyed, intent on goring anything in their path. The horses are safely tucked away in a separate corral, out of harm's way as the enraged cows hook the corral rails trying to get to their bawling calves as they are branded. Smoke, dust, and dirt particles drift thickly across the barnyard and corral as they brand the cows and their calves then release them back to the open pasture.

"That's a good day's drive." Raker dropped the branding iron beside the fire. "We'll make another one come first light."

"What about the Lazy Bar cows you didn't brand?"

"We'll hold them in the corral tonight then push them west toward Lazy Bar range come morning before we start another sweep of the range." Raker toed dirt on the fire. "If we find any of ours off to the west, we'll push them back this way and brand them before we start tomorrow's drive in the east pasture."

Talbert watched the stirred-up cows from a top rail. "Them things sure work up a mad, don't they George?"

"They do Talbert; I'm telling you old son, don't get caught afoot out in the open pasture if they got a newborn calf." Raker warned. "They're faster than a tornado and meaner than a cyclone."

"Whatever."

Talbert suddenly straightened pointing his finger as a lone rider appears far out on the road riding at a slow trot towards the ranch. A wide Mexican hat recognizable even at the distance covers the rider's head, identifying him as a Mexican. All three men stop what they are doing and watch as the rider draws closer.

"It's Miguel Ortiz." Raker walked a few steps from the corral. "Well, I'll be."

The slight rider pulls up and sits silently, staring at the three dust covered men then looked over at the penned cattle. "It is good to see you, jefe."

"And you Miguel, where are Maria and your children?"

The dark eyes sweep over the corral one more time before turning back to where the three men stand. "You have been very busy señor. I see some of your cows have found their way back here."

"They have."

"I think this will cause much trouble with Senor Caldwell." Miguel smiled. "He will say you steal his cattle."

"His cattle Miguel? You know these old cows; we worked them many a time together in the old days."

"Si, I know this is true, but tell me who will take the word of a Mexican over a rich Americano?" The dark skinned man shrugged.

"I would." Talbert spoke up.

"I have come here to work for you jefe to fight if necessary, but until the trouble is over, Maria will stay with the others where she will be safe."

"I understand."

"Then it is agreed, I will work for you." Miguel dropped lightly to the ground. "The other men will come soon if you want them."

"They will have a job here."

"I will send word to them."

As the Lazy Bar cattle broke from the corrals at a dead run, Raker, Bowie, and Miguel rode in behind the small herd whooping and hollering driving the half-wild cattle back towards the west and their home range. Five miles down the dirt road toward Medicine Mound the horses are reined in allowing the cattle that have already slowed to a walk to scatter out on the grassland and settle down to graze.

"You see them." Bowie looked across at Raker, whose attention is on the grazing cattle.

"I've seen them alright."

"Lazy Bar riders." Bowie looked to where the men are sitting. "I recognize them as some of the hard cases that stopped us yesterday."

"Yeah, too bad they don't come and stop us today."

"I figure they'll come soon enough." Bowie waved his hand, making sure the riders know he has seen them. "Soon as we drop our guard, they'll be on us like bees on honey."

"I'll guarantee your right about that, this big he hog Bacon Caldwell will know about the brand changing soon as the Lazy Bar riders get back to the ranch." Raker reined his gelding towards home. "I hope he comes looking for me, I do believe we have something to discuss."

"That outfit must have cattle strung out for miles."

"They should have, seems they've branded every cow they could put iron to for over four years now." Raker shook his head in disgust. "I saw a cow and calf that belong to me a ways back; we'll pick them up and drive them home."

"Si señor, the Caldwell riders have taken many head of cattle on the open range." Miguel removed his sombrero and wiped his face. "These are evil men."

"Does Caldwell have one honest cowboy working for him?"

"No Señor Bowie, I do not think an honest man would work for Señor Caldwell."

The sun has just began to set in the west as the hungry men unsaddle and head for the house. To their surprise Talbert has a hot supper waiting, already laid out on the long table. Small talk settles around the kitchen as the men enjoy their coffee and the hot food that steams from tin plates. Smiling as the men brag on his cooking the old man pulled out a chair and sat down.

"Looks like you boys pushed in several head again today."

Raker nodded as he set his coffee down. "Twenty-two cows and eighteen calves, all told."

"You fixing to brand this new bunch come morning?"

"If the sun comes up and the river doesn't rise, I aim to."

"Have company today, Talbert?" Bowie inquired as he picks up a wedge of cornbread.

"Snake or human?"

Bowie frowned across the table. "They back, again?"

"I seen them early this morning." Talbert admitted. "Some watched you ride out then followed you. Others kept me company until they seen you boys driving in the cows."

"We saw some of them west of here this morning, but we had our hands full trying to drive in the cows we picked up. I didn't see any watching us here as we rode in."

"Well sir, they were here and they were a mean looking bunch I'll tell you." Talbert blinked his eyes as he talked. "Mean looking I'm telling you, and they seem to take a special interest when they saw your new hand riding with you."

"You mean Miguel?"

"Yep, they were looking him over as y'all rode off." Talbert answered. "I couldn't hear what they said, but they were sure wagging their heads."

"Just keep that scattergun loaded and ready." Bowie warned. "It'll knock the meanness out of a rattlesnake."

"Don't you tell me my business, young Mister Morgan." Talbert huffed. "I was taking care of myself before you were whelped."

"Kinda touchy ain't you, old man?"

Talbert grinned. "Nah, just working up a mad so' I'll be ready whenever those fellers come a calling."

"You just be careful." Raker pulled out the makings and rolled himself a smoke. "These boys ain't anything to fool around with."

"He's the one that should be careful right now." Talbert motioned towards Miguel. "Those boys seem a mite peeved that he was here working for you."

Bowie thought over Talbert's words for a few seconds. "George, maybe you should have Miguel bring his family here for their own safety."

"You think they'd be safer here than where they are?"

"At least here we'll be able to watch after them, at the settlement Caldwell could send his men in and do them some harm and they wouldn't have any help at all."

"He's right Miguel." Raker looked over at the small Mexican. "But, it's your call."

"Si patrón, Señor Bowie is right." Miguel rolled himself a smoke. "I will bring them here tomorrow."

"Good, is your woman a good cook? We need one."

"Funny, very funny, Bowie Morgan." Talbert grunted.

"Si señor, my oldest son Carlos will be able to help around the ranch."

"You have a son that old?" Bowie can't believe the young looking Mexican is old enough to have a son in his teens.

"Si he is a good son, if I can keep him here on the ranch."

"What do you mean Miguel?" Raker looked at the man curious.

"He likes to roam the land, he likes to fish and hunt."

"Sounds like he's all boy to me." Bowie grinned. "I was much the same way as a lad."

"Si señor, he is a good son but, the open range is a dangerous place for one so young."

Raker nods. "Good then it's settled, you bring your family here. It'll be like it used to be, at least some of it will."

"Mañana señor, tomorrow I will bring them if you don't need me, and señor it will be like old times again soon, you will see."

"Bring Jackie Harrison and her mother if she will come."

"I will try señor, but she is a very head strong young woman." Miguel shook his head. "Very much woman."

"I'll drink to that." Bowie whispered to himself.

Bowie had slipped out to the barn early to watch as Miguel started the old wagon west for Medicine Mound. Saddling his gelding quickly, he starts to mount up when George appeared from the shadows.

"You want me to ride out with you Bowie?"

Whirling in a crouch, Bowie shakes his head. "You surprised me George, be careful doing that."

"Sorry."

"I just thought I'd shadow Miguel into town and make sure he doesn't run into any trouble from Caldwell's men." Bowie mounted. "Tell Talbert to keep supper hot for us."

"Alright Bowie but you remember, we've been told every one of Caldwell's men are experts with a rifle or pistol." George wets the cigarette paper with his tongue. "Folks say he doesn't hire men for their looks or expertise with a rope, and I believe them."

"Thanks George, that's a good thing to know."

"It is if you want to stay alive." The sulphur lights the area momentarily as it is struck. "I'm telling you Bowie; Miguel says they're the meanest pack of curly wolves he's ever seen."

"Adiós, see you at supper."

George pulled on his smoke watching as the tall man kicked his gelding and loped out across the grassland, shadowing Miguel. "I hope so."

The small, sleepy town of Medicine Mound slowly starts to wake up as Bowie sits his horse in a side alley. He had watched as Miguel passed along its dusty street, driving the wagon straight through town without stopping. Skirting the buildings he followed slowly behind the wagon, staying just out of sight beyond the brush bordering the road. He doesn't figure the Lazy Bar hands will be this close to town so early, but he wants to make sure Miguel and his family get back to the Circle R safely. Pulling up at the edge of the Mexican houses, Bowie sat his gelding and watched as Miguel embraced the small woman then helped load their meager possessions onto the wagon. One older boy about twelve years old, probably the son Miguel mentioned, carried two smaller children and placed them into the back of the wagon. The youngster stood aside as another man and woman with a small baby climb into the wagon bed.

"Well, looks like old Talbert is gonna have plenty of help cooking." Bowie mumbled under his breath as the wagon lurched forward. With all the grown-ups, corn-shuck bedding, bits of furniture, blankets, and children, the old wagon had quite a load as it starts out for the Circle R.

Retracing his path back to the west, Bowie stays as close as he can to the laughing noise of the children wanting to keep the wagon in sight in case they need him. Reining in behind the livery stable as Miguel stopped in front of the mercantile store, he watched as the young boy raced inside and returned with the young white woman, Jackie Harrison. Even from this distance he has to admit, she is a thing of beauty. Tall and willowy with long auburn hair, her teeth shine white as snow when she smiled up at Miguel and his wife.

"You should come with us, Miss Jackie." Miguel pleaded with the girl. "Señor Raker wishes you and your Mother to come to the ranch."

"So does Señor Bowie." Maria laughed. "The tall, handsome Señor Bowie Morgan."

"Maria." The young woman blushed, then turned to where Miguel sits listening curiously. "He didn't say that, did he?"

"Who Señor Raker or Señor Morgan?"

"Maria."

"He is muy handsome for a gringo." Maria laughed again. "Muy handsome, don't you think."

"What are you talking about Maria?" Miguel looked confused at both women. "What are you saying?"

"Oh, it is nothing my husband." Maria smiled coyly. "Just women talking about love."

"Love?" Miguel looked at his wife, then at Jackie. "Who is in love?"

From where he waits, Bowie can't tell what they are whispering about, but he can plainly see Jackie shake her head as Maria pointed off to the east and seemed to plead with her. Finally shaking his sombrero,

Miguel clucked to the team just as the girl called out for him to wait. Disappearing inside the store she returned with an older woman and two bags, then smiled at Carlos as he climbed down and helped them into the wagon. Maria laughed happily as the old wagon rolled out of town with only a farewell wave coming from the Scotts standing in front of the mercantile.

"Perhaps the señorita was already packed." Maria teased. "Perhaps she sees the tall young gringo in her dreams."

"Maria, you hush." Jackie shook her head.

The heavy team of horses is pulling hard, straining, making the trace chains taut as they pass across some of the seldom-used roads. The sand is deep in places, making the heavily burdened wagon wheels sink deep into what passes for a road. Following far off to the side of the trail, Bowie watches as the older son of Miguel and the girl jump nimbly over the side and land on the ground. The other Mexican man follows them lightening the wagon as they start up a small grade. Suddenly, from a heavy stand of Mesquite trees and brush four riders appear in front of the team forcing the wagon to stop. Bowie kicked his horse into a trot and slipped unseen into the same underbrush the Lazy Bar riders have just vacated.

"Where you headed, Miguel?" A heavyset rider comes close to the wagon and leaned from his horse, grinning at the women.

"East, señor."

"East?" The big man eyes Maria and Jackie. "Where east?"

"We're going home." Miguel pulled the frightened Maria closer to him.

"Home? I thought you people were from old Mexico and that is west and south of here." The man pointed over his shoulder then spurred his horse closer to the wagon. "What's your name, honey?"

"She is my wife señor."

"I know who she is." Scraggly teeth show from the ruddy face as the man grinned evilly. "Maybe I'll make her my wife, Mex."

Watching as the riders edge their animals closer to the wagon causing fear to come into the women and children's faces, Bowie nudges his horse and rides up behind the unsuspecting riders. Only the men's geldings are aware of the newcomer as their rider's attention is focused fully on the two women. A surge of relief shows on Miguel's face as he recognized the tall form of Bowie as he moved from his place of concealment and rides into plain view.

The big man started to reach out a hairy hand for Maria when Bowie spoke. "I wouldn't, fat man."

The beefy hand dropped quickly as the command coming from so close behind him temporarily freezes the riders as every head turns. "Who are you, mister?"

"Circle R, name's Bowie Morgan."

"You're the young fellow that rides for Raker ain't you?"

"That'd be me alright." Bowie spoke softly. "Now you boys drop your weapons."

"And if we don't?"

"Well my friend, when you turn that horse you best make your play." Bowie nodded at Miguel. "Drive the wagon out of the way Miguel, far out of the way."

The wagon had barely moved when one of the riders whirled his horse and made a grab for his pistol. Placing two slugs into the man before he can fire his weapon, Bowie turned on the others stopping them from drawing just as Miguel lunged from the wagon and landed on the back of the fat man's horse. The blade of a large skinning knife flashes in the sun as the fat rider pulls at the crazy demon on his back just as the sharp knife plunges deep into his neck. Only a scream comes from the dying man as he falls from the spooked horse. Falling with the wounded man, Miguel retrieved his knife and plunged it deep into the man's stomach.

"Maybe next time señor, you will respect my woman." The small Mexican wiped the blade on the dead body then climbed back onto the wagon.

"Like I said, you boys drop your weapons then take this garbage back to your boss." Bowie pointed his pistol at the two surviving riders. "You tell him he's no longer running this country, tell him he better send Mrs. Raker home or I'll take it personal and pay him a visit real soon."

The riders grudgingly drop their weapons then dismount, starting toward the body of the fat men. One of the men looks up at Bowie and frowned. "You ain't heard the last of this, mister."

Dismounting Bowie motioned toward the man's pistol. "Pick it up and we'll finish it now."

Dropping his eyes to the ground the man shook slightly as the tall man stepped closer to him. The silent watchers hear the hard slap of an open hand as Bowie slapped the man knocking him to the ground. Looking up at the figure looming over him, the man shakes his head. "I ain't fighting."

"What about you?" Bowie glared at the other rider. "Do you think I've heard the last of this?"

"I ain't getting killed for Caldwell mister." The rider stepped backwards. "I'm riding out of here, right now."

"I'd say that's a smart move." Gathering all the weapons the men had Bowie placed them in the wagon then mounted. "You tell Caldwell what I said or I'll look you two up personally."

"We'll tell him."

Maria looked to where Jackie is sitting wide-eyed. "See, what did I tell you, we need this one."

"And I told you, he is a gunman."

"Your eyes say different young one." Maria smiled. "You are proud of him, you cannot deny this."

"Maria, I swear."

Chapter 7

For a solid week, they combed the ranch and surrounding grasslands looking for cattle until only Circle R stock with their re-burned brands are seen grazing on the Circle R. Seventy-one cows, three bulls, and fifty-three calves had been rounded up, driven into the corrals, tallied and now carried the Circle R Brand. Sweeping the range for days, riding through rain and wind no more strays are found, finally Raker halts the roundup; only Circle R cattle now graze the ranch. Life on the Circle R settles down to the normal ranch life of cowmen as the men ride the range checking on the widely spread cattle and pushing them back to their own range. While away from the ranch daily, they leave Talbert to watch over the women and children. With the double-barrel shotgun across his arm, the old soldier prowls the ranch, making sure to keep out of their way as the women cook and clean the large ranch house.

At supper or early morning breakfast, only brief words of greeting have passed between Bowie and Jackie as they meet each other in the kitchen or out on the porch. Both are young, inexperienced, and both seem too embarrassed in each other's presence to carry on much of a conversation of any kind.

"I was hoping to round up more, but I reckon we didn't do too badly." Raker sat leaning against the porch after supper holding a notched piece of wood, showing the cattle count. "But, at least we've got a start of a herd."

"I sure can't figure Caldwell letting us round up cows that he claims." Talbert puffed on his old pipe. "Especially, after Bowie killed his two riders last week."

Raker shrugged. "Me neither, but he did."

"I didn't kill the fat man they called Maxwell, Miguel did."

Miguel looked over at the others. "The other dead man is Burnet, but the fat one Maxwell, is the one people call Brazos Red."

"You sure?"

"Si señor, this is him alright, word is he's has killed over ten men in stand up fights." Miguel nodded. "A real bad man killed by a small Mexican, with a big knife."

"It's hard to figure, alright." Raker rolled his own smoke. "You'd think Caldwell would throw all of his men against us."

"Way I got it figured, he ain't fixing to let you keep them or this ranch, it's that simple."

"You could be right in your figuring, old man." Raker struck a sulphur and looked over at Talbert. "Just could be."

"Could be? They're planning on killing you off George Raker, you better count on it." Talbert smacked his lips as he swallowed coffee. "I believe whoever the feller with the Sharps was that shot you back in Virginia is here now and he will probably try to ventilate that ornery hide of yours again."

"Are you telling me the man with the Sharps is back here in Texas all the way from Virginia?" Raker looked over at Talbert. "That's crazy."

"It may be crazy, but has it ever occurred to you that all the men that rode away from here with you are dead George." Talbert frowned. "Sure wish we had a way of knowing how the others died, I'd bet it was Sharps poisoning."

"You know, he just might be right, there is something odd about all the others being killed." Bowie looked over at the old man. "He may be on to something, George."

"Then all we have to do is find a man with a Sharps rifle and we've got the man that shot me, it's not that simple boys, half the buffalo hunters on the frontier carry a Sharps Rifle."

"Not ranch hands." Talbert argued. "Cowboys don't carry a heavy rifle like that working cattle."

"That's true enough." Bowie looked over at the old man. "Who said you couldn't think for yourself, Talbert."

"I'm telling you George, you better watch your back, I can't figure why, but I've got me a bad feeling about these cattle and Caldwell leaving us alone like he has."

"I'm a hard man to kill you old reprobate."

"Well now, that's downright comforting to know, I'm beginning to like it here."

"It's good you like it here so much, maybe we can find you some work to do." Bowie grinned. "Since the women have taken over your cooking and cleaning jobs."

"Why you young scamp, I'm working like a dog now."

Bowie finished his coffee and looked over fondly at the old man. "Back home our dogs worked hard too, scratching fleas."

"Humph," Is all that comes from Talbert as he gathered the dirty cups and stomped off. "Young whipper snapper."

"Course now, we could always make you our chief snake hunter." Bowie smiled slightly as Jackie walked by shaking her head.

"Yeah, and I could quit."

Jackie stopped in front of Bowie and frowned. "Bowie Morgan, don't you have anything better to do than pick on Talbert?"

"Yes ma'am, I do for a fact." Bowie quickly exited the porch to everyone's laughter.

Brace Caldwell stalked the Lazy Bar like a caged wolf, pacing back and forth across his brother's ample office. The younger Caldwell, along with the other Lazy Bar hands had watched as George Raker rounded up every cow on the Circle R for a solid week. They knew Raker had rebranded the ones he recognized as his or any showing their brands were altered. Several times as he watched the roundup from his place of concealment Brace had raised the Sharps, but each time Bacon had pushed the rifle down, refusing to let him kill the Circle R owner. Caldwell knows the talk is out, people in Medicine Mound have heard that Raker is still alive and has returned to his ranch. To shoot him now, out on the range could cause unwanted problems. People would suspect him especially since the reb soldier had ridden through town and falsely reported Raker's death years before. If Norma ever found out Raker had returned alive from the east and she hadn't been told, she would guess he was responsible for his killing. Lastly there is the law; none exists in Medicine Mound or anywhere near here. Nevertheless, killing a man like George Raker could bring a Texas Ranger or even a Federal Marshal into the Medicine Mound area real quick.

In town, in plain sight, and in front of witnesses, Raker can be killed with no questions asked. People would just explain it as a jealous ex-husband recently returned from the war, mad about his cattle, mad about his wife, and mad about life in general. They will think he has a chip on his shoulder, picked a fight with some of the Lazy Bar riders, and was killed. No law would become involved, no questions asked, just a simple case of self-defense.

Bacon Caldwell grinned as he poured Brace a shot glass full of whiskey. "Calm down Brother, the cattle don't matter. We'll take them back as soon as Mister Raker is out of the way, besides it's just a piddling few."

"I wouldn't call almost a hundred head of cattle a piddling few Brother." Brace cussed. "Now that bunch has gone and done in two of our top guns."

"Brazos Red Maxwell can be replaced." Bacon recalled the fat gunfighter had been a top gun out of Wichita or Abilene he can't remember which, but he was supposedly the best and now he's been killed by an unknown. "Apparently, he was just an overrated fat man."

"Maybe he was a fat man, but he was fast with a gun Brother. He was second man in these parts only to Frank Fisher. You're supposed to have the best gun hands in Texas on your payroll and still Raker is running around healthy as a grain fed horse." Brace shook his head. "Folks are gonna see this and start getting brave again."

"I've got another gun hand, which I'm fixing to send for that is, if things get any worse."

"Just more wasted money thrown on the ground." Brace cussed. "I'm betting things are fixing to get a whole lot worse, I'm telling you Bacon, Raker and his bunch aren't anything to mess around with, they are a rough bunch."

"This man is the best, the fastest man with a gun I've ever seen and he's completely without a conscience." Bacon ignored his brother's words. "I've seen him gun down Stone Wakely in Dodge City last year, that's where I got his name from."

"Who are you talking about?" Brace is curious. "And who the devil was Stone Wakely, never heard of him myself."

"Cord Alvord." Bacon had never forgotten the gunman's name or his cold looks. He even jotted down the town he worked out of and stuck it in his desk drawer. "I'll send for him, if and when we need his services."

"Is he really that good?"

"He is, but he comes high." Bacon admitted. "This Stone Wakely was supposed to be the fastest gun in Kansas when they met. We'll just wait a spell, then if we need him."

"What about all the cattle Raker has rebranded?"

"With what we stand to gain after Raker is dead, a few head of cattle is just a drop in the bucket." Bacon downed a shot glass of whiskey. "We'll get them back, don't fret yourself."

"Does your wife know her ex is back?"

"No, we haven't been into town in three weeks." Bacon shook his head. "I expect she's the only one in the country that doesn't know he's back."

"You gonna have Fisher do it, or do I get the honors?"

"Not you Brother." Bacon sat down at his desk. "You had your chance."

"I told you what happened."

"Just kidding with you Brace; I just don't want you mixing in this in front of the town."

"You don't want your wife finding out your brother killed her ex, is that it?"

"Something like that, it would be better if you weren't a part of the killing."

"You're getting soft, Bacon." Brace shrugged. "But it doesn't matter, I'm sure Fisher can handle one ex-soldier."

"That's what I pay him for." Bacon shrugged. "But then again, I thought Maxwell and three other gun slicks could have handled one man and a wagon load of greasers."

"What about me Brother, am I included in your thoughts too?"

"Truthfully Brother," Bacon sat back down heavily at his desk, "I figured you could have killed him, yes."

"Do you have any idea how hard it was to slip into the middle of a Reb army, ask around for the man, identify him, then hang around until you get the opportunity to kill him?"

"No I reckon I don't, sorry."

Brace nodded, then poured himself another whiskey. "It ain't easy, that's for sure."

Jackie stepped out onto the front porch where she found Bowie sitting alone, his feet dangling off the end of the high porch. Pulling a chair up next to the tall man, she sat down and looked out across the flat rangeland.

"I've always loved this place, almost as much as I do the Diamond H."

Bowie nodded and looked up at her, surprised she is talking to him. "Yes it is beautiful, and peaceful."

"You like peace and quiet, Mister Morgan?"

"Don't you, Miss Harrison?"

"I do very much, but I'm afraid there will be no peace for me until the Diamond H is returned to me and my mother."

"Is it that important to you?"

The girl's eyes flashed across at him. "Wouldn't getting your home back be important to you, Mister Morgan, that is if someone stole it from you?"

"I suppose it would." Bowie nodded. "I would feel more comfortable Miss Harrison, if you would call me Bowie or Morgan."

"Alright then, I'll call you Bowie." The girl stared into his eyes. "If that isn't too personal?"

"Nothing you can say would be too personal, Miss Harrison."

"Then Bowie, you may call me Jackie." Standing she smiled. "Good night, sir."

"Good night, ma'am."

Maria smiled brightly from where she is washing dishes as Jackie entered the kitchen door. "Not a word señora, nada, nothing."

"But Señorita Jackie, I was just going to give you the dish towel."

"In a pig's eye you were." Jackie took the towel and shook her head.

"He is muy bonito."

Jackie blushed, then nodded her agreement. "Yes Maria, he is handsome, now wash dishes."

Early morning found the small town of Medicine Mound shrouded in a quiet mist as Talbert drives the wagon into town and stopping alongside the general store tie rail. Tying the team, the old soldier climbed stiffly down from the wagon.

"We still got money?" Talbert looked longingly to where a man is sweeping the porch outside the only saloon in town. "I need me a drink, riding that wagon is starting to get to me."

"You want to go down to the doc and get you some medicine for what ails you?" Bowie grinned. "Maybe he'll have something to rub on your posterior."

"Funny, very funny." Talbert frowned. "Nothing ails me that a good shot of panther juice won't fix."

"Soon as we get our supplies, we'll have us a drink." Bowie checked the loads in both pistols before dismounting then followed Raker inside the store. "Maybe even two, one for your gizzard and one for your backsides."

This time, the Scotts aren't surprised or shocked as the rancher walked through the door and into their store. Both come over and welcome the three men, especially Raker as the bell hanging over the door jingles. Several old men look up from where they're sitting around the cast iron stove smoking as they push through the door. Curious eyes cast their way, but only one man stood up and greets Raker.

"It's sure good to see you back George, we heard you were dead."

Raker shook hands with the man then nodded at the others. "Seems everybody in these parts thinks I'm dead, Matt."

"No offense old friend, but that was the rumor."

"Well sir, as you can see I'm still alive and kicking." Raker remembered stopping by the man's small ranch for coffee on several different occasions back in better times before the war. "Are you still running cattle down on the Cinnamon?"

Dropping his eyes, the rancher shrugged. "No, Bacon Caldwell put me out of business when he first arrived."

"You sell out to him?"

"I reckon you could call it that." The slender man's face turned hard. "Didn't have much choice, my cattle were rustled and I couldn't get the money to pay my taxes."

"Rustled, who would rustle cattle that weren't worth a copper cent?"

"Don't know, but somehow Bacon Caldwell got his hands on the lien I had signed on my ranch and called it in." Matt shook his head. "That paper was all the way over in Wichita, but somehow he wound up with it."

Motioning the man off to the side of the store out of earshot, Raker looked into the shorter man's eyes. "We go back a long ways Matt Sloan tell me, what has happened around here."

The blue eyes looked up curiously. "You're serious ain't you George, you really don't know. Caldwell has everything sewed up around here, even your wife Norma."

"I know about my wife, I want to know the particulars, tell me."

Looking behind them at the old-timers who are watching and straining their ears to listen, Matt nodded toward the door. "Let's go out on the porch away from prying ears."

Thirty minutes later, Raker stood up and shook hands with the rancher. "Tell me Matt, do you think Norma really believed me dead?"

"She did George, that woman loved you more than life itself, she would never have remarried if there was a chance you were alive." Matt looked across at the saloon. "I talked to her a couple times before she married Bacon Caldwell."

"Matt, why did she do it?"

"She didn't do it for herself, George. She had the baby to consider and there was no one else in this country to help her." Matt shrugged. "She didn't have a choice none at all, we were all destitute and starving, shucks we had potatoes but no grease to cook em with, so we ate them raw."

"Where are you hanging your hat now?"

"I'm wrangling broncs for Caldwell." Matt scowled. "Yes, I'm having to eat crow, but I had to have a job and eating crow is better than starving."

"You don't have to eat crow anymore, we'll be riding out as soon as we re-supply." Raker watched as three Lazy Bar riders dismounted at the saloon. "You've got a job at the Circle R if you want one."

"It could cause you some trouble, hiring me."

"I've already got trouble Matt." Raker's eyes never wavered from the three hard cases. "A little bit more will fit in nicely."

"Alright, you've got yourself a hand." Matt looked across at the saloon again. ""George, I ain't prying, and you don't have to answer if you don't want to."

"What is it?"

"Does Norma know you're back?"

"Caldwell does, I don't know about her." Raker shrugged. "I just don't know for sure if she does or doesn't."

"I'm a betting she doesn't."

"Maybe not." The big man studied the riders. "But she's gonna and soon."

Matt nodded across the street where a tall rider stands on the porch eyeing both of them. "That's Frank Fisher."

"Who is he?"

"He's a fast gun out of Dodge City, brought in here by Caldwell to do his dirty work."

"A real bad man, huh?"

"Bad enough." Matt spit. "He's mean clear through, and there's another bad one out there at the Lazy Bar ranch."

"Who's that?"

"Well, actually there's two bad ones, Brazos Red Maxwell and a gun hand named Burnet."

"Both men you named are dead."

"I hadn't heard that." Matt was surprised. "When, how?"

"Maxwell and some of the other Lazy Bar riders tangled with Bowie and Miguel yesterday on their way home from town." Raker rolled himself another smoke. "Brazos Red and the rider named Burnet weren't fast enough."

Matt looked over to where Bowie has exited the store. "He must be a stroke of lightning with that pistol."

"What about the other one, Brace Caldwell?" Raker didn't mention Miguel killing Maxwell for fear he or his family could become a target for Caldwell.

"Brace Caldwell, he's the younger brother of Bacon Caldwell." Matt's hands clinch into fists. "He's not Fisher or Maxwell by any means. He's a back shooter, a coward, and he's got that long-range Sharps that he favors to do his killings, and that makes him even more dangerous."

"Brace Caldwell." Raker recalls what Talbert had said. "And he carries a Sharps?"

"Yep, I've never seen him without that rifle and he's pure poison with it." Matt built himself a smoke. "Won himself a turkey shoot right here in the street with it couple years back. Blew the bird's head clean off at a hundred yards."

"Well now, seems old Talbert may have been right." Raker nodded. "Tell me Matt, has Brace Caldwell been gone from these parts for a spell?"

"He was gone for over two years, but I seen him a couple weeks back, passing down the west road wearing a Confederate uniform and a long filthy beard, unlike Brace." Matt recalled. "He's all cleaned up now and riding the range every day, I hear he's been watching y'all round up cattle."

Raker blinked, his thoughts turn to Talbert's dire warning about the unknown man and the Sharps buffalo gun. Shaking his head he knows Brace Caldwell was no doubt the shooter back in Virginia. He also remembers the report on several of the local men that rode east with him and Captain Harrison to fight. Sniper, he recalls the word used to describe the deaths of the men that had ridden with them four years ago. Apparently, Talbert might have been right about that too. Shaking his head, he motioned Bowie over to them.

"Bowie this is Matt Sloan."

Shaking hands Bowie nodded, but kept his attention on the tall rider across the street. "Good to meet you, Mister Sloan."

"The handle is Matt."

"Okay Matt, mines Bowie."

"Matt's coming to work for us."

Bowie only nods as he continues to watch the saloon porch. The tall Lazy Bar Rider seems to be intentionally staring across at the three of them like he is throwing out a challenge for them to cross the street. The man's stare never wavers, he is up to something even from across the street, Bowie can smell trouble afoot and on the wind. The man has an intimidating look with his hawk-like face, huge nose, and stooped shoulders. It was a deformed physique and face that would be hard to forget. Only the eyes are hidden, the stooped gunman keeps his felt hat pulled low, hiding his cruel eyes.

"Like I told George," Matt nodded across at the stooped man, "That'd be Frank Fisher standing over there."

"Yeah, I've seen him once, he's the one that done all the tough talking last week at the Lazy Bar."

"Uh huh, I remember that face myself." Raker straightened. "Hard face to forget."

The three men watch as Talbert starts placing boxes and sacks of supplies into the wagon. "Matt, you help that old man over there load the wagon. Just pay him no attention, his name is Talbert, his bark is a lot worse than his bite."

"The way Fisher is watching us I smell trouble George, you watch yourself." Matt repeated. "Like I said, he's a curly wolf with that gun of his."

"Y'all get the supplies loaded then bring Talbert over and we'll wet our whistles before pulling out." Bowie turned sideways as he unfastened his tie down. "He needs some help for his backside."

"Do what?"

"Nothing Matt." Raker laughed. "Just bring Talbert over when you're finished loading."

Matt looked across at Fisher then repeated his warning as he shakes his head. "You're the boss George, but listen to me, Frank Fisher is one salty dog, pure greased lightning with that gun of his."

"Thanks Matt, for the warning."

Frank Fisher turned and followed the other two men back into the saloon as Bowie and Raker step down into the dusty street and start for the saloon. "I doubt you're in his class with a six-gun George, let me handle Fisher if trouble starts."

"No sir, this is my fight Bowie Morgan, my town and my problem." Raker shook his head. "I'm a grown man."

"And I'm your partner, remember?"

"I remember." The rancher growled. "I'm thanking you for your offer; if he gets me you get the whole ranch."

"Matt wouldn't lie about the man, I figure Fisher is a bad man." Bowie followed Raker ignoring his last remark. "By the look of him, I'd say he's on the prod looking for trouble."

"I can't allow you to take my part in this." Raker grabbed Bowie's arm. "It'd make me feel yellow, worse still it would make me look yellow in front of the whole town."

"We've just come out of four years of war, where every day you put your life on the line." Bowie smiled a rare smile. "You know you ain't yellow, and I know you ain't yellow, that's all that counts."

"No it ain't, these town folks count and they've got to know that I'm not scared." Raker stared up at the saloon looming before them. "It's important, we can't let Caldwell get them thinking I am."

"A man's pride can get him killed."

"A man's self-respect and pride is all he's got worth keeping." Raker argued. "Without either, a man might as well be dead."

Pushing into the dark saloon, both men step away from the door and move toward the long bar. A few men sit around the gambling tables, but none stand at the long bar as they approach. Bowie has already spotted the hawk featured Fisher sitting with two others at a rear table. A portly barkeep nodded nervously, then moved slowly down the vacant bar, stopping before them.

"Can I help you gents?"

"You know me Charlie Watson, and don't give me that you're dead bull."

The man looked nervously toward the rear tables. "Yeah, I know who you are George Raker, and right now you look very much alive to me."

"Well, now that makes me feel better, at least you know I ain't a ghost." Raker tapped the wooden bar with his finger. "Two whiskey's Charlie."

"Yes sir." Again, the barkeep looked nervously over at the back table where three men play cards. "Two whiskey's coming up."

"Leave it." Fisher never raised his eyes from where he sits dealing cards as the barkeeper reaches for a bottle. "We don't serve Confederate trash in here."

Raker turned his attention to the rough voice, then back at the barkeep. "I wasn't aware the Lazy Bar owned this saloon, Charlie. Did you sell out to Caldwell?"

The tall stooped man stood slowly scattering the cards across the table as he glared hard at Bowie. "I ain't got a problem with you youngster so step away from him, your boss Mister Raker, now he is a problem."

Bowie turned slightly and studied the man. "I've got a problem with you calling me a youngster."

Raker studied Fisher a minute, then reached with his left hand and unbuckled his heavy pistol belt, laying it on the bar. "You're a witness Charlie, I ain't wearing a gun."

Fisher's face muscles twitch nervously as he looks across at the unarmed man. He can't count the times he has been in a similar situation, but this is the first time a man has removed his weapons and stood disarmed before him. There is no law in the small community of Medicine Mound; actually there is no law in this part of Texas at all. Still, Fisher knows to gun down an unarmed man can get the shooter a tall tree and a short rope real quick by the local citizenry. The gunman isn't even sure his boss Bacon Caldwell would back him if he killed an unarmed man.

Bowie stiffened and watches the stoop-shouldered man closely as Raker reached for the half empty whiskey bottle. "You ain't drinking that Raker, not in here."

"You know mister, you're a curiosity." The rancher turned from the bar. "I don't even know you, yet you seem to know me pretty well."

"Yeah, we know you real well." Fisher is nervous obviously shaken, he has been taken completely by surprise with the move, something he isn't sure how to handle. "You're a cattle rustler and claim jumper."

"Tell me sir, who's this we you speak of?" Raker stepped closer to the gunfighter. "You and Bacon Caldwell?"

"Put your gun belt back on, or are you a coward?"

"Those are hard words, Mister Fisher, now let's see if you can back them up."

"Careful George." Bowie whispered.

Raker faced Fisher and smiled. "He ain't nothing but a tinhorn Bowie, but if he shoots me you have my permission to kill him."

Fisher took a step backward and froze shaking his head in dismay as the big man approaches straight to where he stands. The rancher must be crazy to walk right into a loaded gun, never has he seen anything like this. All his fights have been straight up, gun against gun, yet here is an unarmed man walking right at him. This is still Texas, wild as it is, the law of the land still prevails, a man could still hang for shooting down an unarmed man in cold blood. Sweat beads around the hawk-nose as Raker stops less than three feet from the table where he stands.

"Confederate trash, cattle rustler, those are rough words to swallow, Mister Fisher." Raker looked into the man's eyes and smiled. "Kinda sticks in a man's craw. Why don't you pour me a drink from your bottle so I can wash them words down better?"

Fisher is comfortable being in charge and feared, men have always walked a wide berth around him and here stands an unarmed rancher, challenging him in front of the whole saloon. Suddenly the gunman's hand snakes downward for his pistol. Raker's huge hand anticipates the move and stops the gunman with a powerful grip that wraps around the hand with a cruel crushing hold. Viselike pressure makes the veins stand out on Raker's hand as he squeezes the smaller hand of the gunman causing Fisher to yell out in pain as the hand is crushed under the pressure.

"Now sir, that's a little friendlier." Raker still hasn't released the hand. "Would you pour us a drink so we can become friends?"

"You can go to…" The words are cut off as Raker applies more pressure to the already crippled hand, forcing Fisher to his knees.

"Pour." Raker looked at the two men still at the table. "And pour your friends here a drink too; all of us might just become real chummy once we get to know one another over a drink."

"You're a dead man, Raker." Fisher grabbed his hand as Raker released it after the drinks are poured.

"Well hoss, I'll say one thing for you." Raker picked up his whiskey and sipped on it. "You're a hardheaded cuss, that's for sure, and you seem to have a grudge against me."

Nursing his hand, Fisher looked up at the big rancher and cussed. "Caldwell's gonna kill you, Raker; he's already got your woman."

Raker was standing between Bowie and the gunfighter, but the words could be heard throughout the saloon. Only the form of Fisher's body is seen as Raker flung the man bodily across the floor into a wall, then strides ponderously after the senseless gunman. Bowie steps in trying to keep the enraged Raker away from Fisher only to be flung sideways himself. Again he attempted to pull Raker backward only to be tossed hard against the bar with one swipe of the huge arm. Talbert and Matt step through the door watching in shock as Bowie regained his feet and lunged into the bigger man trying to knock him away from the groaning Fisher.

"You're gonna kill him George, turn loose." Bowie is powerless to pull Raker's powerful hands from Fisher's throat as the big rancher rolled the limp gunfighter around on the floor like a rag doll. "Help me, Talbert."

Finally, with all three men holding onto the crazed rancher they tear him loose. "Get your man and go."

The other two Lazy Bar riders had retreated out of the way, but now step forward nervously to pick up what is left of Fisher. "He ain't left us much to get and go with."

"He asked for it." Bowie hears the gurgling noises coming from Fisher's bruised throat as they drag the man out the front door. "He's lucky to be alive."

"Well now." Talbert released Raker's arm. "Never a dull moment, I'm thirsty."

Bowie motioned to the bartender for drinks then pulled a chair out for Raker to sit down. The big man's brain is still in a dull fog from his adrenaline rush and madness, which still clouds his thinking and his eyes. Bowie pushed the whiskey glass into his shaking hand.

"Drink up George, you've earned a drink."

Nodding slowly as if mesmerized, the rancher lifted his glass. "Did I kill him?"

Talbert downed a whiskey and poured himself another. "Almost George, you sure didn't do him any good. If Bowie hadn't pulled you loose from his neck, he'd of been dead pretty quick I reckon."

"You ready to head for home?"

"I guess I am." Raker nodded. "I'm sure tired, boys."

"Adrenaline does that to you old son, makes you tired and lifeless after all the fun is over," Talbert cackles and motioned towards the whiskey bottle. "That other feller now, he's gonna sure need some of this panther juice."

Digging in his pocket, Bowie tossed money onto the long bar and looked about the room. "We're a peaceful bunch of men when left alone. You people tell Bacon Caldwell to leave us in peace and stay on his own side of the county and we'll stay peaceful."

Brace Caldwell sat watching from his vantage point, expecting gunfire to erupt from the saloon at any minute. He blinks in surprise as they drag the half unconscious Fisher from the saloon and put him on his horse. Clutching the ever present Sharps to him Brace watches from the hay chute opening over the livery stable as Raker and his riders leave the saloon several minutes later. Cussing under his breath as he climbs down from the loft, Caldwell mounts and kicks his gelding into a hard lope to the west. Two miles outside Medicine Mound; Caldwell turned back to the main road and watches the Lazy Bar Riders lead Fisher's horse slowly down the road.

"What happened back there Sandy?"

"Fisher didn't get a chance, the Reb outsmarted him." The blond headed rider shook his head. "Dangdest thing I've ever seen in my born days."

"Outsmarted him, how?"

"You just can't shoot an unarmed man, Mister Caldwell."

"Raker had a pistol on when he came out of the saloon just now." Brace cussed. "What did he do with it?"

"Well he sure didn't have one on when he dang near strangled poor old Frank." The man spit. "He took his pistol off before he attacked Frank, there weren't a thing we could do."

"That Raker's crazy, I've seen his eyes." The other rider looked over at Brace nervously. "If his hired hand hadn't pulled him off, he would have choked the life out of Fisher or kicked him to death."

"Yeah, reminded me of my dear mother wringing a chicken's neck for supper."

"The one that stopped it, was he a tall dark headed younger man?"

"That's him, shucks I think he's crazy too." The rider nodded. "Fact of the matter is I believe he wanted to let the big man kill Frank."

"Yeah." Brace remembered seeing the tall man back in Virginia, remembered watching him whip the Yankee champion. "I've seen him before; he's a bad one to fool with."

"We tried Mister Caldwell." The smaller man called Slim, looked over at Caldwell. "They just had us cold this time."

"Well, bring what's left of him on into the ranch." Brace turned the bay gelding and kicked him into a lope.

Slim watched the younger Caldwell ride away. "Mister Caldwell might have bit off more than he can chew with that bunch Sandy."

"What are you saying?"

The blue eyes of the man look across at the other man. "Sandy, did you see the young man siding Raker?"

"I seen him alright."

"Did you look at his eyes and weapons?" Slim shook his head. "He's a killer if I've ever seen one, he ain't no regular cowhand."

"You're just guessing."

"Maybe, but take my warning and stay out of that man's way, you may just live longer." Slim struck a sulphur to his smoke. "If I don't miss my guess, he's a salty one, a hired gun just like us, but better."

Norma Caldwell watched from the kitchen window as Brace Caldwell raced across the ranch yard and came to a sliding almost colliding with the hitch rack. She has never liked the younger brother of her husband whenever possible she makes sure to stay out of his way, only at supper does she have to socialize with the man. Then she sits with her young daughter Emma at the far end of the long table, letting the two brothers dominate all the conversation. On several occasions Bacon would look at her curiously as she replied snappily to any questions asked her. She doesn't understand her dislike for the man, but something gnaws at her every time they are in the same room together, she simply doesn't trust or like Brace Caldwell.

Slamming the kitchen door, Brace brushed by her without a greeting pushing open the heavy study door leading to his brother's office. Norma can hear the muffled voices coming from the office. For the last couple of weeks Bacon has been acting differently, talking only to Brace and staying mostly in his office letting either Brace or Frank Fisher run the Lazy Bar. Curiosity gets the best of her as she moves quietly to the heavy door and places her ear up against it.

"Fisher didn't get it done." Brace poured himself a drink out of the decanter. "Raker came close to killing him.

"He that fast?" Bacon looked over at his brother. "Tell me, what happened?"

Norma's hands flew to her mouth, trying to stem a gasp as she hears the name Raker through the door.

"He used his bare hands, that's what."

"His hands, why didn't Fisher shoot him?" Bacon's closed fist slams down on his desk. "Tell me, what happened in Medicine Mound?"

Brace quickly tells what Sandy and Slim had told him of the fight in the saloon. He watches as Bacon shakes his head in disbelief. "Which way did Raker and his bunch go after they left the saloon, they weren't heading here were they?"

"Nah, they headed back out to the Circle R," Brace downed a drink. "And Fisher didn't shoot the man because they hang people around here for shooting down an unarmed man."

"This is getting out of hand." Bacon turned to the window. "Folks go to siding with this ex-reb and we may have big trouble."

"That ain't all. Matt Sloan switched sides. He sided Raker in the saloon then rode out with him; looks like you lost two hands today, Brother."

"Sloan!" Bacon swore. "He doesn't matter, I never trusted the man anyway."

"Can't blame you there." Brace grinned sarcastically. "I wouldn't trust a man I cheated out of his life's work either."

"I picked up his ranch for taxes, that wasn't cheating him." Bacon glared at his brother. "It's just good business dealing's is all."

"Good business dealings." Brace repeated. "Well brother, these good business dealings today kinda backfired in our faces."

"Yeah, well I'm fixing to repair that backfire or my mistake if that's what you want to call it."

"Why couldn't you have picked up Raker's place for taxes like the rest?" Brace sipped on some brandy he found in the cabinet. "That would have simplified things."

"I already told you I couldn't; Raker was smart he paid the taxes up before he rode off to the war."

"Why didn't the others?"

"No money around these parts in those days." Bacon shrugged. "Back then, most people stayed behind in their taxes. Most of them had mortgages against their places, so they could only pay the interest each year."

"Harrison and some of the others did keep their taxes paid." Brace patted the Sharps. "But thanks to me, I'll guarantee you they won't be a thorn in your side anymore."

Bacon cussed under his breath. "I wish you had gotten Raker, the woman would never have known anything and all of this mess would have been behind us."

"She ain't gonna learn nothing Brother, at least for quite some time." Brace snickered lightly. "That is if you keep her out of town."

"There ain't no way I can do that forever." Bacon shook his head. "And you know it."

"Well, what do you want me to do?"

Bacon looked at the Sharps then lit up a short cigar. "Don't miss this time."

Hearing the muffled shuffling of footsteps, Norma retreated quickly to the kitchen where her young daughter sat playing with a doll. The words she had heard through the door are confusing and she doesn't understand. Dazed and in shock she can't believe her beloved George is alive, she had heard his name plainly as she eavesdropped through the closed door. Surely he had been what the two Caldwell's were talking about so guardedly. Revulsion hit her in the pit of the stomach as it dawns on her what she has just heard. Her beloved husband isn't dead, now she is married to another man, possibly a killer. Somebody had lied to her about his death, now she knows why the Circle R Ranch and George's cattle are behind it. Bacon has already changed the brands on all the Circle R's cattle, on her trips to town with Bacon she had spotted the changed brands on several of their older cows brought to Medicine Mound by George from south Texas. Norma knows Bacon Caldwell has big plans to own all of the Wichita River Valley; he wants every inch of ground between the Pease and Wichita Rivers. On several occasions, as she cleaned his office she had studied the large map outlining the properties he had already bought up. Looking over at her five-year-old girl George's daughter, she shook her head in shame. What has she done, out of ignorance and deceit she had given up on a good man that truly loved her, for one that has just used her.

Chapter 8

Raker led the wagon from town as several local people stood along the boardwalks, nodding and smiling as the big rancher and his riders passed. Word had spread like wildfire around town of the whipping Raker had given Frank Fisher and though none dare say it, they are all elated. When Bacon Caldwell had first moved into Medicine Mound he had been a pleasant enough sort, but after buying up every piece of land he could, he started to change ruling the surrounding area with an iron hand. He had beaten down any who opposed him and now the locals hold a deep resentment for the Lazy Bar owner and his riders.

Though none dared speak out against the injustices of buying land for pennies on the acre from men behind in their taxes they hated Caldwell. Like Matt Sloan the people had little choice, it was either give in to Caldwell or lose their hard-earned lands to the auction gavel. Later after selling, too many of the same men who lost their lands were found dead along the lonely trails. The locals blamed most of the deaths on hostile Indians, but in their hearts the townspeople knew better. Discovering the bodies most scratched their heads; Indians do not carry a high caliber rifle like the one that killed several of the dead men. None were fooled, everyone knew who was responsible, but none dared accuse Bacon Caldwell or his brother for the killings. His Lazy Bar outfit had too many riders and every one of them was a known gunman carrying a bad reputation and a fast gun. The dead rancher's deaths were final; they would no longer be around to cause Caldwell any trouble in the courts if law ever came to Medicine Mound.

As the three riders follow Talbert and the wagon into the yard of the Circle R, they look over to where the rustic ranch house sits quiet and peaceful under the huge oaks that shade and cool it during the hottest of days. Slowly Raker dismounted and looked up at the coal oil lamp burning in the window of the house like it was beckoning them home. For several minutes he stood deep in thought and stared at the house before leading his gelding on to the corral. Bowie, Matt, and Talbert stood watching their friend walk away, then shook their heads sadly.

"He sure has changed." Talbert unhitched the team and led them towards the barn. "I thought he was gonna kill that feller back there."

"If he had, the man had it coming." As they pass close to the house Matt looked up as Jackie and Maria appeared on the porch. "Fisher has killed many a man, he is a mad dog, mean clear through and I'll guarantee he won't forget he'll be back."

Miguel and Carlos along with the other Mexican man hurry up from the corrals to help carry the supplies into the house. Smelling the aroma of cooking food as he finished feeding the work team Talbert walked with Matt back to the kitchen anticipating a good meal. In all the excitement he had completely forgotten the Mexican women would have supper ready and how hungry he was.

Bowie had listened to the conversation absently, not answering the old man as he unhitched the team and led them toward the barn. But Talbert had been right, George has changed, had become hard. If not stopped he would have stomped Fisher to death back in the saloon. War could make some men hard and cold, but not Raker, it was the loss of his wife and daughter that was foremost on the rancher's mind, what made him hard as he is now. Bowie knew if only he could figure a way to get Norma and her daughter away from the Lazy Bar, maybe then more killings could be avoided. No he knew better, access to the Caldwell Ranch is impossible; there is just no way to get close to her. From what he had seen of the place it is impregnable, guarded with at least thirty riders. Shrugging he turned to where Raker is brushing down his horse and watched him quietly.

"What you thinking George?"

"Nothing much, just that I saw a few more head of my cattle as we were coming home."

"I've spotted them myself."

"I want them, every head and hoof that once carried the Circle R Brand." Raker turned the horses out into the small trap. "They belong to me and I aim to have them."

"We'll make a drive tomorrow if you want."

"Bowie, this is probably gonna turn to more killing sooner or later, I know it and so do you." Raker's eyes followed the horses watching them as they rolled in the sandy lot. "Caldwell ain't gonna just let us keep rebranding cows without a fight."

"I figure you're right about that."

"There's another thing." Raker looked back at the tall man. "Matt told me Brace Caldwell, the younger brother of Bacon Caldwell favors a Sharps buffalo gun, carries it wherever he goes."

"The same caliber rifle that got you."

"And probably Captain Harrison and several of the others." The rancher pulled the corral gate shut. "We were told then it was snipers, but now I figure it was Caldwell."

"Are you saying Brace Caldwell rode all the way east and joined the army just to kill the local ranchers around here."

"That's what Matt thinks." Raker nodded. "Said the man was gone for over two years and just now got back, almost exactly at the same time we did."

"How would it be possible for him to move about the different regiments and shoot these men?" Bowie shook his head. "It would have been quite a feat to just find them, we were so spread out."

"Most of us Texas boys were in the same regiments and the regiments were close together, it would have been possible alright." Raker secured the gate. "It would have taken some time but yes, I believe it could be done."

Bowie stared at the dark outline of the nearby trees. "I guess you could be right, especially if Caldwell never enlisted, just put on the uniform that let him move about freely in the ranks unquestioned."

"Exactly, and I figure that's how it happened."

"All that just to gain control of a few acres of land?"

"More than a few Bowie." Raker rolled himself a smoke. "From what Matt says Bacon Caldwell has control of almost the whole county around here, and he says Brace Caldwell is our shooter."

"Why would he have killed these men if he already had their lands?"

The flare from the sulphur lit up the rancher's face. "Simple, dead men don't talk or ask questions in court later down the road when they get back from the war, providing they get back."

"You're saying some of these land deals were shady?"

"I figure most were." Raker nodded. "Oh, he had the liens bought up on the places around here alright, but most juries in a court of law would still consider it a little shady the way the books were changed."

"Why didn't he try to take over your place?"

The rancher shrugged. "I can't answer that except, I had the taxes paid up and there were no liens against it."

"I figure it was your wife."

"Norma?"

"Maybe he didn't want her suspicious." Bowie hung the work bridles with the harness. "He had plenty of time to get this place, there was no rush."

Talbert walked out on the porch and whistled. "Supper's ready boys, come and get it."

"I'm starved."

"We'll start picking up those cattle tomorrow." Raker started for the house. "We've got Miguel and Matt to help us now, shouldn't take long."

"And Talbert and Jose?"

"They'll stay here and guard the women and children."

"One thing George." Bowie stopped and turned to Raker. "The Sharps is still out there."

"I know it is, and I'm telling you right now." Raker's voice grew hard and cold. "Any Lazy Bar rider I find spying on this ranch, I will shoot on sight. And any man I find carrying a Sharps rifle, I will personally hang."

"You're growing hard, old friend."

"Yeah, it's called survival." Raker looked about the ranch. "This place is all I have left; fifteen men like Bacon Caldwell ain't running me out."

The day grew hotter as Matt, Bowie, Miguel, and Raker trail several head of cows, calves, and one old bull down the Wichita road toward the Circle R. All four men have been in the saddle since daylight, all are hungry and tired.

"That old bull sure seems gentle." Matt studied the huge bull. "Not like most longhorns."

"Matt, don't you remember me telling you about Cisco?" Raker leaned from his saddle and patted the bull. "The calf I raised on that goat."

"That's him?"

"Yes sir, all two thousand pounds of him on the hoof."

"He's got to be ten or twelve years old," Matt looked shocked. "Man, how he has grown."

"Well, that's old Cisco alright." Raker smiled down at the huge animal. "It's good to have him back."

Remaining hidden far back in the Mesquite thickets, Brace Caldwell has been shadowing the four men all day as they pick up cattle on their sweep across the grasslands east of Medicine Mound. Several times during the morning he had sighted down the Sharp's barrel dead center on the big man's back, then pulled the rifle back across his saddle swells and grinned. None of the Circle R hands have any idea Caldwell is watching them as they push almost twenty head of cattle ahead of them. Brace shook his head and grinned knowing the big rancher is his anytime he wants to squeeze the trigger.

Caldwell watched curiously through his long glass as the men point and seem to be talking about the big longhorn bull walking ahead of them. Suddenly it dawns on him, once on a trip to town as they passed close to where the big bull grazed he had heard his brother's wife mention that her ex-husband raised the bull on goat's milk and that he was very proud of the longhorn. Suddenly the Sharps jerked up and roared knocking the bull to his knees. Laughing crazily, Brace Caldwell kicked his horse into a hard run and disappeared into the surrounding mesquites and oaks.

Whirling at the sound of the rifle, both Raker and Bowie charge the thickets, uncertain where the shot came from. "Matt you and Miguel stay with the cattle." Raker hollered over his shoulder.

Spurring their horses hard both men feel the pull of the sharp Mesquite thorns as they separate and push their racing geldings through the surrounding brush. Reining in their blowing horses both men study the ground closely as they try to pick up fresh tracks.

"Here he is George." Bowie lets out with his rebel yell and waits until the rancher rides up. "He's long gone, and it's far too dangerous for us to follow him as long as he's got that Sharps."

"You recognized it too, did you?"

"Same sound as when you were shot, it would be hard not to recognize it." Bowie shook his head. "Only a buffalo gun makes that kind of boom when it goes off."

Heading back, both men stopped alongside the dead bull. "Just plain meanness that's all, killing that old bull was plain cussedness."

Bowie looked down at the bull. "You have any doubt it was Caldwell?"

"It was him alright just like Matt said, he carries the Sharps with him all the time," Raker cussed. "He'll pay if it's the last thing I do, Brace Caldwell is a dead man."

"One thing's for sure, he's a mean one." Bowie agreed. "The skunk deserves whatever he gets."

Raker spurred his horse following the small herd. "Can one man be so greedy that he's got to own everything?"

"Apparently, Mister Bacon Caldwell is."

"What did I do to deserve a man like this in my life?"

Bowie thought back of Louisiana and Landeaux. "Seems like everyone has a Caldwell somewhere in their lives."

Talbert had managed to knock down several rabbits with his double-barreled shotgun and the women have them frying in a skillet atop the wood stove along with a pan of brown gravy. The kitchen also carries the aroma of frying wild onions and boiled beans. Hollering for the men sitting out on the porch smoking, the old man grinned as they stroll through the door.

"You boys sit down and wrap your tonsils around some Texas beef-steak." Talbert laughed. "Maria and Jackie did a bang up job on supper."

Miguel looked over into the skillet and laughed. "It looks like señor rabbit to me."

"Some people just have no sense of smell or taste." Talbert turned to Carlos and winks.

"It's scrumptious, Maria." Matt tasted the rabbit. "Better than steak, and I ain't lying to you."

"Gracias señor." Maria smiled as she carried a pan full of biscuits to the table. "We have at least one gentleman among us."

Talbert smiled as the small woman moved back to the stove. "That's more like it."

"You've outdone yourself, you old goat, we sure didn't know we had a hunter in the group."

"Well thank you, Mister Raker." Talbert pulled out a chair. "There is lots of things about me you don't know."

Bowie kept silent; he doesn't want Jackie accusing him of picking on Talbert tonight. "What's next George, we going out again tomorrow?"

"With that Sharps out there, we'd be taking a chance, we didn't even know he was anywhere about today."

"What happened out there today George?"

"We think the same sniper that got me back at Appomattox killed one of our bulls today."

"A cow, why didn't the man shoot one of you instead of a harmless cow?"

"Good question old man, we'll let you know soon as we figure it out." Matt shook his head. "But, just so you know, it was a bull."

Talbert's question is on the mind of everyone at the table, but for now there is no answer. The men around the table don't understand a greedy man like Bacon Caldwell, they are just small-time cattlemen. None have the crazed driving ambition to cheat, steal, or kill just to accumulate wealth and power.

Bowie finished his coffee and stood up. "I'm turning in wake me up early if we're riding out."

"Just to be sure we didn't miss any maybe we should make another sweep west." Raker nodded. "We did pretty well today."

"How many you figure are still out there?"

"I don't rightly know Matt; I thought we had them all already." The rancher shook his head. "We've collected fifty of my original grown cows. I figure the rest could have died off of natural causes, or Caldwell might have sold or ate them."

"Well, wake me up and we'll make one more drive." Bowie turned toward the barn where his bunk was. "Talbert, we've got a killer out there watching us; you keep your head down and stay inside if you can, and keep the children inside."

"Kinda like playing war again huh Bowie, snipers and all?" Talbert chuckled. "You really think they'd shoot a child?"

"I don't know old man, I just don't know." Bowie stopped at the door. "Anybody that would shoot a harmless bull just might do anything."

Both he and Raker had become fond of the old man and his antics over the last four years. Too old for war, Talbert nonetheless had shouldered his old musket and marched up and down the Shenandoah Valley stride for stride with the young men that were forever kidding him about his age. They knew Talbert always looked at the bright side of everything, hunger, death, even the outcome of the war. Looking at him, you'd think he was not too bright and mainly harmless, but when riled the old man would stand his ground.

"Well, from what I've heard from Miss Jackie there were plenty of civilians killed around here over the last four years." Talbert lifted his coffee cup. "I wouldn't put it past Caldwell to kill one or two more."

"It's kinda like war, but the man with the Sharps has taken a personal interest in us, you keep your head down you hear me?"

"I heard you." Talbert winked over at the tall man. "But tell me, who would waste a shell on an old codger like me?"

Raker slammed down his fist causing plates to jump up from the table. "You heard him Talbert; this man is out to kill anything he can."

"Alright George, alright." Talbert shrugged. "Calm down, I'll keep my eyes open."

"Good, I've got enough to worry about right now." Raker looked down the table at the men and women, then walked outside to smoke.

The sun is just peeking its head in the east as the four men finish pulling their cinches tight, then lead their horses from the barn. Bowie is curious as Raker hands him a Spencer carbine, the rifle doesn't have the long range the Sharps has, but it is a seven-shot weapon with deadly knock down power.

"I want you to cover me and the boys when we start pushing cattle today." Handing over a fist full of shells Raker looked at the old rifle. "She ain't got the range of his Sharps, but before I finally killed its previous owner, he was making us duck for cover, I tell you."

"I remember that day all too clear, he was just a boy, a baby."

"With that Spencer he was a deadly baby, no sir he was no boy, he was a brave man and he died like a man."

Matt is curious about the previous owner of the gun, but he doesn't ask. He knows the things men are forced to do in war is their own private moments, seldom spoken of. Sometimes in the quiet of the evening while they smoked they would tell their stories, but usually they said little about the bloody hardship of war or the men they've killed. Most ex-soldiers just try to let the memories of war fade away, but none ever completely forget the horrors of war. Most men don't find glory in seeing a man's insides strung out for yards behind him as he tries to crawl away looking at something no one else can see, reaching out with his last gasp toward something only he would know.

Bowie mounted then rode to the house and hailed Talbert, who is preoccupied with the breakfast dishes. "Keep your head down Talbert, and keep that shotgun with you all the time while we're gone."

The old man wiped his hands dry and produced a ten-gauge shotgun. "I'm way ahead of you Bowie, thanks for worrying about an old man."

"I ain't worried about you." Bowie looked down at the gray head. "I just don't want to lose a good hunter; those dumplings last night were delicious."

"Why thank you kindly sonny boy, I truly appreciate all compliments."

Jackie had stepped down into the yard beside Bowie's horse and looked up at him. "You be careful today out there."

Shocked as she touched his leg lightly he reached down and placed his hand on her shoulder. "I'll be careful."

"Come home safe."

Maria smiled mischievously and winked as Jackie returned to the kitchen. "Shut up Maria."

Norma had watched as Brace Caldwell rode into the ranch yard the previous evening, just before suppertime, wearing a huge grin on his face. She watched in disgust as he kissed the barrel of the rifle like he would a woman as he dismounts. Worry and fear clutch at her chest, the man is evil and she can tell by his actions he has been up to no good. She is scared, who has he killed this time, George or someone else? Fading back into the large pantry she waited until Brace walked through the kitchen then waits for the door to close. Treading silently across the wood floor once again, she placed her ear against the oak door. "You killed that old bull?" Bacon's voice comes like a whisper through the door then she hears the scrape of his heavy chair. Norma quickly retreats to the kitchen and busies herself peeling potatoes as Bacon looks in on her.

"Is supper about ready Norma?" The voice is gruff, agitated. "I'm hungry."

"It'll be a few minutes yet." She never looked up for fear of guilt showing on her face. "I'll call you."

Letting out a sigh of relief as he turned back to the study, she knows this time George wasn't the target of the Sharps again, at least not today. Born on the frontier only a few years after the Alamo fell, she was raised by her father. He rode at Sam Houston's side during the San Jacinto battle and he taught her to shoot and handle guns. She knows exactly what the rifle Brace Caldwell carries is and how dangerous it can be in the right hands. She remembered the day one of the hands brought it in from town, a birthday present from Bacon to his little brother. The rifle had made a monster out of the younger Caldwell; he started killing almost anything that moved. Hour after hour, she watched him practice with the weapon until his shoulder became too sore to fire the heavy caliber weapon for a few days.

Calling the two men in for supper she watched as Brace stood the weapon gingerly beside the doorframe in the hallway, just out of sight as he takes a seat at the table. At least Bacon had a little upbringing his mother wouldn't allow guns in her kitchen. Looking across to where the men sit Norma pulled down a small bowl from a cabinet containing forty-five caliber round steel balls. Retreating to the kitchen she quickly mixes cornmeal and milk together until it makes a thick dough. Holding a wooden spoon, she places several pieces of shredded cloth in the bowl with the dough.

"And how is my favorite little niece this evening?"

Norma listens as Brace speaks to Emma then sets the bowl down and starts bringing steaming food to the table. Bacon always insisted on a family dinner, at least at suppertime. Most any other time of the day the house remained empty, except for the girl. Bacon himself stayed locked up inside his study busy with paperwork.

"Fine, Uncle Brace." Little Emma smiled happily. "How are you?"

"Well little Missy, I sure ain't as pretty as you are."

Bacon watched as Norma moved about the room quietly keeping her eyes averted as she passed both men. "Is something wrong, Norma?"

"No, I was just thinking about going into town in the morning. I need thread material, and a few things."

"I'm busy tomorrow, just make a list and have Happy Gillum ride in and get it for you."

"He can drive me in, but I want to pick out the material for myself." Norma looked across the table. "You know a man doesn't like shopping for frills and such."

Brace grinned and looked over smugly at his brother; he actually enjoyed seeing Bacon pushed into a corner. "Not tomorrow dear, perhaps next week."

"But…"

"That's final Norma I'm busy tomorrow, a little material cannot be all that important."

"Maybe not to a man, but to me it's very important." Norma stood up speaking sharply over her shoulder as she left the kitchen with the small bowl grasped tightly in her hand. "You are treating me like a prisoner, locked up on this ranch."

Brace raised his eyebrows as he grinned over at Bacon. "Well now, Brother."

"You have Happy keep a close watch on her." Bacon doesn't notice, but he had bent one of the spoons in his rage. "A very close watch."

"She can't get far without a wagon." Brace whispered as he picked up the bowl of potatoes. "You want some spuds, Emma?"

Norma looked back at the table before slamming a bedroom door, pretending to enter. Stepping out of her shoes she tiptoed back to the Sharps and quickly shoves strips of cloth down the long barrel, then tamps them further down with the skinny handled wooden spoon. Tipping the bowl she holds it steady as the doughy concoction runs slowly down the barrel. Pushing several more strips into the gun she tamped them down tightly so none can spill from the barrel until it sets up and hardens. Wiping the gun clean so it shows not a trace of the cornmeal she sets it down gently, then retraces her steps to the bedroom door and slips her shoes back on.

Raker motioned Bowie forward as the four clear the boundaries of the Circle R and start down the west side of the pastures leading toward Medicine Mound. Pulling the Spencer from its leather scabbard, Bowie kicked his bay gelding into a lope. He will scout ahead of Raker, Matt and Miguel so they can put their full attention on hunting for Circle R cattle that were rebranded. Working in a wide arc, out in the heavy mesquite, Bowie keeps just far enough ahead of the three men to keep them safely in his sight as best he can.

Several times he circles the entire area, working both front and back. Today if it is in his power, Caldwell will not get a free shot with the Sharps. Several times he reins the horse in hard as his sharp eyes pick out movement ahead in the trees. Every time as he watches it turned out to be a cow and calf or a deer. Once it was a lone coyote, a good sign to Bowie. He knows if a human were out there, the wild dog wouldn't be. At his approach startled jackrabbits with their big ears and powerful hind legs bound out from the tall grass and skip out of sight.

At noon Raker waved his arm and motioned Bowie in where the men set resting close to a small stream of water. The small herd is pushed into a curve in the river bed, a natural corral to hold the cattle while they let their horse rest and graze a few minutes. Twenty head of longhorns with a few calves stand grazing in knee-deep grass alongside the stream as Bowie rides in and dismounts.

"See anything out there Bowie?"

"One lone coyote is all."

"That's good we've done well this morning." Raker nodded. "There can't be too many of my cows left, let's call it a day, we're finished."

"Sound's good to me."

"Alright then, you wait here a few minutes then follow us." Raker looked at the others. "Stay alert and stay alive."

"Shucks Private Raker, sounds like you're back in the army again."

"At least the army was at war head on, not the back shooting we have here."

The drive back to the Circle R stayed quiet and uneventful as Bowie circled the herd on his tired gelding watching for any sign of Brace Caldwell or any of the Lazy Bar riders. He is suspicious, he just can't figure why Bacon Caldwell is not challenging them over the cattle. It had been two weeks since the start of the roundup and rebranding, Caldwell had to know Raker was reclaiming his stolen cows. Why hadn't he made a move? Matt had estimated Caldwell's cattle herds in the hundreds, maybe the man is holding back because he thinks a few head of cattle he originally rebranded aren't worth the trouble. Caldwell can't be scared, four Circle R men against thirty Lazy Bar gunmen isn't much of a match, even if it is a straight shoot out which Bowie knows it wouldn't be.

The tall man rode slowly watching in all directions, he knows the Circle R will soon be coming into view. He is tired and hungry from the long day of hard riding and he has worried all day about Talbert and the women, and their safety. He knows the old man is dependable, but also set in his ways. Talbert fears nothing and will do whatever he wants, when he wants, without listening to anybody. It probably wasn't wise to leave him alone at the ranch guarding the women and children, but the younger men were needed to help round up the cattle. Bowie is straining his eyes to see the ranch gate when suddenly, from less than a mile ahead, the heavy roar of a rifle booms out across the flats. Yelling like banshees, Bowie and Raker whip their tired horses hard, putting them into a full out run toward the ranch buildings, leaving Matt and Miguel behind to bring in the cattle.

Racing into the yard, both men rein in hard bringing their blowing geldings to a sliding stop. They let out a sigh of relief as Talbert stepped from the house with the double-barrel cocked and ready. "Are you alright old man?"

"Just fine George?" Talbert grinned as he lets down the hammers of the shotgun. "Why, is something wrong?"

"Are the women and children okay?"

"They're fine, everybody's fine, what's wrong?"

"You didn't hear that roar?"

"I was just funning y'all, yeah I heard it, then a horse took off at a hard run to the south." Talbert pointed towards the heavy timber. "Don't know exactly where it was, but it came from somewhere right in those live oaks over there."

Riding their horses slowly toward the trees, each man comes in from a different side with Talbert following on foot behind them. Quickly Bowie spots the smoking remains of what was a Sharps rifle. The end of the barrel is split and smoke still filters from the ruined barrel.

Dismounting, the tall man picked up the heavy weapon by its wooden stock and examined the hot barrel. "This gun exploded, the barrel must have gotten plugged up."

"I reckon its owner was a little negligent in keeping his weapon clean and oiled." Raker grinned. "Hard to believe a man like Caldwell would let his prize rifle get dirty."

"I believe you're wrong George." Bowie studied the ground. "Somebody deliberately fouled this barrel so it would explode when fired."

"Who would do something like that?" Talbert scratched his chin and shrugged. "But whoever it was, I love them for it."

"It had to be somebody with an axe to grind in this mess, and who sure didn't want Caldwell killing with the Sharps again."

"And somebody who doesn't like Mister Brace Caldwell." Raker examined the rifle then handed it back to Bowie. "If somebody did pack that barrel, they meant to give Mister Caldwell a bad headache for sure."

Bowie lifted the heavy weapon higher and examined it closer. "Amen to that."

"Well, one thing's for sure." Talbert spit. "This little old gun won't kill again."

Running his hands over his blowing horse, Bowie shook his head. "My gelding is done in, I don't want him wind broke or I would try to run that drygulcher down."

"I don't see how he's riding, that rifle barrel blowing up must have gotten a piece of his face, maybe even blinded him some." Raker shook his head. "You remember what happened to some of the boys that had guns blow up in the army."

"Y'all remember the youngster from Richmond that had twelve balls shoved down his rifle barrel and it hadn't been fired once."

"That was a good feat for a fact," Raker laughed lightly. "The youngster thought he was firing every time he shoved another ball down that old gun."

"You know, he made a captain?"

"You're joshing?" Talbert looked bewildered as he turned to walk away. "As scared as he was that day he still got promoted to captain?"

"Nope, I ain't joshing he made a fighting machine after that little embarrassment."

"What happened to him after that?"

"The lad was killed at Gettysburg near Little Round Top." Bowie followed the old man. "Won himself a medal that day, he did."

"He wasn't alone; we lost many a good man at Gettysburg."

Bowie walked beside George. "Talbert's getting old."

"Yes he is, and I want him to get older." Raker added. "You know Caldwell meant to kill him today."

"Well he didn't, and I doubt he'll be looking to kill anybody else for a spell if he can still see to kill anything at all." Bowie looked down at the ruined weapon he holds. "Talbert is right; Brace Caldwell sure won't be using this gun again."

Raker and Bowie had figured right as the barrel of the Sharps exploding in his face had done its damage. Caldwell has powder burns across the left side of his face and a piece of steel from the busted barrel sticks from his side. Disoriented, bleeding, and half blinded, his eyes won't focus, everything before him is only a blur. Kicking his horse, he gives the gelding his head, his only chance of getting back to the ranch in his condition is to let the gelding find his own way home unless one of the Lazy Bar riders finds him. Hurting too bad to turn in the saddle, he wonders if any of the Circle R outfit are following him. If they are he knows he will be an easy target, he is in no shape to fight or defend himself. He meant to kill the old man back at the ranch house as a warning to Raker and to scare the Circle R owner into clearing out. When the old man finally appeared on the front porch late in the day, he had sighted in on him and squeezed the trigger only to have the weapon blow up in his face. His head and eyes are foggy, he's disoriented, he squeezes the saddle horn hard trying to stay in the saddle.

Chapter 9

Shaking his head in shock and revulsion Happy Gillum reins in beside Brace Caldwell's meandering gelding and looks unbelieving at the man hanging from the saddle. Taking the horses reins he dismounted and tried to right the moaning man in the saddle.

"Who is it?" Brace gasped, to weak and in too much pain to try and straighten up or turn his head.

"It's me Happy Gillum; Brace." The rider looked at the once handsome face in horror. "Just sit tight, I'll get you home."

"Water."

The little rider uncorked his canteen and placed it to the burnt lips. "We're almost there."

In view of the Lazy Bar; Gillum fired his pistol to announce their arrival and send out a call for help. Quickly every hand on the ranch turned out armed to the teeth, ready for trouble. Bacon Caldwell reached the two riders first, then recoils in shock at his brother's appearance. Quickly ordering several riders to carry the wounded man into the house he hurried ahead.

"Gillum, you're well mounted get to town and bring Doc Evans back, fast."

"Yes sir." Happy whirled the red roan he is astride, a horse well known on the ranch for his endurance and running ability. "I'll get him."

"Hurry Gillum."

Norma stood by the kitchen door as they carry Brace into the bedroom and lay him gingerly on the bed. Smiling slightly she knows exactly what has happened, she also knows Brace Caldwell has been up to no good again and got precisely what he deserved. She has seen weapons explode from fouled barrels before; she knows the Sharps rifle he has been so proud of would kill no more innocent men.

"Get some hot water Norma, while I get him undressed." Bacon pushed by her without a sideways glance.

Fisher stared down at the jagged piece of steel protruding from the naked torso as Bacon places wet compresses across the ripped and burned face. Another bad slash showed across Brace's upper arm, probably caused by a sliver coming from the exploding gun. Bacon is no doctor, but he knows stemming the blood flow is the main concern as the two wounds bleed freely.

"Should I try to remove the piece of steel from his side?" Bacon looked up at Fisher. "I ain't sure what to do."

"I'd leave it until the sawbones gets here." The gunfighter has seen arrow wounds exactly like the one in front of him. "If it's deep and he starts to hemorrhage after you remove it and the doc ain't here, he's a goner for sure."

The thin mouth tries to make words, but the man is in too much pain to speak. Bacon wants to ask him what happened, but he knows Brace is far too weak to answer.

"What do you think happened, Frank?"

"We can't be sure until he comes around." The stoop-shouldered man shrugged. "That sure looks like a piece of metal from a rifle barrel."

"Like the Sharps?" Bacon felt the hand on his arm grasp him a little harder. "Was it the Sharps, Brother?"

Fisher watched as the hand squeezed slightly then relaxed. "Sure enough, it looks like a piece of barrel."

"That was a new gun and he kept it clean enough to eat from." Bacon covered the piece of steel sticking from the man. "How could it blow up?"

"Well, I couldn't say for sure what caused it, but I've seen the damage a plugged rifle barrel can cause when it discharges." Fisher looked down at the shallow breathing man. "A plugged barrel from mud or a dirt dobber will blow almost every time."

"Brace treated that gun like his right arm, he cleaned it every night." Bacon dabbed at the wounds worrying as he looked up at the ticking clock. "He wouldn't let it get fouled."

"Just my opinion is all Mister Caldwell." Fisher fidgeted. "Apparently, he didn't clean it last night."

"Yeah, seems that way, don't it?"

Happy Gillum raced up the stairs to the doctor's office and pushed through the door without knocking. The young man sitting at the desk turned from his paperwork and stared at the excited man.

"Doc, they need you out at the Lazy Bar quick as we can get there." Gillum looked around the office. "We got a man hurt bad."

"Alright, settle down." Evans stood up slowly. "What's wrong with him?"

"He's been burned, has a piece of steel sticking in him, and he's bleeding like a stuck pig." Gillum poured himself a tumbler of water from the water pitcher. "I don't think he'll make it."

"I'll get my bag; you go to the stable and get me a saddle horse."

Doc Evans ordered everyone from the room except Norma then started removing the blood soaked bandages. "Get me plenty of hot water."

"It's on the stove already."

"Hurry woman."

Evans hand moved deftly as he removed the steel sliver from the wounded man's side and cleaned the puncture wound. The wound looks bad with all the blood that has soaked Brace's clothing, but luckily the sliver only penetrated the fatty tissue of his body missing any vital organs. Quickly stitching the ugly gash closed, the young doctor turned his attention to the arm wound quickly sewing up the second wound. The face is another matter, powder burns cover the entire left side of the face and Evans knows the younger Caldwell has lost the use of his left eye and possibly the right. Swabbing out both eyes he spreads a cream across the face, then wraps gauze over the entire burned area and covering the eyes as well.

Only an occasional moan sounds from Brace as they raised his head from the pillow to allow the gauze to encircle his head. After patching the man back together, Evans took two pills from his bag and slides them inside Brace's mouth.

"I know you're in pain Mister Caldwell, but you'll have to swallow them." The young doctor touched a cool glass of water to the burnt lips. "They will help with the pain."

Exiting the bedroom Evans finds Bacon and Fisher sitting silently at the kitchen table. Closing the door quietly, the Doctor moves towards a chair that Bacon has motioned him to. "Is he…?"

"He's alive, but he's gonna be in considerable pain for a while." Evans looked about the room tiredly. "Quite a long while, I'm afraid."

"Then he'll make it?"

"He will, with no complications." Evans seated himself at the table and took the coffee Fisher pushes in front of him. "The wounds look terrible, but they aren't serious if he doesn't develop blood poison."

"What else?"

"It's his eyes, the left is gone and his vision out of the right could be blurry at best." Evans tasted the hot coffee. "Only time will tell."

Bacon turned pale and slumped in his chair. "How much time, Doc?"

"It's hard to say, but we'll keep the eyes covered and the bandages on for at least six weeks before we remove them and find out exactly how much damage was done."

"That's a long time for a man to be in the dark, Doc."

"It's a short time if it helps." Evans looked over at Bacon. "Hopefully, your brother won't be in the dark for the rest of his life."

"Are you riding back to town tonight?"

"Yes, there is nothing further I can do for now." Evans nodded his head. "Mrs. Kincaid is in the family way and I need to check on her, I'll be back first thing in the morning."

"I appreciate that Doc; I'll get the missus to fix up a bite of supper for you." Bacon stood up. "Can I go in?"

"Yes, but don't try to talk with him. I gave your brother a heavy sedative that'll make him sleep for several hours." Evans opened his thin hands. "Here's a curiosity, didn't I hear you men say the weapon in question was a heavy caliber Sharps?"

"What about it, Doc?" Bacon watched the hand as it opened letting a small, round smoothbore lead ball roll onto the table.

"I took that from your brother, along with that sliver of steel."

Bacon's eyes narrowed. "How could that be, are you sure?"

"I'm sure it came from the wound." Evans shrugged. "But, I'm a doctor Mister Caldwell, not a gunsmith."

Bacon held the lead ball in his hand and studied it absently for several seconds before looking over at the wall cabinet where he keeps most of his shells. Walking to the hutch, he pulled down the bowl holding the round shot and took another rifle ball exactly the same size and caliber from it. Gripping it tightly, he replaced the bowl and started for the bedroom.

Norma listened through the door as the three men talked, then moved back to the bed as Bacon entered the bedroom. Looking up as the big man comes through the door; she is shocked at the haggard look on his face. Walking to the end of the bed, Bacon shook his head slowly then looked over at her.

"Norma would you fix the doctor something to eat before he leaves?"

Nodding, she turned for the door. "You want anything?"

"No nothing."

As the sun slowly sets in the west, tree frogs begin their singing from the surrounding live oak trees. Whippoorwills call to one another down along the small creek bordering the large ranch yard as Bacon and Fisher walk toward the corrals.

"What do you think happened out there Frank?"

"I don't know Mister Caldwell, only thing I do know is the rifle exploded in his face." Fisher shrugged, he had no answers. "That Sharps was like new, and you said he cleaned on it every night."

"I believe the rifle was deliberately fouled." Bacon held the two lead balls out to Fisher. "I believe someone plugged the barrel of my brother's rifle on purpose."

"Dat burn, if it don't look like it for sure." Fisher studied the balls. "Who would do such a thing here on the ranch?"

"Tell me Frank, do you think some outsider could have slipped in here during the night and done it?"

"That'd be a slick piece of footwork if he pulled something like that off." Fisher shrugged. "He'd have had to get in the house while Brace slept, but I reckon anything's possible."

"I agree, getting in here unseen isn't possible." Bacon looked toward the kitchen. "Someone who works here must have done it."

"What do you want me to do?"

"Do you think, come morning you could take Gillum and backtrack Brace to wherever he dropped the rifle?"

"I can give it a try."

Bacon nodded. "Fisher."

"Yes sir?"

"This time if Raker gets in your way, kill him whether he's armed or not." Bacon looked toward the east. "Don't let him get close enough to get his hands on you, I want the man dead."

"You're the boss." Fisher touched his throat. "That man is strong; you can bet he won't get close enough to grab me again."

Norma watched from the kitchen window as Bacon and Frank Fisher stood in the ranch yard talking. She noticed how Bacon kept looking toward the house and frowning. Could he suspect she was the one that plugged the Sharps? Nervously she pulled paper and pencil from a drawer and quickly writes down a few words. Placing the short note in an envelope she walked into the bedroom where Doc Evans is checking the bandages on Brace Caldwell's wounds one last time before leaving the ranch.

"The wounds are all clean, Mrs. Caldwell; I'll check in on him again tomorrow. If he needs them, give him two more of these pills tonight."

"I'll do that Doctor." Norma quickly slipped the envelope inside the leather medical bag as Evans leaned over Brace. "Is there anything else I can do?"

"No, other than keeping him comfortable and trying to get him to drink plenty of liquids." Evans turned to her. "And give him one of these other pills three times a day."

"Yes sir." Norma studied both sets of pills. "These are different from the others?"

"One is for pain, the other is for infection."

"How long will he be bedridden?"

"He's young and strong, providing he doesn't get blood poisoning or bad fevers, he should be up and about in a week." The young doctor snapped his bag shut. "I'll be back tomorrow. Mrs. Kincaid is fixing to have a baby so I best be getting over there."

"I have you some food on the table."

"I better be going, but thank you anyway."

Following the doctor outside, Norma watched the man mount and ride away without a backward look.

"Well that's good news, isn't it my dear?" Bacon startled Norma. "Brace is gonna be okay."

"Yes it is." She turned to go inside as his next words stopped her.

"Norma you didn't see anyone around the house in the last couple of days did you, a stranger maybe?"

"In the house of course not, I would have told you." Norma looked at him without blinking. "Why do you ask, who would be in the house?"

"I said anyone around the house." Bacon dropped his gaze and turned away. "Just wondering."

The Sharps' mangled remnants stood against the doorframe, a sad reminder of what a beautiful but dangerous weapon it once was. Bowie sits at the supper table studying the blown up barrel wondering if Brace Caldwell survived. Whoever had plugged the rifle barrel rigging it to explode when fired sure meant business. Yes sir, whoever done it sure meant old Brace bodily harm.

"What you thinking about Bowie?" Talbert noticed how preoccupied he is with the ruined rifle.

"He's thinking the same as I am." Raker answered. "Who would have it in for Caldwell bad enough to plug that barrel?"

"Exactly, but my question is who could have gotten close enough to do it?" Matt bit into a piece of squirrel. "Caldwell never let that Sharps out of his sight and far as I know none of the hired hands except Frank Fisher, ever went to the house."

"That only leaves two people." Bowie poured gravy over his pan fried biscuits.

Matt nodded. "Norma and Bacon Caldwell himself."

"It can't be." Raker looked across the table at the man. "Norma would never harm a soul in any way."

"You're wrong there George, if she found out about you still being alive and that Caldwell is trying to kill you." Matt shook his head. "She just might."

"No way, not my Norma."

"She's been through a lot." Matt picked up his coffee cup. "She ain't allowed to talk to any of the hands and she ain't allowed to go into town unless he's with her."

"Why?"

"I don't know why, all I know is she's practically a prisoner out there." Matt shrugged.

Raker pushed back his chair and walked thoughtfully from the kitchen out onto the porch. Leaning against a porch column he struck a sulphur to his smoke then turned as Bowie took a chair behind him. "You want a smoke, Bowie?"

"No thank you."

"You think it was Norma don't you?"

"It's hard to say." Bowie shrugged, then straightened as he hears a horse coming down the road in a hard lope. "Somebody's sure in a hurry."

Raker stuck his head in the doorway. "Talbert blow out the lamp and you boys get a hold of your guns."

Bowie had already reached inside the door and pulled down his Colts. "Whoever it is, they're traveling late."

The horse slowed to a walk as it approached the darkened house, then stopped fifteen feet from the front porch. "You there Circle R; I seen your lights go out, I come in peace."

"Who are you?"

"Doctor Evans, from Medicine Mound."

"Okay mister, keep your hands clear of any weapons and come on in where we can see your face." Bowie stepped from behind a heavy porch post. "Talbert, strike a light."

"It's Doc Evans alright, I recognize the voice." Matt spoke up from the shadows.

Evans nodded his head as he looked at all the weapons pointing down at him from the porch. "You boy's always this careful?"

"We are when a stranger comes riding in here after dark like you did just now." Matt stepped down next to Evans. "Boys this is Lionel Evans, the best sawbones in these parts."

Dismounting; Evans took the extended hand. "Matt forgot to mention I'm the only sawbones in these parts."

Matt introduced everyone as Evans enters the house. "What you doing way out here, Doc?"

"Just delivered a baby over at the Kincaid's and I have a delivery for a George Raker. Being this close, I figured I'd just drop it by and maybe get a free meal out of the deal."

"Well Lionel that was some pretty good figuring." Matt laughed. "Have a seat while the ladies fix you a plate, if it's okay, Boss."

"That's fine." Raker looked over at the doctor curiously. "You've got a delivery for me?"

"I sure do, found it in my medical bag when I got to the Kincaid's." Evans pulled the letter out from his vest-pocket and handed it to the curious rancher. "I was over at Caldwell's fixing up Brace Caldwell when someone slipped it into my bag."

"How bad is Caldwell?"

"Cut up pretty bad from flying steel." Evans stopped talking as his eyes settle on the blown up Sharps. "I doubt if he'll ever see too shoot again."

"Do say." Talbert grinned. "Well, I'd say a man needs to be more careful what he's shooting at."

Raker stepped out on the porch stopping under the glowing lantern that hung from a peg. Holding the letter up to the light he nodded thoughtfully, it was her handwriting, of that there is no mistake. Tearing the envelope open carefully, he read the few words twice before returning it to the envelope. The words had leapt from the pages, tearing at him.

"I want to come home my love Norma." Was all the letter said, in those few words.

Looking off to the west, toward the town of Medicine Mound and further along toward the Lazy Bar range, the big man swore. "And you will, that I promise."

"Is old Brace gonna live Doc?" Matt poured another cup of coffee.

"I figure he will, providing no infection sets in."

"You boys turn in early tonight." Raker's big frame appeared in the doorway and looked about the room. "Doc, you're welcome to stay the night and ride in with us come morning."

"I'm sure enough tired I'll take you up on the invite." Evans nodded. "Thank you."

"What's the occasion George?" Matt looked up from where he and Talbert sit smoking. "Me and Talbert were just fixing to sit down for a game of stud poker."

"Tomorrow at sunup, we're riding into Medicine Mound." Raker looked around the room. "You boys will have to postpone your game tonight, Talbert tell the women to have breakfast on the table long before daybreak."

Bowie looked over at Raker curiously; his friend seems in a good mood, even happy. Whatever was in that letter must have been good news. "You want me to ride with you?"

"I may need you, we'll leave Miguel and Jose here to protect the women while we're gone, Talbert and Matt will ride in with us."

Daylight finds Medicine Mound waking up as businesses start opening doors and setting out every sort of hardware the local farmers and ranchers use. Raker reined in at the mercantile and dismounted as the others spread out beside him. Entering the store Raker finds Tom Scott at the rear of the store weighing some nails for a farmer he doesn't recognize.

"Morning George," The store owner greeted the big man.

"Good morning Tom."

Turning as the farmer starts for the front with his supplies, Scott looked up at the big man. "Now George, what can I do for you this morning?"

"First I need a saddle for Talbert, we can't have him driving that wagon all the way into town or riding bareback."

"I've got several, some new, some used, and some really used." Scott pointed to a side room of the large store. "Take your pick."

"It may be a day or two before I can pay you."

"Your credit is good George, you know that." Scott glanced over his spectacles. "Are you forgetting who helped me get my start when I first arrived in Medicine Mound?"

"Thank you Tom."

"And the second?"

"I need to get a letter out to Norma at the Lazy Bar." Raker reached inside his pocket for Norma's letter. "Today."

"She's remarried George."

Handing the letter over to the store man, Raker studied his face as he read the few words. "She didn't know I was alive, Tom. If she had, she wouldn't have married Caldwell."

"I know." Scott looked toward the front where Bowie and Matt were examining a brand-new Winchester repeating rifle that had just arrived. "You know, Bacon Caldwell and some of his men just rode in; they're over at the Doc's office now."

"Doctor Evans just rode into town with us."

"I watched Caldwell and his men ride by earlier this morning." Scott nodded. "He came to town looking for Doc Evans for some reason, sure didn't look any too happy."

Raker didn't wait for Scott to finish as he walked from the store and crossed the street to the building with the medical shingle hanging outside the door. Two Lazy Bar riders standing outside the doctor's office tried to block Raker's advance as he crossed the sidewalk. Putting their hands out to stop him they find themselves slung sideways like they were children as the big man walks past them both. Evans is just handing Bacon a small envelope containing pills as Raker walks unobserved into the small office.

"Sorry Doc, my brother knocked a water glass over on the ones you left yesterday." Bacon looked sideways as he notices Raker standing near the door. "We'll be more careful with these, I promise."

"I'll be out to check on Brace this afternoon." Evans glanced over at the hard face of the Circle R owner. "Just as soon as I take care of any patient's here in the office."

"Looks like you have a patient already." Bacon had no doubt who Raker is, but he's never seen the big man before. "Maybe he needs a pill."

"I'm not here to see the good doctor." Raker glared hard at Bacon. "I have business with you, Bacon Caldwell."

The Lazy Bar smiled calmly. "Well sir, it seems you have the advantage on me, I don't believe I know you."

"You know me alright; you stole my wife and sent this skunk here to gun me." Raker pointed at Fisher. "I warned you once Fisher, not to let me find you in Medicine Mound again."

"Gentlemen please." Evans stepped between the two big men. "Take your argument outside; I have valuable equipment and medicine in here that I cannot replace. Please, for my other patient's sake, let's have no trouble in here."

With all the talking neither Bacon nor Fisher hear Bowie slip quietly into the room behind them. Nodding at Caldwell; Fisher started to move his hand slowly down to the forty-five he wears when he feels the barrel of a pistol pushing into his back.

Bowie whispered softly into the gunman's ear. "You just let them handle their own differences or I'll blow a hole through you big enough to walk through." The pistol prodded harder into the gunfighter's back. "You understand?"

Sticking his thumbs into his gun belt Fisher nodded. "Yes sir."

"Alright Doc, we'll take it outside, thanks for the pills." Bacon pushed Raker aside as he left the office. "I'll see you this afternoon."

Raker followed the Lazy Bar owner across the porch, and out into the dusty road. "Turn around, Caldwell."

Bacon stopped, then slowly turned looking over to where his other two men are covered by Matt. "Well you must be Mister Raker?"

"I'm Raker."

"Seems you have the deadwood on me and my men, well what can I do for you?" Bacon sneered. "This must be about my sweet wife, Norma?"

"I want her and my daughter brought to Medicine Mound today."

"And if she doesn't want to come?"

"She does." Raker stepped closer to Caldwell. "Bring her in then keep to your own side of the Cinnamon."

"Why don't you just come and get her, if you're so sure of yourself."

"I don't want them caught in any gunplay, Caldwell."

"Do you think I'd start trouble and get my wife accidentally shot?" Bacon smirked, goading Raker. "Or get my daughter hurt?"

"No, maybe not you, but that back shooting brother of yours sure wouldn't have any problem shooting a woman."

"My brother!" Bacon's eyes hardened. "Did you have anything to do with his rifle blowing up?"

"Did that Sharps belong to your brother?" Raker smiled slightly. "We found the rifle after someone tried to back shoot my cook."

"You're a liar."

"Drop your gun belt Caldwell, now." Bowie cocked the Navy Colt. "Or I'll blow you into next week."

"No Mister Caldwell, I'm not a liar." Raker unbuckled his gun belt. "I figure it was your brother that shot me back in Virginia, probably Harrison and several others that owned land around here as well."

"That's absurd Raker; you're crazy." Bacon grinned into the cold eyes of Bowie then unbuckled his own gun belt. "Why would he do that?"

"You know maybe I am crazy, but now I want to hear you say you'll bring my wife back or I'm aiming to beat you half to death." Raker released his belt. "The second question is simple; you wanted every acre of land around these parts and with the men that had legal claim to the land dead, it would be easy."

"That's an out-and-out lie big man, and I ain't bringing Norma anywhere."

Raker started forward. "Then I'm gonna whip you until you squeal like a pig, Mister Bacon Caldwell."

"That's mighty big talk." Caldwell kicked his pistol belt out of the way. "Mighty big, you sure you're man enough to back it up?"

With a roar Raker charged across the narrow space separating them barreling into Caldwell with both fists swinging. Both men are closely matched in height and weight. Like two powerful giants the men fight back and forth in the wide street like two longhorn bulls, pushing and shoving. Neither backs up nor tries to duck a punch as both land punch for punch against each other. Hammering club like fists rain down as blood starts to flow from noses and cut faces. Hate emits from both red faces as the men hit and claw at each other like wild animals. Several town people appear on the sidewalks watching in shock as the big men battle back and forth in the middle of the wide street.

A hard right from Bacon brings Raker to one knee, but only for a second as he shakes his bloody face and lunges to his feet. Catching Bacon with a punch of his own, Raker knocks the Lazy Bar owner into the dirt, then kicks the down man hard in the rib cage causing several ribs to crack. Regaining his feet slowly, Bacon holds his side with one hand as he turns to meet the charging hate crazed man before him. Both men have expended much energy causing extreme fatigue to set in, but the raging hate in Raker gives him the edge. Nothing is gonna stop the Circle R owner as he savagely rains down vicious and savage blows onto Bacon Caldwell's broken face.

Using head butts, gouging fingers, and hard elbows, Raker fights like a crazy man. His way of fighting may be dirty in some watcher's eyes, but this isn't about fair or clean. His fighting is all about beating Caldwell within a minute of his life as he said he would. The Lazy Bar owner is finished, down on his knees trying to ward off the heavy blows of Raker who continues without letting up to punish a man that has stolen everything from him. Rolling painfully sideways Caldwell rights himself only to receive another fierce blow to his right eye crushing the socket, almost knocking the eye out of his head.

Bowie can see the Lazy Bar owner is finished as he rolls in the dust trying to regain his feet. He has to admit Caldwell has guts, he isn't gonna quit or ask for mercy. "He's had enough, George."

"I ain't." Raker's voice is hoarse from exertion, barely audible. "Not by a long shot, I ain't."

Bacon tries to stand but he is finished, blinded by blood flowing in his eyes, hardly conscious of his whereabouts. Where he finds the courage to try to get to his feet, Bowie doesn't know. "That's enough, George."

One final blow lands as Bowie with Matt's help pulled Raker from the bloody pulp that once was a man. Motioning Fisher and the other Lazy Bar riders forward Bowie watches them carry Caldwell into the doctor's office.

"We'll see you again, tall man." Fisher turned around in the door and pointed at Bowie. "This ain't finished by a long shot."

"Right now gunfighter, right now would be a good time as any to finish it." Bowie squared off against the man. "If you've got the guts?"

"Soon, very soon." Fisher followed the riders carrying Caldwell into the office.

As with most men witnessing a fight the battle's excitement makes any man watching want to get into the fight himself. The smell of blood, adrenaline rush, or just the age-old fighting instincts revive as they stand watching two combatants battling each other. Bowie Morgan is no different, watching as the two men fight and bleed he feels the same, his blood races, his fighting spirit surges.

The long ride back to the Circle R is silent as a cemetery. Neither Bowie, Talbert, nor Matt speak a word as the horses plod slowly east. Before leaving Medicine Mound; Raker had washed his face in the horse trough at the local livery washing away the blood. The big face is slightly puffy and beginning to turn bluish in places, but other than those few blemishes, the big man shows no other signs of the fight. Bowie knows from experience that come morning, Raker's muscles will probably be sore all over from the exertion of the fight. In a dog eat dog, no-holds-barred fight a man unconsciously uses muscles he never knew he had, straining them to the breaking point. The morning after a fight, a man is so sore, he can hardly move about and it is sometimes a month before the effects of a hard fight wear completely away.

Riding into the ranch yard they are met by Miguel and his family. The small Mexican stared curiously at Raker; he can tell the big man has been in a set-to with someone. The little man cusses, if Raker had been fighting with Caldwell he would have loved to have seen it.

"I must have missed a good one señor?"

Matt shook his head and laughed. "You did Miguel, but I watched it for you."

Carlos stood quietly in the yard waiting as Raker disappeared into the house, then followed Bowie as he leads the horses away. "Who was it?"

"The he hog himself, Bacon Caldwell."

"Señor Caldwell?" The boy exhaled sadly. "And I missed it, who won the fight?"

"It sure wasn't Caldwell." Matt walked toward the barn laughing. "He looks like he has been in a fight with a five-legged grizzly bear."

"Ah señor, I sure wish I had seen it."

"You sure missed a good one alright, if Bowie hadn't of pulled George off Caldwell, he would have killed him." Matt laughed again. "It'll surprise me, if he lives through that beating."

Talbert stood off to the side, listening and remembering the Sharps and the good men Brace Caldwell probably killed. "You should have let him finish the job, Bowie."

"He came close Talbert, real close."

Norma looked on in shock as Fisher helped Bacon into the house. Already the beaten man's face was swelled twice its normal size and had turned a blackish blue. "What happened?"

Bacon pushed the gunman's hands away then slammed the door as he disappeared into his bedroom as Fisher turned to the curious Norma. "Your ex-husband is what happened lady, that man's crazier than a stirred up hornet's nest."

"Fisher, get in here." The words seem feeble, barely audible coming through the heavy door.

The stooped gunman took a final look at the smiling woman then walked into the bedroom to find Caldwell already lying on his bed, his eyes closed. The face was a mess; stitches show where Doc Evans had sewed up deep cuts over both eyebrows and one deep cut along his left cheekbone. Evans had warned Caldwell, come morning even with cold compresses applied continually, both eyes would be swelled shut, the cheek and both eye sockets will swell and cause extreme pain. His broken ribs would make breathing almost impossible, and any movement from the bed will cause intense pain, the good doctor was blunt he had said Caldwell was a complete wreck.

"Fisher, you hear me and hear me good." Bacon's words come out barely audible. "Put a rider on the road to Wichita tonight."

"For what?"

"You ever heard of a man called Cord Alvord?"

"Who hasn't?" Fisher shook his head. "He's one man I don't want any truck with."

"You know him personally?"

"Personally no, but I know him alright." Fisher admitted. "He killed a friend of mine in Dodge a couple years back."

"Then you'll go, you know what the man looks like, go bring him here." Bacon eased his head on the pillow. "You hear me go yourself, pay his fee whatever it is, just get him here."

"He's gonna come high Boss." Fisher shook his head. "And Alvord ain't a man."

"What do you mean?" Bacon moved his head slightly.

"He's a crazed killer worse than a rabid wolf, Mister Caldwell." Fisher shook his head. "I sure wouldn't bring that bloodthirsty killer here."

"Get him." Caldwell opened one eye and looked across at Fisher. "And send Happy in here to me."

Fisher looked at the beat up man lying on the bed. "Are you sure you want me to leave you alone with both you and Brace in the shape you're in?"

"We'll be alright." Caldwell motioned with his good hand. "Get riding, there's travel money in the top drawer of the desk."

Fisher took one final look at Bacon Caldwell, then shaking his head he walked over to the huge desk. "I'm going but, he'll want to know what the job is."

"You know the job; killing is the job, killing George Raker."

Norma stood over the bed looking down at Caldwell; she had heard Fisher's remark as he followed Bacon inside the house, there is no use asking what happened. "Can I get you anything, Bacon?"

Caldwell's one good eye focused on her standing at the end of his bed. "Have you been in contact with your ex-husband?"

"I want to leave this place Bacon." Norma turned her head, ignoring the question. "I know you lied to me about George's death, and I know you sent Brace east to kill him."

"You seem to know a lot about my affairs, my dear."

"I've heard you talking, and finally realized what you are."

"And what is that?"

"A monster of some kind, greedy, and land hungry." Norma looked down at the bruised face. "You're no account, Bacon; I should have realized that sooner."

"I asked you, did you contact Raker?"

Norma raised her head proudly. "I slipped a note to him."

"How?"

"I did it; I won't tell you who carried the letter." Norma shook her head. "I'm leaving here today."

"You ain't leaving this house or this ranch woman, you're my wife." Bacon tried to sit up then slumped back in pain. "You hear me Norma? You're staying."

"I'm still the wife of George Raker."

At the words Caldwell's tried again to rise. "I'll be out of this bed in a few days woman, then we'll see how tough you talk."

"You touch me and I'll kill you myself."

"Get out."

As Norma left the bedroom and returned to the kitchen, Happy Gillum stepped quietly through the back door. Hat in hand he stood looking over to where she stood close to the wood stove, unaware of his presence. "Pardon me ma'am, Mister Caldwell sent for me."

"In there." Norma pointed at the closed door, she had been so deep in thought she didn't hear him enter.

"Yes ma'am." Happy Gillum is only a line rider for the Lazy Bar and not too smart a one at that, finding someone to hire him had been hard. Riding for Bacon for years he always did exactly as he was told, when he was told, no questions asked just to preserve his job. Tapping lightly the cowboy opened the door slowly peering into the study then stepped inside the room.

"Close the door and come over here."

"Yes sir."

"I've got a job for you Happy, you do it without asking foolish questions and you'll get a five-dollar a month raise." Bacon watched the man's face out of his one good eye. "That's a lot of money for a cowhand."

"Yes sir Mister Caldwell, you know I always do as I'm told."

"I know that Happy, but this is a little different work than punching cows or riding fence." Bacon motioned the man closer.

Gillum wasn't in town when the fight had taken place, he had heard of the fight but he is as shocked as Norma was when he moved closer to the bed and got a good look at Bacon's face. He can't believe how beat up the man is. His slow mind can't comprehend how anyone would dare lay a hand on Bacon Caldwell, a man who he thought of as a giant.

Blinking in fright as he listened to the words of the rancher, Happy stepped back. "I can't do that Mister Caldwell, she likes me."

"It's for her own good Happy, at least until me and Brace can get on our feet and Fisher gets back so we can protect her." Bacon looked up and smiled at the scared man. "You like your job here, Happy?"

"Yes sir, a lot."

"Then you get Little Tom and take her to the line shack up on Dry Creek until I come for her." Bacon patted Gillum on the arm. "It'll be okay, I know she'll be safe with you."

"Yes sir, if you're sure it'll be okay."

"It'll be fine, her mother knows all about it." Bacon lied. "Just don't say anything more about it right now, we don't want anybody upset."

"Yes sir."

"Get enough supplies for a week and after dark, slip in and take her." Caldwell looked up at the confused Gillum. "Be real quiet like."

"Yes sir, if you say so."

"I'll keep the missus busy in here until you get the girl and ride away."

"You don't want me to take Mrs. Caldwell with her?"

"No, not this time." Bacon shook his head. "I'll bring her to the line shack in a couple days."

Chapter 10

Norma tried to listen through the door, but the voices are only muffled whispers, too soft for her to understand. Watching out the front window as Happy leaves without speaking or looking at her she notices two riders posted at the front and back doors of the house. Never has the house been guarded before, her heart misses a beat as she realizes the men are posted on the porch to watch her. There is little doubt now she is a prisoner in her own home. What happened in town, what had started the fight? Did Bacon know about the note when he rode into Medicine Mound, was the note the reason for the fight?

Stepping through the back door and starting off the porch, Norma found one of the riders blocking her path. "I'm sorry ma'am, but you're not to leave the house until Mister Caldwell is back on his feet."

"Get out of my way Sandy."

"I'm sorry Mrs. Caldwell; I can't let you leave the house."

Whirling Norma stomped back into the house and pushed the bedroom door open. "Is this your idea Bacon, keeping me prisoner in my own home?"

"There have been threats my dear." Bacon looked over at the woman. "It'll only be until I get back on my feet to protect you."

"Threat's against who?"

"Have you checked on Brace?"

"He's resting." Norma knows he is trying to throw her off. "What's going on Bacon?"

"The good doctor should be here soon." Bacon turned his head slowly. "Fix him up a good dinner, then we'll talk about this again."

After changing the bandages on Brace's wounds and persuading him to swallow several pills, Evans walked into Bacon's study and pulled a chair up close to the daybed.

"How are you doing Mister Caldwell?"

"I hurt Doc, my ribs, face, I ache all over." Bacon tried to ease himself. "How is Brace?"

"His wounds are clean, with no apparent signs of blood poisoning."

"And his eyes?"

"I won't know until I unwrap them."

"How long did you say?"

"At least six weeks to be safe." Evans leaned over Bacon. "Now let me take a look at you."

"I'm alright Doc." Bacon turned his head and looked out the open window. "I've taken beatings before."

"Not this bad, I hope." Evans examined his patient. "Look into this lamp and let me see your eyes."

Frowning, Caldwell turned his head and stared into the coal oil lamp. "I'm fine, I tell you."

"Any headaches or pain?"

"Plenty of pain and a small headache, why don't you spend the night Doc, it's late."

"No thanks, I need to be getting back." Evans closed his bag. "Here's a couple pills for when your face really starts hurting."

"Thanks." Bacon looked at the pills Evans placed on the table. "Norma has supper on the table she made special for you, at least eat before you leave."

"Thank you, I will take you up on that offer, Mrs. Caldwell is an excellent cook."

"Tell me Doc, did you pass a note from Norma to Raker?"

"I found a letter in my bag addressed to George Raker." Doc Evans straightened his shoulders and stared down at the man. "I don't know how it got in my medical bag but yes, I gave it to Raker. You know Mister Caldwell, tampering with the mail is against the law."

"Thank you Doc, for coming out." Bacon nodded slowly. "Now, go have yourself some supper."

"Thank you."

"When will you return?"

"Your brother seems to be out of danger from infection; I'll ride back by this way and check on both of you in a couple days."

"Good, leave a bill with Norma and I'll have your money ready when you return."

"Good evening Mister Caldwell." Evans turned to the door. "And thanks for your hospitality."

"Oh Doc." Bacon raised his head slightly and looked over at the doctor. "From now on it might be safer for all concerned if you just stick to your medical profession and leave the mail to me."

"Seems Mister Caldwell, you have enough enemies already without adding me." Evans frowned. "Just keep your mail and your problems out of my medical bag."

"Good day, Doctor." Bacon turned his head, surprised at the spunk the slender doctor showed.

Placing his bag on the table, Evans sat down before a steaming plate of steak and potatoes Norma had prepared. Nodding as he took a bite of the food, he smiled over at her. "This is delicious, Mrs. Caldwell."

"Thank you Doctor." Norma looked at the open doorway of the bedroom knowing Bacon is listening to every word. "I'm glad you like it."

"It sure beats the town cooking I've been eating, by a long shot."

"Why isn't a young man like yourself married?"

"Just haven't found the right girl yet I reckon, or the time for courting."

Norma looked at the open door again, then refilled Evans' coffee cup. "Well like I said, you're young yet, you have plenty of time for such things.

"Yes ma'am." Evans can tell she is afraid the way she keeps looking at the open door, then back at him. "Well I reckon I better start back, I've got to stop by the Kincaid Farm and check on the new baby."

"Tell Martha I'll come over and see the baby as soon as Bacon gets back on his feet."

Evans looked closely at the frightened woman, but doesn't ask what is on her mind. He too is aware of the open door and he knows Caldwell can hear their every word. "I'll be sure to tell her, ma'am."

"Just call me Norma, everyone else does."

"Yes Miss Norma, and thanks again for the fine meal." Evans stood and retrieved his hat and bag. "I best be going."

"Good day Doctor, we'll see you soon."

"Yes ma'am."

Happy Gillum shook his head sadly as Little Tom took the reins of his horse then made his way slowly along the outside of the large ranch house. He doesn't like what he has been ordered to do, but he likes to eat and that means he has to have his job at the Lazy Bar. He is well aware he is a weak-minded man, not the brightest, just a hired hand. Being slow since childhood, he has always been taught to do as he was told. This time it is no different, even though he knows something is wrong and he has no stomach for the job, he will follow Bacon Caldwell's orders just as he has always done.

Removing his hat Gillum looked through the half open window where the moon had lit up the small bed Emma was peacefully sleeping in. Raising the window until it is fully open Gillum eased through the window and crept to the side of the bed. Shaking his head sadly he pulled the small frame into his arms then hugged her to him as she struggles, frightened by being awoken from a sound sleep. Quickly he exits the window hurrying with the small bundle to where Little Tom is waiting.

"Ride out quiet Little Tom." Gillum whispered, covering the struggling girl's mouth with his hand as they clear the ranch buildings, finally removing it when they are out of hearing. "It's just me Emma; Happy Gillum, don't scream."

"You scared me Happy." The youngster is afraid, but she likes Happy Gillum, he had always been a good friend to her. "Where are you taking me?"

"I'm sorry Emma; I didn't want you to yell out and wake the whole ranch."

"Where are you taking me?" She asked again. "I want my Mama?"

"We're going camping for a couple days is all." Happy looked down at her smiling. "You're gonna have fun."

"Does my mother know you've taken me?"

"Sure she does Emma, it was her idea for you to go fishing with us," Gillum lied. "She knows how you love to fish."

"Well, I guess its okay, I do like to fish."

The early morning warmth of the kitchen with its aroma of fresh baked biscuits cooking on the huge wood stove normally brings Emma sleepy eyed from her room, hungry and ready to eat. When Emma doesn't make her usual morning appearance hollering she is hungry, Norma laid down her dishrag and opened the girl's door only to find the bed empty. Turning her eyes to search the room, she suddenly focused on the open window and the lace curtains blowing in the morning breeze. The window puzzles her, she knew it was only half open when she had tucked Emma into bed last night and she knows the child is too small yet to open the heavy window by herself. Quickly moving to the bed, she places her hand on the bedding only to find it cold and barely slept in. Putting her closed fist to her mouth in rage she raced to Bacon's bedroom where he is lying on his bed holding his ribs as he tries to breath.

"She's gone, my baby's gone." Norma glared at the man's swollen face. "What have you done with her, Bacon Caldwell?"

"Why do you think I have anything to do with her not being in bed?" Bacon spoke hoarsely through his swollen lips. "She's probably just outside playing."

Turning, Norma retreated to the dining room and the gun rack that hung on the wall. Retrieving a shotgun, she walked back into the bedroom and approached the bed. "Bacon so help me, I won't ask you again."

"Have you taken leave of your senses woman?" Caldwell eyed the shotgun with his one open eye, then looked into the crazed face before him. "You know I've been right here in bed."

The cocking of the shotgun hammers resonates loudly through the room as the hysterical woman ears back both hammers. "I know you Bacon, and I know your men don't make a move unless you tell them."

"Be careful with that cannon woman." Caldwell stared into the seemingly insane eyes. "You shoot me and the girl is good as dead."

"I aim to kill you Bacon Caldwell, right here and right now, unless you get Emma back in here to me before I count to five."

"I can't Norma; some of the boys took her fishing for the day."

"One!"

Sweat beads on Caldwell's face, he can see the woman he thought he controlled has gone completely crazy. "Alright Norma, put that gun down and I'll get her in here."

"Two!"

"Norma, for pete's sake give me a minute and I'll send for her." For the first time in his life Bacon Caldwell is afraid. His broken ribs prevent him from moving fast enough to get away from the shotgun's twin barrels that are pointing right at his midsection. Caldwell swallowed in fear, at ten feet the barrels look like cannon's, there is no way she can miss.

"Three." Norma inched the big gun up a notch. "Good-bye, Bacon."

Bacon cringed on the pillow; he had seen the wild look that had come over the woman just as she pulled the trigger causing the shotgun to belch fire and lead. The shotgun's roar reverberates throughout the house, shaking chinaware, windows, and anything that will rattle. Wood splinters and wallpaper floats from the ceiling where the heavy pellets have blown several holes through the roof. Just in time, only seconds before the discharge Sandy had heard screaming and arguing from the house and slipped in silently from the porch. Wrenching the shotgun from Norma's hands as she pulled the trigger caused the big gun to discharge harmlessly into the ceiling. With the force of the hard wrench Norma had fell backwards onto the floor, regaining her footing she lunged crazily forward at Bacon as Sandy grabs her from behind.

"I'll kill you Bacon, if it's the last thing I ever do," Norma screamed across the room as Sandy restrained the fighting woman. "I'll kill you."

"You cut that close Sandy." Bacon wiped his face trying to compose himself. "Real close."

The Lazy Bar rider looked across the room at Caldwell's wet, pale face, shaking his head in disgust. He has to be careful not to betray his thoughts or feelings. He has his job to protect, but he knows now the boss of the Lazy Bar, the man who has ridden roughshod over the entire county is a coward. Yesterday, Caldwell stood his ground and fought George Raker taking his whipping like a man. The blond rider doesn't know for sure, perhaps the severe beating had taken the courage and fight out of the man. He has heard of things like that happening, but today he had seen as Caldwell cringed in fear. He heard the man whimpering and pleading for his life like a woman as the gun roared. Bacon Caldwell, despite all his bravado and swaggering is a weak man. Sandy thought he smelled fear in the big man the day of the fight in Medicine Mound with Raker, now he knows his suspicions were right.

Suddenly Caldwell's beefy hand strikes forward knocking Norma to the floor, causing blood to flow from her split lip. "Ain't no need in that Boss." Sandy bent to pick Norma up from the floor. "She can't hurt you none now."

"I thank you for saving my skin Sandy, now get out and leave me and my loving wife alone." Bacon glared down at Norma. "Load that shotgun and leave it here with me."

From the next room comes the sound of crashing bottles and glasses as a table goes over, then they hear a muffled voice through the thin board wall. Forgetting Norma for the moment, Sandy rushed into the next room where Brace is trying to pull the bandages from his face so he can see what is happening.

"Here stop that Brace, your eyes aren't healed yet." Guiding the blind man back to his bed Sandy laid him down then pulled the heavy quilts over him.

Looking over to where Norma stood watching at the door, Bacon pointed his finger at her from the bed. "Clean that mess up in there woman then get out of here."

"You want me to help her Boss?" Sandy waited in the doorway.

"Just help me get dressed then come outside with me." Bacon pointed his finger at Norma before leaving the room. "You pull another stunt like this Norma and so help me, I'll beat you half to death."

"What about your ribs?" Sandy tried to get Caldwell's mind away from Norma.

"I'm getting up; I almost got killed just now lying in that bed like a helpless baby."

Norma whispered to herself as Sandy helped Caldwell from the house and over to the corrals. "I swear Bacon; I'll kill you if anything happens to my baby."

"What was the shooting about Norma?" Brace reaches blindly with his hand, feeling for her, trying to find someone in the dark.

"Nothing Brace, try to get some sleep."

"It durn near scared me out of a year's growth, whatever it was."

"It was nothing, I dropped the shotgun and it discharged is all."

"You best be careful with guns, you see what one has done to me."

Normally, Norma is a soft, gentle loving woman; she shook her head almost feeling sorry for Brace. Now he's blind and she was the cause of it, shaking her head she wondered what has Bacon Caldwell turned all of them into?

Early morning against his father's wishes, Carlos Ortiz slipped away from the Circle R to go fishing. His favorite fishing hole is at a bend in the small clear Cinnamon Creek that runs west of Medicine Mound. Slipping off without permission from his folks always gives him guilty feelings, but he always returns safely bringing fresh tasty fish for supper. Anyway, his chores are done up, so Carlos sees no harm in spending at least one day alone fishing and enjoying the freedom he always feels far out on the grassland. They are used to him being gone a day sometimes two, but they still worry. Though still very young, Carlos is an excellent woodsman and he knows all the dangers lurking out in the wild. Always with his safe return, they forgive their son as they are happy to see him home again.

Hearing the hoof beats of two horses then the sound of voices, Carlos steps from the trail he is on and hides in the thick bordering bushes. His dark eyes watch as two riders from the Lazy Bar ranch trot by with a little girl sitting in the saddle in front of one. Carlos doesn't know the men by name, but he has seen them around Medicine Mound and he recognizes them. The men work for Bacon Caldwell, who dismissed his father from the Raker ranch as soon as he married Norma Raker. His father had always worked for George Raker and was left to look after the Circle R Ranch in his absence. Carlos was about eight when the baby girl was born, right after the war started. He had been with his mother the day she helped deliver the little baby girl Emma. The girl's mother Norma Raker had married Bacon Caldwell shortly after the girl's birth, so he hadn't seen much of her except when they came to town occasionally for supplies. Knowing Emma all her young life, he recognizes her right away.

Carlos can see plainly as the horses pass his place of concealment the small face is smeared by tears. He couldn't help but notice the dirty stains on her as they ride by, telling him something is very wrong. For some reason she has been crying. Why did these men have the little girl far out here away from the Lazy B ranch headquarters and without her mother? Carlos has no way of knowing what is happening, but whatever is going on he can tell by Emma's face, she isn't happy.

Laying aside the fishing pole he had just cut, the young Mexican follows carefully behind the two men and the girl, careful to keep out of their sight. Looking off to the east to get his bearings, he guesses the Circle R Ranch is at least five miles away cross country, as the crow flies. The Lazy Bar ranch is much closer, but Carlos doesn't know Bacon Caldwell or his brother Brace. He heard his father and others speak very badly of the brothers several times so he doesn't dare go to the Lazy Bar to tell them what he has just seen.. He judges the distance, then quickly makes up his mind. He will race back to the Circle R and tell his father what he has seen, but first, he will follow the riders, he has to know where they are taking the girl so he can lead the men back.

Late afternoon finds Happy and Little Tom dismounting at a small line shack that was once a part of the old Eagle Ranch now another of Bacon Caldwell's holdings. Carlos hides behind the tall grass and brush, watching as the smaller man looks around carefully then takes Emma inside. The other rider unsaddled the horses and turned them into a corral behind a small lean to shelter. Looking up at the sun, Carlos guessed it is still at least six hours until full dark. He had followed the men for many miles, so he knows he cannot reach the Circle R before morning, even if he travels all night. Slipping up alongside the cabin as the second rider closed the rough plank door; Carlos crouched under an open window and listened to the men's conversation.

"We'll fix you up some supper right quick Emma." The short rider talks softly to the girl.

"I want to go home Happy; I want my mother."

"You be a good girl Emma, and she'll be along any minute."

"You promise you ain't lying are you?" Her voice brightened a little.

"No missy, I sure ain't lying, she'll be here soon, you'll see."

"Okay, in that case I guess I am a little hungry."

"You just play a little while and old Uncle Happy will fix you up some flapjacks in just a jiffy."

"Okay."

The two wranglers walked out on the porch for some stove wood, stopping exactly above where Carlos is hiding under the porch. "What are we gonna do Gillum, when her ma don't show?"

"The boss said he'd be along to take her off our hands."

Little Tom shook his head. "You know as well as I do, he's too stove up to ride way out here for a few days."

"He'll be here Tom, or he'll send someone." Happy stooped and picked up several sticks of wood, then straightening; he shook his head and grinned. "I reckon, he sure didn't figure on Raker being that rough."

"That feller he's a big 'un for sure, but so is Caldwell."

"He wasn't big enough." Happy turned for the door. "Let's get the girl something to eat."

Raising his head Carlos peered cautiously through the window where Emma and the two riders are sitting at the table eating. He had given thought to taking her home as soon as it is dark enough to sneak her out, but the girl is too small to travel five miles on foot. And she also doesn't know him very well, only seeing the young Mexican on a few occasions. She sure wouldn't leave with a stranger without a fight and maybe get him caught. Munching on stale biscuits he had brought he waits until both men have retired to their bunks, then slipped back to the small corral and bridled one of the horses. Leading the animal through the gate and far away from the corral before swinging up on the horse Carlos heads east. Grinning, he knows what his saintly father would say about him stealing the horse, but he has no choice. For sure he will be lectured; Miguel will say he is far too young to become a horse thief. Nevertheless if he is to get back to the Circle R he must hurry, that means taking the animal. After listening to the two men talking on the front porch, he knows the girl has been taking without her mother's knowledge.

Out of hearing of the line shack Carlos kicks the gelding into a hard lope. It will be morning before they miss the horse, by then he should be back at the Circle R to tell Senor Raker of the girl's abduction. If the Circle R men are at the ranch they will have plenty of time to return to the line shack before daylight comes on the land again.

Early morning light filters through the door and open windows of the cabin as Happy coaxes life back into the dry kindling he has placed in the belly of the old wood stove. Looking over to where Emma is sleeping soundly he smiled then placed the blackened coffeepot on the stove before waking Tom. Slicing bacon into the skillet, he nodded as the skinny rider pulled out a chair and yawned.

"How long before the coffee boils?"

"Thirty minutes." Happy looked out the open window. "See to the horses Tom, and I'll cook us up some breakfast."

"Alright."

Happy had just shoved a pan full of biscuits into the hot oven when Little Tom motioned to him from the doorway. "Come out here a minute."

"What's up?"

"We got a horse missing, taken during the night." Tom shook his head.

"Was the gate open, maybe he just wandered off?"

"Not unless he can work a sliding pole gate, he didn't."

"Who you reckon took him?"

"Barefoot tracks of a small person were left in the sand."

"Indians maybe?"

"I don't think so." Tom shook his head again then studied the ground under the window. "Happy look here, the same tracks as in the corral, a kid's track."

"Some youngster probably spotted us yesterday, then for some reason took the horse after we turned in last night." Happy looked down at the tracks. "Just a horse thief maybe, but I don't like it."

"What would a barefoot kid be doing way out here alone?"

"Hard to say." Happy was worried as he looked across the tree covered flats surrounding the cabin. "Saddle the horse we've got to make tracks outta here fast."

"You think the kid is headed to tell someone we've got the girl?"

"Maybe, I don't know." Happy turned for the cabin. "We sure ain't waiting around here on our backsides to see if someone shows up."

"You know what folks around here would do to us if they catch us with the girl?" Little Tom is nervous. "They'd string us up to the nearest tree and Caldwell wouldn't help us one bit."

"I know."

"Let's leave her and ride."

"Where, if we ride out and leave her Caldwell would kill us." Happy shook his head. "No sir, with only one horse our only chance is to hide her out, then ride to the Lazy Bar for help."

"Where we gonna hide her?"

"Get saddled, I'll think on it while I roll up some biscuits and side meat."

"Save me a cup of coffee."

Waking Emma; Happy handed her a hot biscuit and some bacon while he filled a flour sack with the rest. Pouring two cups of hot coffee, Happy sips on his while watching the trails as Little Tom saddles their lone gelding.

"Are we going home Happy." Emma munched slowly on her biscuit.

"Yes Emma, we're going home soon as Little Tom saddles the horse."

"Good, I miss my mother."

"I do too," Happy mumbled under his breath, wondering why he ever let Caldwell get him into this mess?

Ground tying the gelding, Little Tom hopped up on the porch and took the extended coffee cup Happy held out. "Thanks Happy, I can't hardly get through a day without my coffee."

"Yeah, well you better drink up." Happy surveyed the flat pastureland that surrounds the shack. "Cause we just may not get through this day, coffee or not."

"I hid the extra saddle, you figure out yet where we're headed?"

"You know that little line shack down on Rock Creek?"

"I do."

"We'll take the girl there, then you'll ride on to the Lazy Bar and let Caldwell know what's going on."

"That's at least ten miles so we best get to riding, I'll brush out any tracks we leave so no one can track us."

Raker, with Bowie and Matt following him, rode slowly into the yard of the small line shack on the old Eagle Ranch and dismounted Stepping into the cabin with their weapons drawn the three men quickly survey the vacant room. The recent occupants are gone, no evidence remains of their presence in the line shack except a pile of kindling lying in the wood box.

"They ain't been gone long George." Bowie touches the still warm stove. "Couple hours or so I'd say."

Matt entered the cabin and looked around. "Someone wiped out most of their tracks, but they missed some, one horse left here heading southwest."

"I reckon Carlos left them short a horse when he stole the bay from them." Raker nodded. "The girl is too small to ride alone and they didn't bring along enough supplies to need a pack animal."

"Apparently they weren't planning on being out with her for very long, when the horse came up missing they figured they better hightail it out of here quick."

"Carlos did a good job, for a young'un he's a steady lad with plenty of guts." Bowie holstered his pistol.

"Yes he is, same as his old Pappy." Raker retreated from the building. "We were fortunate he discovered Emma with the two men and came to tell us."

"Do you think Caldwell is behind this, or have they taken her for ransom or something like that?"

"We won't know that until we catch up to them." Raker's face turned hard. "And we will catch up I guarantee it, even if we have to follow them to hell."

"We'll catch them, a cowboy doesn't walk well and one of them is afoot." Matt laughed. "He sure won't travel far walking in high heeled riding boots."

"Let's ride."

Finally picking up the trail a mile away from the shack Matt finds it easy to follow until it reaches a deep rocky gully two miles from the line shack. The tracks lead down a narrow cow path down into the arroyo which is covered in small rocks, making it impossible to follow.

Climbing out of the deep gully, Raker and Bowie follow its course looking for any tracks leaving the arroyo, while Matt stays down in the wash looking for any sign of the men ahead. The small gully meanders through the grasslands where it finally flattened out and dumps into Cinnamon Creek.

"Whoever has the girl sure knows how to hide a trail," Matt sat looking at the small creek. "I'll say that for him."

"We'll get him if I have to follow him all over this country."

"I ain't no tracker, but I know cowboys." Matt lit up a curlie. "They all hate to walk, I say again whoever is afoot ain't going far."

"You boys search this side." Bowie kicked his horse into the Cinnamon and started across. "I'll take the other side."

"You think they went up stream or down?" Raker looked across the creek.

Turning in his saddle Matt looked up and down the stream. "I think they'll head downstream, there are no cabins or line shacks back that way."

"We got company." Bowie stopped his gelding knee deep in the creek and is looking behind Raker and Matt.

Trotting toward them with a big smile on his face Carlos Ortiz came riding down the trail straight to where the three men sit their horses. Grinning broadly as he rode up, the young Mexican reined in close to Raker and smiled at the men.

"I thought you were headed back home Carlos?" Raker looked over at the youngster who was supposed to go back to the ranch after making sure they were on the right trail.

"Si señor, I said I would, but maybe you need Carlos' help in finding these bad men from the Lazy Bar."

"Do you know these parts?" Bowie splashed back onto dry land.

"Si, I fish this place many times." Carlos waved his small hand. "All along the Cinnamon is good fishing."

"Your old pappy might not like me putting you in danger."

"Perhaps Señor Raker, but I think he would want me to help get the young one home safely." Carlos shrugged. "I will find them for you."

"You a tracker Carlos?" Matt eyed the young boy. "A good tracker?"

"I will find them for you." Carlos slid from his horse and handed Matt the reins. "I tracked you here."

Slipping into the water he waded along both banks of the creek, then pointed a slim brown finger downstream. The three men spread out on each side of the small creek following Carlos. The youngster's dark eyes surveyed every possible place the Lazy Bar riders could have exited the water. Cattle trails leading in or out of the creek are muddy, any man leaving the water afoot or on a horse would leave tracks that couldn't be missed.

"There!" The brown hand shoots out pointing to tall weeds that lay bent over across the cow path leading out of the creek. Still wading in the clear creek Carlos was able to spot the almost hidden horse tracks where they exited the water. "They ride to the south now."

Raker looked up at the setting sun. "We'll follow them as long as we can."

Lunging up the slick trail leading away from the creek bed, Matt handed Carlos his horse reins and rode over to where Bowie and Raker are waiting. "It's getting too late to follow them much further boys."

"Alright." Raker slowly nods his head. "Let's make camp, we'll get after them come daylight."

Little Tom raced his lathered horse into the ranch yard and dismounted at the porch railing where Sandy is standing guard. "Where's Mister Caldwell?"

"In the house." Sandy stepped down from the porch. "Where is Happy and the kid?"

"At the Rock Creek Shack." The rider started for the door. "Cool out my horse and feed him, will you Sandy? He's been rode hard."

"I will, you watch the woman."

"She ain't gonna try nothing with us holding the kid."

"Don't bet on it." Sandy laughed. "She almost blew Caldwell into next week after y'all left with the girl."

"You're joshing."

"No, I ain't joshing Tom." Sandy shook his head. "I'm telling you; when that shotgun went off Caldwell almost wet his pants."

"How'd she miss him?"

"I grabbed the barrel just as she pulled the trigger."

"What do you know about that?" Tom grinned. "How's the boss doing?"

"He's up and about, but he's moving mighty slow, he ain't over that whipping by a long sight I'm telling you."

Little Tom looked around making sure no one is listening. "I'll tell you Sandy, this whole business with Raker is dangerous, that man's crazy."

"What can we do?"

"We could climb on our horses and ride while we can."

Sandy shrugged. "We could Tom, but ride where?"

Norma glanced up from the table as Little Tom pushed the door open and walked into the kitchen. Always before the hired hands on the Lazy Bar had the courtesy and respect to knock, not anymore. They sense she has lost any control and authority she once had over Caldwell, now she is little more than a prisoner in her own home.

"Mrs. Caldwell." Tom touched his hat.

The blue eyes look up at him. "Is she safe, Little Tom?"

"She's just fine, ma'am." Tom always liked the woman. "She thinks she's on a fishing trip and you'll be coming soon."

"Take good care of her please."

Tom nodded. "She's with Happy Gillum and you know how much he thinks of her."

"Bring her home to me, Tom please."

"I need to see the boss."

"He's in his study." Norma pointed toward the closed door.

"How is he and Brace?"

"I could care less, but I'm afraid they're both alive."

"Yeah." Tom grinned. "I heard you tried to ventilate Mister Caldwell."

The blue eyes blaze as she stares toward the closed door. "Too bad I didn't."

Opening the door Little Tom finds Bacon sitting at his huge desk, staring at a ledger. "It's me Mister Caldwell; Little Tom?"

"Tom Hodge!" Bacon looked up from his books in surprise. "What are you doing here?"

"We ran into a little problem." The rider looked over to where Brace sat with his head cocked, listening. "Maybe a big problem."

"What's happened?" Bacon stood up slowly. "Is the kid, okay?"

The rider quickly tells of being discovered by some unknown person just as soon as they rode into the line shack, then the horse being stolen sometime during the night. Fearing whoever took the horse might ride back to Medicine Mound to spread the word and not wanting to be found with the girl, Gillum moved on down to the Rock Creek line shack. Both men know what the penalty would be if anyone discovered them with a stolen child. Swirling his hat around his hand, Tom finished his report by telling Caldwell about seeing four riders headed south as he made his way back to the ranch. The riders were following the same trail he and Happy had taken on their way to the line shack on Rock Creek.

"Who do you think they were?"

"Can't say for sure the distance was just too far, but one of the men was big enough to be Raker and it could have been that Ortiz kid leading them." Tom looked about the room. "Whoever stole the horse from us was barefoot just like most of them Mex kids run around."

"Pour yourself a drink, Little Tom." Bacon stared hard at the rider then looked across the room where Brace sat listening. "So you're thinking the kid stole your horse, then rode to Raker and told him about seeing the girl?"

"Thanks Boss." Tom picked up the decanter of whiskey. "Yep, that's the way I have it figured, it was Raker back there on the trail alright, I'd bet a month's pay on it. They passed me at a pretty far distance, but I'd know my own horse at any distance."

"How long do you figure it'll take them to reach the line shack?"

Tom shrugged his shoulders. "It's hard to say for sure with the Mex tracking us. He was moving pretty slow, but he was sticking to our trail like a tick on a hound's back."

Bacon frowned in deep thought. "How far away from the line shack were they?"

"Five miles, give or take."

"You reckon you could take riders and get back to the line shack trail ahead of Raker?"

"It'll be awfully close, but with fresh horses and them having to stick to our trail and sort it out, I may be able to beat them there." Tom finished off the whiskey. "Providing I leave now and wear out some horses getting back there."

"Ride."

"And if we catch up?"

"There'll be a bonus for every one of you if Mister Raker gets himself shot dead along with the others with him, while trespassing on my land and rustling my cattle."

"Yes sir." Tom set down the glass softly and looked across the room. "How you doing, Brace?"

"I'm blind."

Nodding Little Tom looked curiously at the bandages, then without speaking again turned for the door closing it behind him. Stopping in the kitchen he shook his head at Norma then pushed open the outside door. Never would he have believed Bacon Caldwell could look as broken as he did in that study. The owner of the Lazy Bar talked tough, but Little Tom could tell by the nervous twitch of his eyes, the Lazy Bar owner was a beaten man. The slender rider knew he is no longer the arrogant iron fisted ranch owner he was before the terrible beating Raker gave him days before.

Little Tom Hodge has been in several fights in his days on the range. He had given and taken his fair share of whippings both in the bunkhouses and saloons, but none were personal, just drunken cowboys blowing off steam. This fight was different; Caldwell had taken a severe beating at the hands of Raker in front of the whole town. The Lazy Bar owner lost prestige and even worse, he now fears Raker and maybe fighting itself. Tom has seen Bacon bully smaller and lesser men, but this beating by Raker has marked him, no longer would men cow down to him. They know now, he could be beaten.

Chapter 11

Quickly gathering together six riders from the bunkhouse, with rifles and fresh horses, Little Tom leads the curious men toward the Rock Creek line shack at a hard run. He has no idea how close Raker and his men are to the cabin, but he aims to intercept them as he was told to do. Tom has killed men before and it will not bother him to kill again, and he could use the bonus Caldwell promised. With the money he could clear out of this part of the country and ride back to his home in south Texas, he misses the flat grasslands he should never have come north. Looking at the riders following him he nods, most of them have ridden with him before and they are good men.

Turning to the southwest to intersect the trail he and Gillum had taken to Rock Creek; Little Tom slowed the men down to a slow lope, saving the horses. He has ridden this land for several months and is aware of a shortcut that will cut off several miles, possibly putting him and his men between the line shack and Raker. Thirty minutes later, he pulled his blowing horse in and dismounts to study the small worn trail leading to the cabin, just a mile farther along.

"We've got them boys." Tom can't see any other tracks other than his and Happy Gillums' on the sandy trail. "We'll slip into that stand of blackjacks and hide our horses."

With one man holding the horses, Little Tom quickly spreads the others out behind the tree line and settled down to wait. Each rider levers a shell into his rifle letting the hammer down as the men focus on the trail that passes only yards from their hiding place.

"We gonna shoot them from ambush, without any warning?" A younger rider asks.

"That was Mister Caldwell's orders Jeb, they're trespassing on Lazy Bar land and probably rustling more of his cattle." Tom looked sideways at the man. "You got a problem with killing rustlers?"

"Beats hanging them, I reckon." The rider dropped his eyes. "It sure don't feel right though, shooting men down in cold blood without warning."

"How does a big bonus for stopping the rustling sound to you Jeb?"

"I'll back you Little Tom, you know that." The young man looked off down the trail. "I don't need blood money to do my job."

"I know that boy." The small man nodded then cocked his head as the sound of walking horses and squeaking leather sound back along the trail. Still out of the waiting men's sight, the muffled sound of movement carries to where they are hiding among the scrub oak and mesquite trees.

Fisher walked into the plush Alhambra Gambling Parlor and looked around the quiet saloon where several men sit playing poker. A tall, thin man sits with his back to the wall his snakelike black eyes studying the fanned cards in his strong hand then looking around the table. Fisher knows Cord Alvord the minute he lays eyes on the gunfighter. The trademark black vest with large silver Conchos running down the front, the black hat with the same Conchos on the hatband, and the ever present black cigar hanging from the thin, cruel lips can only belong to the Kansas gunman who keeps a room at the Alhambra.

Frank Fisher is a fast man with a gun, but he has seen Alvord in action when he gunned down his friend, Sun Haskett in Dodge. He fears the man in black and he cannot help it, he knows he is no match for Alvord in a stand-up gunfight. He remembers well, that day two years ago when Haskett pushed his luck too far and challenged the tall man. It wasn't even close and the black cigar was still clenched tightly in the thin lips as the cold eyes looked down at Haskett, then over at him. Not a word was spoken between the two men, but Fisher knew all too well the gunfighter had his number. As Alvord's eyes met his, Fisher was the first to blink.

Walking to the long, well-polished bar, Fisher ordered a whiskey then turned to where the poker game is being played. Several times, Alvord turned his black eyes in Fisher's direction then returns his attention back to the game. Finishing off his drink Fisher walked to the table and stood across from Alvord. Nodding as the man in black looked up at him, he waited until the hand is finished before saying a word.

"When you get a minute, Mister Alvord, I'd like to have a word with you." Fisher can tell the tall man is trying to place him.

"What's on your mind?"

"Business, in private if you don't mind."

Alvord nodded. "Have yourself a drink I'll be with you directly."

"No rush."

"I never rush." The voice is ice cold the cold eyes never look up. "Rushing can get a man killed."

Fisher is on his third whiskey after waiting almost an hour when Alvord quit the poker game and walked to where he is sitting. Circling around so his back would be to the wall, the gunman pulled out a chair and sat down. The gunfighter moves with the fluid grace of a mountain cat, reminding Fisher of a predator looking to spring at any moment.

"I'm sorry to keep you waiting Sir, but the cards." Alvord doesn't finish as he waved off the bartender. "Don't I know you from somewhere?"

"Dodge City, you killed a friend of mine there a couple years back."

"Oh yes." Alvord nodded, his eyes narrowing. "Now I remember you, why didn't you help your friend that day?"

"Weren't my fight."

"And today, mister?"

"Fisher, Frank Fisher."

"I've heard of you Mister Fisher tell me Sir, what's so important that you have to interrupt my afternoon poker game?" Alvord seemed agitated as he looked back toward the table where money is being tossed into the pile. "What business do we have?"

"My boss has a job for you Mister Alvord."

"Isn't gun fighting in your line of work?"

"My boss is Bacon Caldwell; he wants you to handle this particular job."

Alvord nodded thoughtfully. "I've heard of a Bacon Caldwell, I hear he's throwing a wide loop down along the Pease River, he's from Texas isn't he?"

"He is."

"What's the job?"

"A little competition he wants removed."

"Straight up, I don't want any law problems."

Fisher smiled slightly, he's found Alvord's first weakness, fear of the law. "Straight up, but it really doesn't matter there's no law in our country."

"None?"

"Not within a hundred miles."

"When does he want me?"

"Yesterday."

Alvord smiled coldly. "In a hurry is he?"

"A mighty big hurry." Fisher reached for the makings in his vest, hesitating as he saw Alvord tense. "You want a smoke?"

Relaxing, the gunman brings out a black cigar from his vest-pocket. "It'll cost a thousand to go that far."

"Done." Fisher agreed. "Can you leave tomorrow?"

"After breakfast." Alvord struck a sulphur and exhaled smoke into the air. "Tell me sir, what am I up against?"

"After breakfast will be just fine." Fisher ordered another whiskey, then explained about Raker while leaving out most of the facts, only adding the part about the rustling. "It's a pretty simple job."

"That's pretty steep pay for me to kill one lone rustler." Alvord is a natural distrusting soul and something sounds mighty fishy here. "Finish it, why don't you do it yourself and save the thousand?"

"Mister Caldwell doesn't want the Lazy Bar involved in the killing in any way."

"Something personal is it?"

"Yeah, Mrs. Caldwell used to be Mrs. Raker."

"Now that's mighty interesting," Alvord nodded. "Two jealous men, and one woman."

Shrugging, Fisher told about Bacon's fight with Raker and Brace's rifle exploding leaving the man blind. He omits the shady land deals or Brace's part in several killings. "This Raker isn't gonna be easy."

"I don't fight with my hands like an animal sir." Alvord leaned forward. "I am a gentleman and I fight with pistols, like a gentleman."

"Word is you're a gentleman from Louisiana; Mister Alvord."

"I'm afraid someone told you wrong sir." The black eyes never waver.

"Mister Caldwell doesn't expect you to fight the man at all; he wants you to kill him."

"Alright then, I'll be ready come morning." Alvord stood up and holstered his drawn weapon. Fisher hadn't even seen the tall man pull it out as he sat down. "Would you care to join us in a little poker Mister Fisher?"

"No sir, I've ridden many a mile today. I figure I'll see to my animal, get a hot bath and shave then turn in." Fisher declined the invite looking over at the well-dressed men at the table. "Besides, I believe I'd be a little outclassed over there."

"Then, good night to you sir." Alvord turned and walked proudly back to his table.

Fisher watched the straight figure closely; the tall man dressed in black is a curiosity with his gentleman's manners and the carriage of a proud aristocrat from the south. Only the pearl handled forty-five strapped to the gunfighter's side impresses him more. He has seen the deadly weapon in action. Finishing off the rest of his drink, he pushed back his chair and returned to where he had left his horse tied. It might just get interesting when Mister Alvord meets Mister Raker, mighty interesting indeed, he sure didn't want to miss it.

Gunfire erupted from the line of oaks as Carlos Ortiz leading the others following the tracks Gillum and Little Tom had left earlier ride into sight. Their attention fully on the trail, no one knows they are in danger until the rifles roar and lead starts whizzing past them. Matt swore and fell sideways as a slug takes him in the side knocking him from his spooked horse. Another slug knocks him back to the ground as he tries to rise. Rushing to Matt's side, Bowie dragged him behind a small tree the only cover he can find. Slightly wounded Raker rolled from his horse and took cover in a small hog or buffalo wallow.

"Where's the kid?" Bowie yelled across at Raker as bullets tear bark and kick up dirt all around the tree.

Ducking his head as lead rips into the dirt around him; Raker cannot raise his head to look. "Don't know for sure, last time I saw him he was riding south like a banshee."

"Sounds like five or six rifles out there." Bowie tried to spot the ambushers as steady fire from the rifles keep him pinned behind the tree. "We were mighty lucky they didn't get us all the first volley."

"I reckon they were excited, how's Matt?"

"He ain't good." Bowie looked down at the wounded man. "He took one in the side and one in the leg."

"We need to get him out of here."

"True enough, but how are we gonna do that?"

Using a stick, Raker started digging a small trench he can stick the barrel of his rifle through so he can shoot with less risk of being seen. "Send a shot their way Bowie, maybe they'll return your fire and let me get a shot at one of them."

"Kinda like the wilderness huh?"

"Yeah, let's just hope it works better on these men than it did on them Yanks." Raker remembered the bitter battle with its fires, burning bodies, some still alive, and the screams of terrified men.

"Here goes." Bowie quickly snaps two rounds off blindly in the general direction of the ambushers.

Several rifles respond gouging chunks out of the tree, then Bowie hears the closer sound of Raker's rifle discharging. A volley of rounds poured into the hog wallow as Raker laughed.

"There's one low down skunk that won't be shooting at us again."

"You get one?"

"Yeah, believe I did at that." Raker hollered loud enough for the ambushers to hear. "Right twixt the eyes, I hope."

"Get yourself ready." Bowie lunged from behind the oak and raced to another one as bullets hit all around him. Again Raker's rifle sounds as the Lazy Bar riders try in vain to figure out how he is firing at them without showing himself.

"Stay down Bowie, before you get yourself killed." Raker cussed then laughed. "You young fool."

Again rising to his feet and racing toward a closer tree to the ambushers, Bowie dives for cover as bullets again clip the limbs all around him. "It won't be long until I flank them."

"Or they'll have you shot to pieces.

"Just be ready George." Bowie is trying to keep his body out of sight, hidden behind the small tree. "Here I go."

Bowie felt the bite of hot lead from a bullet grazing his leg as he lands behind the last oak tree. Peeking around the larger tree he opened fire on the exposed riders as they run for their horses. Holding fire as he recognizes some of the Lazy Bar riders he stands up, his rifle cocked and ready.

"You boys hold it right there or I'll open up on you." Bowie stepped out into the open. "At this range, I sure can't miss like y'all did."

Raker stood up and advanced on the four standing men who are dropping their weapons. "I ought to shoot all of you."

"You've done kilt poor old Abner and wounded young Jeb, real bad." Little Tom held up his hands. "Ain't that enough?"

"You're making me cry." Raker raised the rifle. "I'll only ask you one time little man, where's my daughter?"

Little Tom swallows hard as he focused on the deadly bore of the rifle. He looks into the hard eyes of the big man and knows Raker isn't bluffing, one wrong word from him and they will all die. He can't blame the rancher; they ambushed the rancher like cowards after taking his young daughter. No, there is little doubt the man will kill him without a second thought if he doesn't answer the man's question.

"She's down the trail about a mile or so." Little Tom looked down at Jeb, the young man who didn't want to ambush Raker and his men to start with. "She ain't harmed any."

"How many with her?"

"Just one, Happy Gillum." Slim looked down at the moaning Jeb. "Is it alright if we get him to a doctor?"

"I ought to kill all of you." Raker raised his weapon.

"Let them go George." Bowie stepped forward and placed his hand on the hot rifle barrel. "We need to get Matt back to the ranch before he bleeds out."

Nodding slowly as the film of rage leaves his eyes, Raker nodded. "You men take your wounded and ride, all except you little man."

Little Tom watched in fear as the rifle again centered on his chest. "What do you want with me?"

"Bowie take Matt home and send Talbert after the doc."

"What are you fixing to do?"

"I'm taking this man and going after the girl and Carlos." Raker looked over at Little Tom. "Mister you better lead me straight to them, and pray they are okay."

Little Tom looked over at Bowie and pleaded. "You can't leave me alone with this crazy man, mister."

"Well cowboy, you stole his daughter and ambushed us, now you pay the consequences." Bowie turned. "Watch them George, while I get Matt on a horse."

"Please mister, we didn't take the girl on our own, Caldwell ordered it."

"And my wife Norma?"

"She was fine last I seen of her, just worried about the girl is all." Tom squeaked. "I swear mister, she's fine."

"Did she know you were taking the girl?"

"She found out the next morning, when she found out what Caldwell had done she tried to shoot him." Tom nodded. "Would have too if Sandy hadn't of hit the gun away, blew a hole in the roof a horse could get through."

After bandaging Matt's wounds as best he could Bowie helped the wounded man onto his horse and started back for the Circle R. The Lazy Bar riders had already loaded their dead and wounded on horses and after sending one man to Medicine Mound to get the doctor they headed for the Lazy Bar. Bowie hated letting Raker ride out alone after his daughter, but Matt had to have his wounds looked after. Turning one last time as Raker and Tom ride out of his sight, he wished him well then headed for the Circle R.

Talbert watched from the window as the two riders come slowly toward the ranch. Warning the women to take cover he pointed the shotgun through the half-open window and waited. Bowie rode in close enough with Matt until Talbert finally recognized them.

"What's happened now Bowie?" Talbert hurried from the porch and helped lift Matt from the horse. "Let's get him inside."

"Get a bunk ready, I'll carry him." Bowie pulled the half-conscious man in his arms.

"Where's George?"

Laying Matt on the bed Bowie removed his boots. "He went after his daughter."

"Is he okay?"

"He was okay last I seen of him, get some water boiling."

"You want me to go after the doc?"

"Wouldn't do any good, he's probably already headed for the Lazy Bar."

"They get shot up too?"

"A little."

The wounds Matt had taken are nasty looking and painful, but not serious if they don't become infected. The wound to his side went plumb through the fatty part of his right side. The one to his leg is just a bad tear where the slug ripped his flesh as it passed through his chaps and pants. Quickly cleaning both wounds with hot water Talbert stitched the torn skin back together then smeared salve onto the wounds before wrapping them with clean bandages.

"That's all I can do for now." Talbert walked over to the stove and poured a cup of coffee. "We need to get the doctor out here."

"We will, soon as we can."

"What now?" The older man pulled a blanket over Matt. "You going after George?"

"No, I don't dare leave the ranch for you and Miguel to defend alone." Bowie walked to the door and stared out at the road leading toward Medicine Mound. "When Caldwell sees his dead men, he could send more of his riders here."

"What happened to Carlos, señor?" Miguel asked from behind Bowie.

"I don't know Miguel." Bowie looked down into the concerned face of the short Mexican. "That young man has more guts than any man I know."

"Si Señor, more guts than brains." Miguel crossed himself.

"George will bring him home okay."

"I pray this is so, I will tell his mother."

Happy Gillum paced the floor of the small cabin nervously as he listened to the gunshots sounding across the flats. He can tell there is a shootout going on, but he has no idea who is in the fight. Looking to where Emma played in the corner with the dishes he gave her, Happy shook his head sadly. There is no horse for him to escape and he knows the girl can't walk all the way back to the Lazy Bar. Walking outside Gillum blinks in surprise as a saddle horse trots up to the line shack, the saddle covered in blood. Talking softly to the spooked animal as it fidgets and starts to turn away, Happy grabbed the dragging reins and turned the sweaty horse around to face him.

Touching the bloody saddle, Happy ran his hand over the brand. "You ain't Lazy Bar old boy, you must be from Raker's ranch, but you're my way out of this mess."

Quickly wiping the saddle clean, Gillum entered the shack and gathered what food and water he can find. Turning to where he left Emma playing in the corner, he blinked the girl is gone. Looking out the open back door he called out, then stiffened as he finds the same barefoot tracks he and Little Tom had discovered back at the line shack the night the horse was stolen. Pulling his weapon Gillum followed the footprints to the corrals where he finds more tracks of a single horse. Whirling in fear as the horse tied in front of the shack knickers, he forgets about the girl. Gillum likes Emma, but now he knows his life is in danger, now his only thoughts are to escape. The girl and the rest of the trouble Bacon Caldwell saddled him with, will be left far behind, mounting up he turned the gelding south headed back to South Texas.

Little Tom with Raker following closely behind him followed the small trail to the Rock Creek line shack. He knows without a doubt, the big man riding behind him will shoot him dead if he tries to deviate from the trail in any way. He can sense the anger in the man, he knows one wrong move and he will be a dead man. Reining in across a small creek from the line shack, Little Tom looked back where Raker sits his horse.

"That's it."

Raker studied the open line shack door for several minutes where everything is quiet and still. "It looks vacant, you sure this is the place?"

"It's the Rock Creek shack alright; it's where I left Happy Gillum and the girl." Little Tom swallowed hard, he knows Raker is crazy mad over his daughter. If the girl isn't in the cabin, he could easily be a dead man. "I swear, mister, I ain't lying."

"You better not be, let's take a look." Raker dismounted and motioned with his rifle. "You walk ahead of me."

"They were here, Mister Raker." Little Tom pointed out Emma's small shoes on the floor, where he had seen her playing with dishes. "They must have heard us coming and lit out."

Raker can plainly see the tracks made by Carlos and the smaller footprints of the girl as he stepped out the doorway. Kneeling, he tried to sort out the tracks as boot prints mingle with the others. Following the tracks to the corral, he finds where a horse was tied and the barefoot tracks of both youngsters show plainly in the barnyard's smooth sand beside the horse. Looking about the ground he sees where whoever wore the boots had turned and walked back toward the shack. Raker isn't a tracker, but the tracks are plain, Carlos has taken the girl and ridden off.

The big rancher in his hurry to sort out the tracks and worrying about his daughter temporarily forgets Little Tom who is standing close behind him. Whirling at the sound of a footstep Raker gasped as the tines of a pitchfork stab him in the side. Firing twice into the man, Raker pulled out the imbedded pitchfork then staggered painfully against the corral fence.

"You killed me." Little Tom gasped as his eyes roll. "I'm too young to die."

"You asked for it mister." Raker looked at the small holes where blood trickles through his shirt. "I would have let you go, but now you've caused your own death."

"I didn't know that." The small head rolled sideways as he uttered one last sentence. "I figured you'd kill me sure with the girl gone."

"I know who's got my daughter and I know she's safe." Raker mumbled more to himself than the dead man.

Holding his side Raker walked back to his horse, stopping to pick up Emma's shoes as he passed through the house. The pitchfork he had been stabbed with is old and rusty, he knows from the war without proper medical treatment, blood poisoning could kill him the same as a bullet. He wants to follow the girl and Carlos, but now with two wounds and bleeding he can do her no good. Mounting slowly, he turned the gelding toward the Circle R and home.

The day after returning to the Circle R with Matt, Bowie sent Talbert to Medicine Mound hoping to find the young doctor and bring him back. Now he waits by the door watching as Doctor Evans leans over the wounded man and examined the wounds. Walking outside to the corral he whistled the saddle horses in then tossed them a few ears of corn. Closing the corral gate he stood looking at the road and wondered if Raker had found the girl. Toeing the corral's soft sand, he tried to decide if the ranch is safe enough so he can go in search of Raker and the girl.

"Bowie look, someone's coming." Talbert hollered from the house pointing at a rider far down the trail.

Squinting through the gloom, Bowie smiled. "It's George, he's back."

Minutes later as he stepped down stiffly from the saddle, Raker nodded at the two men who stand smiling at him. "Is that the good doctor's buggy?"

"It is." Bowie stepped forward noticing the pain in Raker's voice. "You hurt George?"

"A little, take my horse will you Talbert?" The big rancher handed the older man his reins, then moved slowly toward the porch.

Looking down at the small spots of blood Bowie frowned. "What got you, a shotgun?"

"No sir, a rusty pitchfork."

"Bring him in here." Evans had been listening from inside the house.

"How's Matt?" Raker looked over where the wounded man waved his hand.

Evans opened the bloody shirt as Raker sat in a chair. "He'll be fine, he had some good doctoring."

"What you think Doc?" Talbert had returned and was looking over Evan's shoulder.

"It's not good; a puncture wound is hard to take care of, especially one made by rusty tines."

"Can you tell how deep they went?" Talbert watched as Evans probes the wound.

"No, not really without operating."

"You gonna operate?" Talbert leaned closer.

Bowie pulled the old man back out of the way. "Fix us some coffee Talbert."

"I'm just trying to help is all." Talbert hesitated. "My Uncle Dorcell fell on a fork once and stuck tines into himself just like George has done."

Evans looked over at the man. "What happened to him?"

"My grandma soaked them holes with coal oil and he was good as new, sore for a while, but he mended up just fine." Talbert placed a coal oil lamp beside Evans on the table. "She said coal oil seeps in and kills any poisoning where normal medicine can't reach."

Evans studied the lamp for several seconds as he swabbed the wound. "Well I have to admit, this is the first time I've ever treated a pitchfork wound."

Talbert shook his head and grinned. "Yeah, I reckon men don't get themselves stuck with a rusty fork every day."

Pulling the globe from the lamp, Raker pushed it toward the doctor. "He's a crusty old cuss Doc, but I've seen him heal up many a man and I trust his judgment."

"I'm not too proud or egotistical to listen to any man."

"Well, I sure don't know what that word ego means, but I think it's worth a try Doc." Talbert piped up. "My grand mammy was a good healer."

"Sure can't hurt anything." Evans pulled another swab from his medical bag. "I do remember my mother soaking my foot in coal oil once when I stuck a rusty nail in it."

"George you just keep away from the stove for a while." Talbert laughed at his own joke.

Bowie listened as Raker questioned the doctor about going to the Lazy Bar and if he saw Norma. Shaking his head Evans told them about riding into the Lazy Bar and finding two men dead from the shootout near the Rock Creek line shack. He told how Norma Caldwell seemed to plead to him with her eyes, but she had said nothing. Lastly, he told about Bacon Caldwell's face still being badly swollen from his beating and Brace Caldwell being practically blind.

"You boys have sure done a job on Mister Caldwell since you came home." Evans worked over Raker. "I don't figure a man like him will forget it."

Raker nodded. "I agree with you, Doc, but I don't really give a hoot what he plans to forget or remember."

"He could get rough."

"Rough!" Talbert swore. "Look around Doc; we've got two wounded, a missing girl and a missing boy. It can't get much rougher."

"I know what you're saying sir." Evans closed his medical bag. "I'll be back in a couple days to check on you men unless you send for me sooner."

"Watch yourself Doc." Raker stood up slowly. "Caldwell has eyes everywhere."

Evans started for the door. "I'm the only sawbones in a hundred miles or more, no one will do me any harm. They just might need me."

"Thanks for coming Doc." Bowie watched as Doc Evans climbed into his buggy and turned the wagon down the sandy road towards Medicine Mound.

Carlos spoke soothingly to the scared girl as he pushed the horse back toward the south, trying his best to convince her he is taking her home. She knows who he is, but she is still afraid. Sniffling softly she doesn't understand what is happening to her, why she can't go to her mother. Carlos reins the gelding in several times listening to make sure no one is following him and the girl. When all the rifles started firing back on the trail Carlos had kicked his horse into a hard run, figuring all the Circle R riders were killed. Riding up to the lonely line shack at Rock Creek he had reined in his gelding at the corral and slipped silently towards the cabin. Peering through the window and seeing Gillum pre-occupied out front with the far off gunfire, Carlos found his chance to grab the girl.

No longer does he hear the rifle's booming gunfire so he fears when Gillum discovers the girl gone, he and the other Lazy Bar riders will be on his trail in a hurry to find her. With Raker and the Circle R Riders dead; he doesn't know where to turn for help, finally after riding in a large circle trying to hide his tracks he makes up his mind. He will take Emma back to the Circle R where he knows the old man and his father should be waiting.

The ride back from Rock Creek is a long hard night for Emma, who finally leans back against Carlos and falls asleep. Occasionally she whimpers in her sleep as the horse follows the dark trail to the east and home. Finally Carlos reined the tired gelding onto the weed-grown road near the gate of the Circle R, they are almost home. As he stops the horse behind the dark corrals and barn, Carlos looked up at the single light shining from the house. Pulling Emma sleepily to the ground, he crouched beside her and looked toward the house. Carlos turned his attention as several horses wander into the corral, curious about the newcomer. It is so dark he can hardly see his hand in front of his face, but he thinks the bigger horse in the corral is the same horse Raker always rides.

The youngster's dark eyes turned back, searching out the quiet ranch house, watching and listening for any sign of life before moving forward. One of the horses squeal and paw, laying his ears back at the unfamiliar horse Carlos had taken from Rock Creek. Quickly backing the gelding away from the corral before the other horses wake up anyone sleeping in the house, Carlos tied the gelding to a small tree.

"You're covered mister." The voice sounds in the dark beside the corral. "Stand up and identify yourself."

Jumping at the sound of the voice, Carlos quickly pushed Emma behind him. "It is I; Señor Bowie, if that is you."

"Carlos, I almost shot you." Bowie stepped from the shadows into what light there is. "How did you get here?"

Picking up the sleepy Emma, Carlos started forward. "I didn't know what else to do, I brought her here hoping one of you still lived."

"We're all alive." Bowie took the sleepy girl from Carlos. "A little shot up, but we're all still kicking."

"There was so much shooting." Carlos smiled, his white teeth showing in his dark face, even in the black of night. "So much noise."

Bowie started for the house. "There was that alright."

Pushing open the back door of the ranch house, Bowie called out to Talbert in the dark. "Light a match you old goat."

"What for?" The sleepy voice sounded from the dark. "I'm asleep."

"Strike a match, we've got company." Bowie waited in the dark room holding Emma as Talbert fumbled to light a lamp.

Raker rubbed his eyes as they focus on the small body that Bowie holds out to him. Rising slowly he looks at his daughter, then over at Carlos. "You brought her here to us, all by yourself?"

"Si señor, I knew of no other place to take her where she would be safe."

"You did right, Carlos." Raker took the little bundle from Bowie. "I will be forever in your debt."

"You owe me nothing."

"You're wrong there Carlos, I owe you her life and you will be paid."

"Her name is Emma." Carlos smiled as the girl's brown eyes blinked sleepily and focused on Raker. "Emma this is your real father, Senor Raker."

Shaking her head, the girl pulled back from the big man. "No, he isn't."

"Yes little lady, I am." Raker sat the cringing girl on his lap. "I know your mother very well."

"I want to go home to her."

"We're gonna bring her here very soon."

"Here?"

"Yes Emma, this used to be her home." Raker smiled down at the timid girl. "Would you like Talbert to fix you and Carlos something to eat?"

"I'm hungry and so is Carlos." The small head nodded. "But, he's a boy and he won't tell you he is."

Raker laughed and hugged the small body. "I'll bet he is too."

"How did you get her Carlos?" Talbert poured a half cup of warm coffee and handed it to the boy. "What happened to the rider watching her?"

The boy moved closer to the table and accepted the coffee cup. "I was watching from the corrals when a horse came trotting up to the cabin and while the short rider from the Caldwell rancho was trying to catch him, I took Emma and ran."

"It must have been Matt's horse; he bolted down the trail when Matt was shot from him."

"The saddle was very bloody." Carlos looked over to where Matt is listening from his bunk. "Is he hurt bad?"

"Not if he stays in bed like the good doctor told him." Talbert grumbled. "But he won't."

"I thought with all the shooting, you were all dead." Carlos dropped his head. "That is why I ran away Senor, not because I was afraid."

"You did right Carlos, you were very brave." Bowie turned as Miguel, Maria and Jackie entered the room. "What did you do then?"

"I took the girl and ran away." Carlos embraced his folks and waited for the rebukes he knows are coming from them. "I was afraid the man Gillum would chase after us, but I guess he ran away too."

"Yeah, I figure he's clean out of the country by now."

Talbert placed two plates of beans, cornbread, and side meat on the table, then smiled down at the two youngsters. "Come and get it before I throw it to the hogs."

Emma slipped from Raker's lap and walked over to Talbert. "What hogs, I don't see any hogs."

Several laughs sound around the room as the small girl pulled herself up on the chair at the table. Bowie isn't sure, but Emma seems to recognize Jackie, or maybe it is because she is a woman the girl feels safer near her. Looking over at Raker he nodded, for the first time in years he actually sees a smile on his friend's face. Motioning at the big man, he walked out on the front porch as Maria and Miguel talk with Carlos.

Turning to where Raker limped after him, Bowie stopped. "I'll be riding out before dawn."

"Where you headed?"

"To the Lazy Bar, with all the confusion and their men shot up, maybe I can get close enough to the ranch to get your wife away from Caldwell."

"It'll be mighty risky, they're probably stirred up like a hornet's nest and the Lazy Bar has many riders." Raker shook his head.

"I'll be careful."

"Well I can't stop you, nor do I want to." Raker blew smoke across the porch. "Just be careful and come back safe with her."

"From what the Lazy Bar rider said back there, she will probably come with me willingly."

Raker smiled. "Norma was always a strong-willed woman."

"I wouldn't want her mad at me."

"She's been mad at me a time or two, but never mad enough to shoot me."

"I can see why she got so riled, that's quite a little angel in there." Bowie looked over to where the girl is eating hungrily. "Well George, you got one back, soon we'll have Miss Norma back too."

"You ride easy Bowie; I wish I was going with you." Raker nodded over at the tall man then flipped his smoke into the yard. "We're a fine bunch, two wounded, one old man, two kids, and women."

"I wouldn't count Miguel or that boy of his out." Bowie smiled. "No sir, we've got a crew I would want at my back in any fight."

"I'll never be able to thank you enough, Bowie Morgan."

Chapter 12

Frank Fisher and Cord Alvord have been on the trail for several days, both are tired and dirty. They are within a few miles of Medicine Mound when they approach six mounted riders blocking the road. Alvord smiles, his whip thin lips spreading back into a cruel snarl.

"Friends of yours, Mister Fisher?"

Fisher studied the faces of the rough looking bunch and shook his head. "Nope, they ain't."

"Well, you best loosen that hog leg of yours and get ready, cause they sure ain't friends of mine." Alvord kicked his black gelding and started forward. "I do believe they aim to relieve us of our valuables, maybe even our lives, Mister Fisher."

"You boys pull up." The biggest of the six men ordered. "Rein in right there."

"Why?"

"Cause I told you to tinhorn." The beefy fist moves back to the man's saddle horn. "We want everything you've got."

"Well, here it is big mouth." The pistol is only a blur as it spits fire and lead into the short space separating the two groups.

Fisher pulled his own weapon as Alvord's gun sounds. The others, watching their leader knocked backward from his saddle, raise their hands. "We're out of it, mister."

"Do say?" Alvord cocked his pistol deliberately. "You're still here."

"We're gone." All five men whirl their mounts and kick them into a hard run back to the north.

"Cowards!" Alvord laughed wickedly. "I believe those boys are in the wrong line of work."

Fisher shook his head as he holstered his weapon. Pulling the makings from his shirt pocket he looked over at Alvord. The man had said hardly anything; he had just calmly shot the man from his horse. Alvord is fast, real fast, Fisher knew his pistol hadn't even cleared its holster before Alvord had drawn and shot the leader of the gang. There is no way he is in the gunfighter's class with a pistol, he's not even close.

Alvord looked down at the dead body, as he reloaded. "How much further is this town of Medicine Mound, Mister Fisher?"

"Tomorrow will see us there, we'll stop at the next water we come to and make camp, then ride out early come morning."

"Very well Mister Fisher, I do need to tidy up a bit."

Fisher can only shake his head, whatever else Alvord is he is a man of few words as the dead man just found out the hard way. "Yeah, me too."

"Well sir, I suggest we ride."

"I know Mister Alvord; a man doesn't ask another about his personal life." Fisher hesitated as they rode off.

"Go on, Mister Fisher."

"I'm just curious is all."

"Curiosity can get a man killed."

"I know sir." Fisher nodded. "But, I'm the curious type."

"Alright sir, one question is all."

Fisher smiled slightly. "I know you're an educated gentleman, how did you ever turn gunfighter and gambler?"

"It's simple, a man likes to eat and survive." Alvord looked off down the road. "I cut my eyeteeth on a pistol since I could walk so I survived, and a hired gun pays well, so I ate."

"And the gentleman part?"

"I believe that's two." Alvord looked over at the man. "Yes, at one time I was a gentleman so they say, but that was many years ago I'm afraid."

"Thank you sir, but somehow I believe you are still a gentleman." Fisher has come to admire the gunfighter in just a few days.

"No Mister Fisher, I'm a hired gun and a gambler."

"That you may be sir, but you're still a gentleman as well."

Alvord looked over at Fisher and nodded. "Thank you for that, sir."

Norma watched from the kitchen as the remaining men had returned to the ranch, then listened as Bacon fired questions at them. One rider is dispatched at a hard run to Medicine Mound for the doctor.

"Where's Little Tom Hodge?" Sandy dropped from the porch.

"Last we saw of him that big rancher Raker was riding toward Rock Creek with him." A rider shrugged. "You should have seen the look in that man's eyes; I wouldn't have wanted to be in Little Tom's shoes no sir, Raker's crazy."

"Yeah he's crazy, and he's coming after all of you." Norma walked out on the porch and picked up on the last of the conversation. "If I were all of you, I'd ride out of here like the devil himself was on my tail."

"Shut up, Norma." Bacon glared as he stepped toward the woman. "And get back inside."

"Why don't you hit me again Bacon?" The woman laughed. "It may put a little spine in your men."

"Take her inside Sandy." Bacon shoved Norma toward the house. "The rest of you men spread out around the ranch and keep a good look out for Raker."

Brace feeling his way to the kitchen door had listened as the men told what had happened at Rock Creek. He blamed himself; he knows all this is because he missed Raker back in Virginia. He still can't figure the rifle blowing up in his face, making it twice the Sharps rifle had failed him. Turning back into the kitchen he fumbled in the darkness, finally finding a chair.

Seeing his brother sitting at the table, Bacon noticed the bandage is pulled up uncovering Brace's good eye, leaving the damaged one still covered. "You must be feeling better, brother."

"Some, I'm still mighty sore but the burning is gone, and I can see okay out of one eye." Brace nodded. "How about you?"

"I'm alright."

"Raker sure has made a mess of our plans around here since he returned."

"That he has, he's been lucky."

"What are we gonna do?"

"I've got help coming." Bacon looked over to where Norma worked at the stove. "Bring us some coffee, woman."

"What kind of help?"

"I've sent for Cord Alvord." Bacon knows the woman is listening, he wants her to. "Yeah, I sent Fisher after him a couple days ago."

"If what I've heard of that one is half right, he won't have trouble with Raker. From what's said about him, he's a rough one to mess with." Brace swore as Norma placed coffee before him. "They say he's fast with a gun and a cold hearted killer."

"Cord Alvord is an outcast, a loner." Bacon sipped on his coffee. "Yes, he's a killer the man has no qualms about killing a man, but on the other hand, he's a gentleman from the old south who believe it or not, lives by a code of honor."

"What's that supposed to mean?"

"Well for one thing, if he comes to kill you he'll be facing you, from what I've heard he ain't a back shooter."

"Like me, is that what you're saying brother?"

"I wasn't talking about you Brace. I was speaking of Alvord."

"I know who you were speaking of." Brace raised slowly and headed for his room. "You sent me to do a job brother and I did it the only way I could."

"I appreciate what you have done."

"Do you Bacon, now that I'm a cripple?"

"You're still my brother and always will be."

Brace turned before leaving the kitchen. "You've done real good here, let's sell out and ride before it's too late."

"Sell everything we've worked for here, land, cattle, everything?"

"We've still got the ranch down south."

"Tell me, Brother Brace, just who around here would have the money to buy me out?"

"I meant gather the cattle, drive them north and sell them." Brace shrugged. "Let the land lay idle for a few years, then sell it."

"I'm not leaving here, Brace." Bacon stood up and pointed at his office. "You can go south if you want; the deed to the folks place is in the safe, I'll go get it for you if that's what you want."

"I can't ride yet."

"Then don't tell me to sell out and leave."

"You should listen to Brace." Norma grinned smugly from where she has been listening. "He shows more sense than I thought he possessed."

"Shut up, Norma."

"I've been listening and I think I have it figured out now."

"And what's that wife, what have you got figured out?"

"I watched your men ride out, then when they came back they were all shot up, now you have sent for a gunfighter."

"So?"

"You ain't man enough to kill George Raker by yourself so you've sent for a killer." Norma smiled, "I think your men got themselves all shot up trying to keep George from his daughter."

"If it makes you happy Norma, he has the girl," Bacon cussed. "Good riddance as far as I'm concerned."

"I already figured that Bacon, he's a real man," Her short laugh was harsh. "A real man, not just a shell of a man."

The slap sounds all the way to the front porch, where two men are stationed.

"Leave her be Bacon." Brace spoke up. "She's showing more sense than any of us."

"Brother Brace, if you care about her so much why don't you take her and leave." Bacon motioned at the door. "When Alvord gets here, this is gonna get a little messy."

"I'm not going anywhere Bacon." Norma straightened. "I wouldn't miss this little set-to for the world."

All day Bowie rode across the Lazy Bar range without seeing a single rider anywhere on the vast grassland. Nothing or no one is moving anywhere, not even a jackrabbit, something is amiss. Pushing his gelding on to the west, the tall man studied each pasture before crossing it. Two hours riding finds him sitting his horse in a thick stand of oak and mesquite only a few hundred yards from the ranch house. Several minutes pass as Bowie surveys the ranch buildings; finally he knows where all the riders are. Around the ranch and out-buildings they are thick as flies, Caldwell has a rider posted at almost every barn, corral, or building. He grinned to himself, Raker is worried Caldwell will send his riders to the Circle R to burn them out and here sits Caldwell worrying about Raker coming against them.

Dismounting, Bowie sat back against a small oak in plain sight of the ranch thoughtfully surveying the Lazy Bar for several minutes. Watching the place a blind man could see there is no way he can slip in there and take the woman in daylight or dark. With the loss of the girl and the death of his riders, Caldwell has become wary like a crippled bear. There is nothing he can do but ride back to the Circle R to report what he has found. Until the ranch hands go back to riding the range to ride closer to the Lazy Bar would be suicide. Bowie knows they can't all keep guarding Caldwell and the ranch forever and just let the vast herds of cattle roam at will.

Shaking his head in disgust Bowie tossed down a branch he has been whittling on and stood up slowly. There is no way of knowing how long Caldwell will keep the ranch under guard, but there will be another time, there always is and he will return.

"You see him out there, Mister Caldwell?" Sandy looked as Bacon crossed the porch.

"I see him."

"Who is he?"

Sandy shrugged. "Can't say, but he sure isn't riding in to introduce himself."

"I figure it's one of Raker's riders spying on us."

"You want me to go find out?"

"No, it looks like our friend is leaving." Caldwell watched as Bowie mounted. "Let him go."

"We need to send Raker a message, Mister Caldwell." Sandy argued. "He's rubbing our noses in it; we can't let him get away with that."

Bacon Caldwell studied the rider closely. Every hand on the Lazy Bar is watching the man, but he doesn't seem concerned. Caldwell knows Sandy is right, all of his ranch hands are watching he needs to do something. If he doesn't, he could lose more of their respect and maybe the men themselves.

"Take Slim and bring him down here or kill him."

"I'll get his hide for you." Sandy waved over to where Slim is sitting with the other riders. "He's already in the bag."

Bacon Caldwell stood on the porch and watched as the two riders mount and ride toward the grassland at a slow lope. Somehow he feels he just sent the men on their last ride.

"You're sending them to an early grave Bacon." Norma stood in the doorway listening then turned back into the house. "And I think you know it."

"Shut up woman and tend to your own business."

"She's right Brother." Brace grinned as he walked out on the porch. "I figure that one out there is the man that gunned the Kansas Marshal up in the territory."

Bacon Caldwell glared at Brace then stepped into the ranch yard. "That's what I pay them for."

Bowie watched as two riders whipped their horses into a hard run as they race up the grassy hill where he has been observing the ranch. Searching the surrounding pastures making sure no other riders are trying to circle him, Bowie turned his horse and waited for the riders to approach him. Both riders are coming hard eager to reach him, they know Bacon Caldwell is watching everything from the ranch porch. Maybe there will be a bonus for them if they kill the man.

"Dang fools." Bowie whispered the words shaking his head as the blowing horses of the two men stop a few feet from him.

Several seconds pass as Sandy leisurely rolled himself a smoke and lit it. "Who are you mister and why are you here spying on the Lazy Bar?"

Bowie stared across the few feet separating him and the two men then smiled a rare smile. The challenge this time is mostly unspoken. But, it is still a challenge the same as the confrontation and duel with the young Landeaux under the great sagging Sycamore trees, in Louisiana. Both sides sit studying one another, both sides know they are here to fight and both sides know someone will die this day.

"The name's Bowie Morgan, I've come here for Norma Raker."

Sandy nodded slowly and exhaled smoke to the wind. "You mean Mrs. Caldwell, don't you mister?"

"No, I spoke clear enough." Bowie tensed. "I've come for Mrs.

Raker, you produce her and I'll ride out peacefully, otherwise you and your friend there tuck your tails and ride back."

"That's mighty tough talk Mister Morgan. Can you back it up?"

Bowie can see the man is ready to pull his weapon, his eyes and actions betray him. "You can open this dance and die anytime you want cowboy, it's your choice."

The distance from the house to where the men talk isn't far, close enough for Caldwell who watches from the porch to see plainly. Suddenly guns roared from the hill and Sandy pitched sideways from his horse, dead before he hits the ground. The report fades away on the air, leaving only the drumming of the dead man's loose horse racing back to its home corral. Hearing the gunfire, Norma stepped back onto the porch looking up at the small knoll where two men face each other.

"What happened Bacon?"

"Your husband's paid killer just shot, Sandy." Brace snickered.

Bowie held the smoking pistol ready as he stares across at the remaining rider who has relaxed, resting his hand on his saddle horn. "I'd toss that hog leg if I were you friend."

Slim looked down at Sandy, then tossed his pistol onto the ground. "You killed Sandy."

"No sir I didn't, he didn't have to grab for his iron." Bowie holstered his weapon. "You tell Caldwell to return the woman and we'll call this madness off."

"I'll tell him."

"You do that, and you tell him to bring her to the Circle R or Medicine Mound pretty quick."

The long shadows passing over the ranch yard are replaced by the darkness of night as Bowie rode slowly into the corral and dismounted. Turning his tired gelding in with the others, the tall man walked slowly back to the house where he finds Raker sitting on the porch. Quickly telling about the Lazy Bar and killing one of their riders, Bowie accepted the hot coffee from Jackie and pulled himself up a chair.

"What am I gonna tell Emma?" Raker looked off into the dark. "I promised to bring her Mother here today."

"Promises sometimes are made to be broken George, you know that." Bowie sipped on the hot coffee. "I sent word for Caldwell to bring her home, we'll just have to wait and see what happens."

"He ain't gonna do that. I've broken my first promise to my daughter."

"There was no helping it; you'll have a lifetime to make it up to her."

"And I will." Raker promised. "I think you're probably right, but what if he doesn't bring her?"

"Then we won't be able to help your wife until Caldwell puts his men back to work on the range." Bowie set aside his cup. "Then I promise you, I'll bring her back home to Emma."

"I know you will." Raker hollered for Maria. "Fix Bowie up some grub please, Maria."

Fisher reined in his gelding at the edge of Medicine Mound and studied the small town for several minutes, stirring Alvord's curiosity. "Something wrong, Mister Fisher?"

"Just checking the street is all." Fisher looked over at Alvord. "Caldwell wants you kept under wraps until he's ready for your services.

"I see, well lead on."

It's early afternoon, still the streets of Medicine Mound seem almost deserted. Reining in at the lone hotel in the small town the two men dismount and tie their horses. Fisher notices Alvord looking about the small hotel as they enter and smiles. Reserving a room in his own name for Alvord; Fisher smiles and points up the stairs.

"It sure isn't the Arcadia, but it is respectable."

"I'll take your word for that Mister Fisher."

"Thank you."

"You don't mind if I hunt me up a poker game tonight?" Alvord pushed down on the mattress, testing it as he tossed his saddlebags and war bag on the bed.

"Just don't use your real name and don't tell anyone who you're working for." Fisher stared out the open window.

"Why don't we just ride out to the man's ranch and finish this today?"

Fisher shrugged. "Sounds good to me, but the boss says to do it this way."

"Fine with me, long as your boss is picking up the bill, and it doesn't take too long."

"He is and it won't." Fisher turned for the door. "I'll ride out to the ranch and let Mister Caldwell know you're here."

"Take my horse to the livery."

Fisher looked across at Alvord. "Glad too."

"Tell Mister Caldwell he's only got a week, after that it'll cost him another thousand."

"I'll tell him."

Hardly had Fisher unsaddled when Bacon sent Slim to the bunkhouse to bring him to the main house. Closing the office door after seeing where Norma is Bacon poured both of them a drink, then listened while Fisher tells him of his trip to Wichita and the shootout on the road outside Medicine Mound. Listening quietly with only a nod of his head Bacon proceeds to tell Fisher everything that has happened while he was absent.

"Alvord is at the hotel." Fisher accepted the whiskey. "I told him not to let out his identity."

"Good, now all we have to do is get Raker into town and we've got him."

"How are you fixing to do that?"

"That will be my little secret." Bacon smiled as he poured Fisher another drink.

"Tell me, what do you have in mind?"

"Alright I'll tell you, it's simple. When Raker finds out his ex-wife is in Medicine Mound, he'll come on the run." Bacon tipped his glass. "Then shall we say, Mister Alvord can earn his money."

"How are you planning on getting Miss Norma into Medicine Mound?"

"That's simple too, when I tell her Emma is waiting on her in town, she'll race to Medicine Mound."

Fisher grinned. "Pretty shrewd Boss."

"It'll work, I'm betting on it."

"When are we riding in?"

"Before we take care of Mister Raker, I've got a job for you Frank." Caldwell turned back to his desk.

"Yes sir."

"I understand from some of Doctor Evans people that Raker has been wounded."

"How bad is he hurt?"

"I don't know, but with Raker laid up and unable to ride that only leaves the tall one they call Bowie able to function."

"What about Matt?"

"Matt's hurt too, now I want you to do some riding." Caldwell tossed a stack of bills on his desk. "This ought to satisfy your hunger."

"You want this Bowie out of the way?" Fisher questioned. "Spell it out for me Mister Caldwell."

Caldwell pushed the bills toward Fisher. "Like you said, I want Morgan dead."

"Why him, he's just a hired hand." Fisher remembered the day of the fight in Medicine Mound and the way the young man stopped Raker from beating Bacon more than he did. "He ain't worth bothering with."

"Maybe, but I want him out of the way just the same." Bacon grinned. "Then Mister Raker will be all alone."

"Alright, when do you want him dead?"

"You've been paid take care of it, now."

"You're the boss." Fisher looked around the plush room. "When are you planning on taking the woman into Medicine Mound?"

"Kill Bowie first, then I'll move." Bacon poured them both another drink. "Then Mister Raker will have to fight his own fight."

"I'll head out at daybreak."

"You do that Frank." Bacon lit up a cigar and offered the box to Fisher. "He's been keeping a close watch on the ranch for a couple days, he killed Sandy so he shouldn't be hard to find."

"Sandy is dead?"

"This Morgan ambushed him, got him in the back." Caldwell lied; he doesn't dare let Fisher know that Sandy was killed in a stand-up fight.

"What's he watching the ranch for?"

"Who knows, maybe to bushwhack another one of us."

"What for, he sure can't kill all of the men."

"If he shows up again tomorrow, you shouldn't have any problem bracing him."

Fisher picked up the roll of money and thumbed through it. "You must want him pretty bad Boss, don't worry I'll find him."

"I do want him." Caldwell admitted. "You stay here at the house tonight in case I need you, then ride out tomorrow."

Caldwell wanted Fisher close, he doesn't dare let his gun hand talk with his other hands for fear of him finding out the truth about Sandy. He doesn't want Fisher to find out he had lied to him about the shooting. Sandy had been a top hand with a pistol and Morgan had killed him before he even got off a shot. No, Fisher doesn't need to know how dangerous Bowie Morgan really is.

"Oh yeah, Alvord said your thousand is only good for a week."

Raker leaned back in a cane back chair, sipping on a steaming cup of coffee as Bowie led his gelding to the house and dropped the reins. "I see you're riding out again today?"

"I'm planning on it." Bowie listened to the call of a bobwhite quail then the answering call of another as the sun starts peeking through the large oaks. "You have a beautiful place here, George."

"It was at one time."

Bowie smelled the fresh morning air and listened to the soft southerly wind as it blew the leaves on the large oaks shading the house. "It'll be again, she'll be back."

"I wish I knew that for a fact." Raker smiled as Emma appeared in the doorway. "Well now, what have we here?"

Carlos pushed her softly toward the big man. "She wants to know Señor Raker, when her mother will come?"

"Soon little lady, very soon." Raker lifted the small frame onto his lap and squeezed her. "You're right Bowie; maybe soon this will be a beautiful place again."

"I'll guarantee it."

"Ride careful my friend, we'll see you at supper."

"I'll be here."

For two days, Bowie circled the rangeland of both the Circle R and the Lazy Bar. Daily he checked to see how many hands are working the herds and how many are guarding the ranch headquarters. While most of the riders have returned to their day work with the cattle, Caldwell still keeps several posted close to the house. Unknown to Bowie he has been observed watching the ranch and riding the Lazy Bar range again. Caldwell knows he is out there somewhere and he knows why, now he has sent Frank Fisher on his trail with orders to kill.

It is almost midday as Bowie sits watering his gelding on the banks of the Cinnamon, three miles east of the Lazy Bar headquarters. The land in this section is mostly flat, covered in deep grass, a ranchers dream. The slight breeze has stopped blowing, permitting the day to warm slightly causing Bowie to remove his light jacket and tie it behind his saddle. His thoughts turn to Carlos as his sharp eyes take in the catfish swimming lazily along the bottom of the clear stream, their tails and fins moving slightly in the current. Looking across the grassy, tree dotted flats, he nods in appreciation, it is a beautiful piece of land, the air is fresh and clean, the water clear, and he has to admit a man would have to ride far to find another place such as this. Maybe someday he will own a piece of land just like this to call his own, a piece of land a man can be proud of.

Before him Fisher had found his quarry, now he waits behind a stand of oaks and watches as the tall man sits his gelding knee deep in the Cinnamon, apparently lost in thought. For two days he has ridden the range searching for Bowie Morgan, just waiting for such an opportunity to earn the money Caldwell had paid him. Now here right before him sits the man he has been searching for. Kicking his horse, Fisher rides slowly toward the unsuspecting rider halting less than fifty yards away. Bowie's gelding raised his head from the water turning slightly. Looking back to where Fisher waits with his hands resting across his saddle swells Bowie picked up his reins.

"For a man trespassing on the Lazy Bar you're kinda careless ain't you Mister Morgan?"

"I've been waiting for you to ride out from behind those trees Fisher." Bowie turned his horse to face the man.

"You knew I was watching you?"

"I did."

"And you remember my name?"

"I know who you are don't you remember I warned you once about letting me find you in Medicine Mound?" Bowie kicked his gelding forward and stopped the gelding thirty feet from the man. "You looking for me?"

"S'pect I am at that."

"Caldwell send you?"

"S'pect he did." Fisher kicked his horse and moved forward a few more feet.

"For what reason?"

"Well it doesn't matter much now, but he paid me real well to kill you." Fisher stepped down from his gelding. "A job I don't relish, but I took it."

"Why didn't you shoot me in the back when you had the chance?"

Fisher pulled the makings from his pocket and rolled himself a smoke. "Ain't my way of doing things, young feller."

"Exactly what is your way?"

"Light down from that horse and we'll have at it, straight up." Fisher blew smoke from his nose. "That's my way."

"A man should be careful what he wishes for, Mister Fisher." Bowie dismounted. "Unless you're a whole lot faster than your friend Sandy was."

"Story is Sandy took it from behind, in the back."

"Whose story?" Bowie studied the man before him. "Caldwell or the one called Slim."

Fisher looked over at the tall man. "Caldwell."

"What about Slim."

"I didn't get a chance to speak with him." Fisher shifts slightly. "Let's get to it, Mister Morgan."

"Caldwell kept you away from Slim I bet." Bowie shook his head. "Like I tried to tell Sandy, I wouldn't be in such a hurry to die if I were you."

"You sure it's me that's gonna die?"

"Like I told you, unless you're a whole lot faster than Sandy was, I'd be careful if I were you." Bowie shrugged. "I believe if I was you, I'd just get back on my horse and ride, just clear out of this country."

"I consider myself a careful man sir." Fisher tossed his smoke. "But, I can't do that."

"Suit yourself Mister Fisher." Bowie took a quick look around the area. "It's your funeral."

"In my line of work when a man's been paid, he can't just ride away."

"I reckon you're right sir." Bowie stepped away from the horse and undid the thong from his pistol. "Well, I'll say this for you Mister Fisher, you've got respect. You sure ain't like the rest of the varmints you run with."

"I'll take that as a compliment." Fisher seemed to smile. "In the last few days, I've learned some about being a respectable gentleman."

"It was meant that way." Bowie watched the man set himself. "Who taught you to be a gentleman?"

"Feller named Alvord."

"Well sir, for what it's worth you are a gentleman in my book." Bowie was sincere. "I wish you'd reconsider."

"For that I'll tell you something." Fisher nodded. "If this doesn't turn out to my advantage, it's something I want you to know."

"What would that be?"

"If you know you'll be able to warn Raker; Caldwell has imported a gunfighter to kill your friend."

"A gunfighter? Who?"

"The man I just told you about." Fisher nodded "He's hired Cord Alvord, fastest man with a pistol I have ever seen and a true gentleman of the south."

"What is Caldwell planning?" Bowie watched the hawk like face. "How does he aim to get Raker to face a real gunfighter?"

"Alvord is already in Medicine Mound where Caldwell plans on luring Raker." Fisher stepped away from his horse. "He's planning on using Raker's wife to get him to come to Medicine Mound."

"Well, I thank you for telling me Mister Fisher."

"Ain't gonna do you any good." Fisher squared himself spreading his feet. "I just thought you should know before you die."

"You seem pretty sure of yourself, why don't you just ride on out of the country?"

"You worried youngster?"

"No sir I ain't, I just don't want another killing on my conscience."

"I like you Mister Morgan, but like I said I took the man's money." Fisher tensed. "I can't go back on my word."

"It's your call then."

Several shots reverberate loudly across the small meadow, melting away on the breeze as Fisher sinks slowly to his knees in the tall grass, a look of surprise covering his face. Looking down at the forty-five lying beside him in the grass, he raised his head slowly and watched as Bowie approached him.

"Who are you?"

"Just a man like you, Mister Fisher."

"Not like me boy, you're still alive and I'm dead." Fisher coughed slightly. "You're fast son, real fast maybe faster than Alvord."

"I'm sorry Mister Fisher." Bowie watched as the man stiffened and breathed his last. "You had your chance to walk away."

Tying the dead man to his fidgeting horse Bowie led the gelding toward the Lazy Bar, then slapped him on his hip sending him into a slow trot toward his home corral. Mounting, he kicked his own horse into a slow lope back to the Circle R. With Fisher dead, Caldwell will only have the new gunfighter he imported to depend on. Bowie knows Raker is no coward that he will face Alvord if called out, he also knows Raker is no gun hand and will be no match for the man. It isn't hard to figure why Caldwell wants Raker dead and out of the way, besides the beating he took Raker is the only real landowner left blocking the Lazy Bar from owning most of the ranch land between the Pease and the Wichita Rivers. Marrying Norma Raker and getting control of the Circle R hadn't worked out as he had planned. Brace Caldwell had missed in his attempt to kill Raker; Fisher had missed in his attempt also, now the only option left to Bacon Caldwell is to have Alvord kill the big rancher. Well, as a man once said, the show isn't over until the fat lady sings, Bowie grinned a rare smile for him; he sure hasn't heard any singing yet.

Chapter 13

Slim raised curiously from a chair on the Lazy Bar ranch house porch and looked out across the flat pasture where a riderless horse is walking slowly toward the corrals. Still too far out across the grassland to see plainly, he knows something is wrong; the horse is saddled but has no rider? Finally as the horse comes closer the watching rider finally makes out a body lying across the saddle. Hollering for Caldwell; Slim trotted across the yard to intercept the slow moving horse. The dead man had shifted to one side of the saddle, pulling the weight of the body sideways making it hard for the tired horse to balance itself.

"Whoa son." Slim reached for the bridle reins, stopping the horse.

"Fisher!" Bacon gasped in shock as he recognized the bloodstained body. "He's been ambushed."

Slim looked closer at the stiff body and shook his head. "No sir Mister Caldwell, he took them in the front close up at least three slugs, he wasn't ambushed."

Bacon wiped his hand slowly across his pale face well aware he had sent Fisher to his grave by not warning him of Morgan's speed with a pistol. "I say he was ambushed."

"Well sir, you're the boss."

"Who killed him?"

"Rumor is he's been looking for several days now for the young man from the Circle R that killed Sandy, sure looks like he found him, don't it?"

"You mean Bowie Morgan outshot Frank Fisher in a stand-up fight?"

"Looks that way to me Mister Caldwell, cause he sure wasn't ambushed."

"You heard me Slim, I say he was ambushed." Bacon glared hard at the man. "You could get run off the Lazy Bar going against me and doubting my word."

"I reckon you can run me off Mister Caldwell, but you better count your losses. You've already lost several men, Sandy dead, Fisher dead, your own brother blinded, you may need me." Slim nodded and pushed the dead body back atop the horse. "Yes Sir Mister Bacon Caldwell, I think you're gonna need me bad before this is all finished."

"Forget it." Bacon turned for the house. "Have some of the boys bury Frank, then come back to the house."

"Yes sir." Slim took the reins and started off, then stopped. "Oh, this money was tied in the horse's mane; you reckon Fisher was saving it?"

"I reckon he was." Caldwell whirled away as the rider flipped him the roll of money. "We're riding into Medicine Mound tonight."

Slim shook his head and smiled, he knows even on a foreman's wages Fisher could never have saved that much money. "Yes sir, I'll bring the horses around."

Cord Alvord sat with his back to the wall playing poker as Bacon Caldwell and Slim entered the saloon and look about the large room. Four men sit in on the card game being played at the back of the room still Bacon has no trouble picking out the gunfighter. Fisher had described the way Alvord dressed down to the black hat with the Conchos. Bacon studied the slender well- dressed man for several minutes until the dark eyes looked up and locked onto his. Not a blink came from the dark eyes as the tall gunman looked across the room. Nodding slightly Bacon sent Slim over to the table then pulled out a chair against the far wall, away from all listening ears.

Alvord watched the cards as they fell seemingly ignoring the slender cowboy as he approached the table. Not wanting to challenge the gunman in any way Slim stopped well back from the card table and waited until the well-dressed man looks up at him.

"Mister Caldwell would like a word in private with you sir." Slim has been down the trail, he knows a killer when he sees one and this one appears as the law says to fit the description. "At your convenience."

Only a nod comes from the black hat as Alvord continued to play his cards. Nodding, Slim walked back to where Bacon waited. "I told him, Boss."

"Yea, I seen him nod let's have a drink."

"Sounds good to me." Slim is a steady gun hand, but the aura Alvord emits without even speaking gives him the shakes.

Caldwell had just ordered another round of drinks when Alvord pushed back from the card table and walked across to where they sat. Quickly Slim moved to the bar with his drink as the tall gunman stood looking down at Caldwell then surveyed the room.

"Where's Fisher?"

"Dead." Bacon leaned forward. "Got himself shot dead this morning."

"In our business, it happens."

"I reckon, but he was killed by a man that shouldn't even know how to handle a handgun."

"Raker?"

"No, a young feller that rides for him."

"Ambushed?"

The Lazy Bar owner shook his head. "That's what I told my men to keep them from stampeding back to San Antonio, Slim over there knows the truth, Fisher took three shots in the chest that a silver dollar would cover."

"Frank Fisher had a big reputation; they say he was a pretty good man with a gun." Alvord is curious. "Who is this man that killed him?"

"Can't say, all I know is that he fought with Raker in the war, then brought him back here all shot up."

"Raker must have healed pretty well word is he gave you a good shellacking a few days back." Alvord looked closely at Caldwell's face where some of the bruising is still apparent. "It still shows."

"He did that for a fact." Bacon blushed. "He seems slow, but don't let that fool you, that man's rough as a cob."

"I don't let anyone fool me, Mister Caldwell." Alvord leaned forward in his chair. "I told Fisher, I don't fight with my hands like an animal."

"Fisher said you are a gentleman, Mister Alvord."

"What's your plan?"

"As of right now I'm paying you double." Caldwell looked across at the gunman. "Morgan is dangerous to me, he's killed several of my men and I want him dead."

"I don't ride around the countryside looking for men to kill."

"You won't have to leave town, I'll get both of them into Medicine Mound day after tomorrow."

"Alright, tell me how do you plan to get them here?"

Bacon motioned to the barkeep and ordered another drink, then explained his plan to use Norma to lure Raker into Medicine Mound. Only Alvord's eyes move in the least as the woman's name is spoken.

"Surely you can find another way to get Raker here without using a woman as bait." Alvord fingered his whiskey glass. "It seems a cowardly thing to do."

Bacon sipped his drink slowly looking over at the gunfighter. With Fisher and Sandy dead, he needs the man. Every man on his payroll is handy with a six-gun, but none can stand up to the man that somehow downed Sandy and Fisher and they all know it. Frank Fisher was the fastest gun on his payroll; if Bowie Morgan killed him in a fair, stand-up fight none of his men would stand a chance against the man. Caldwell shook his head in disgust remembering Brace had shot one harmless bull instead of taking out Raker or Morgan.

"I'll get him here, but I want them both dead right out there in the street for everyone to see."

"I understand what you're paying me for." Alvord's hard eyes settled on Caldwell. "They'll be dead when I ride out."

"It's agreed then, now I'll let you return to your game."

"Mister Caldwell, I believe you owe me another thousand dollars."

"I'll have Slim bring it back in; I don't want anyone seeing money pass between us." Bacon pushed to his feet. "You understand my position."

"I do sir; an outsider doing your killing wouldn't sit well with the locals."

Bowie unsaddled slowly at the Circle R Corrals and watched as Raker walked toward him from the house. "Evening, George."

"Bowie." Raker placed his big foot on the lower rail. "Nothing today?"

"No, they're back to working cattle, but they're watching the place real close." Bowie turned the gelding into the corral. "How's Matt?"

"He's sitting up and talking."

"Then he'll make it just fine."

Raker nodded. "I figure he will, Doc Evans was here today and gave him a clean bill of health."

"Good." Bowie hung his bridle on a peg and closed the gate behind him after tossing the horse three ears of corn. "How's the side?"

"Just fine." Raker looked at the tall, quiet youngster closer. "What's wrong?"

"Nothing is wrong." Bowie started for the house. "Except I'm hungry."

"I've known you through five years of war Bowie." Raker grabbed the tall man's arm. "I asked what's wrong?"

Turning to face the big man Bowie nodded then related what had happened earlier in the morning with Fisher and what the dead gunfighter told him of the imported gunman Cord Alvord. "Dead men don't normally lie, George."

"So Caldwell is planning on using Norma to lure me into Medicine Mound."

"That's how Fisher laid it out."

"What do you think?"

"From what Fisher said, Alvord is a bad man with a six-gun."

"And I'm not in his league?"

"As a man you are, but you're no gunhand you'll only get killed if you try to face this Alvord or Bacon Caldwell."

"I don't have any choice; if he calls me out I'll have to fight."

"George, you're a cattleman, not a gunfighter."

"Maybe, but gun hand or not I'm obliged to fight him."

Bowie stepped onto the porch. "Don't fool yourself into thinking Alvord will let you get close enough to get a hold of him like you did Fisher."

"You mean he'd shoot down an unarmed man?"

"He probably knows what you did to Fisher, then to Caldwell."

Bowie shrugged. "He'll shoot you down like a rabid dog, then walk away from Medicine Mound scot-free."

"I can't believe that."

"You better old friend." Bowie turned to Raker. "Ain't a man in that town with the guts to buck Caldwell, now with Alvord backing him, he's even stronger. Let's eat, I'm hungry."

"You reckon they're gonna send word when Norma will be in Medicine Mound?"

"You can bet on it, you're the only man left in Caldwell's way to owning this whole country. He wants you dead, and out of the way."

"But why the Circle R, it's just small potatoes?" Raker shook his head. "He owns almost the entire country now."

"It's simple enough to me, the Circle R splits Caldwell's holdings down the middle and you have water rights to a lot of the Cinnamon." Bowie watched as Jackie moved about the kitchen. "He knows you won't let him cross the ranch with his cows so he'll have to trail them several miles around the Circle R to get them to his home corrals."

Leaving Alvord; Bacon Caldwell walked from the saloon and studied the almost deserted street. It is past sundown, and most people are home having supper or at one of the eating places. Motioning at Slim, he stepped into the street and untied his horse.

"I'm riding back to the ranch." Bacon mounted then leaned over and handed the rider a roll of bills and a twenty-dollar gold piece. "You stay in town tonight, grab yourself a room, have a good supper and a few drinks."

Slim looked at the money then at Caldwell, he knew the rancher wasn't being so free with his money for nothing. "Then what?"

"Come daylight you ride out to the Circle R and tell Raker his wife Norma will be in Medicine Mound in two days, that'll be day after tomorrow." Caldwell looked down at Slim. "Tell him to bring the girl and come into town and get her."

"I'll get the word to him Boss." Slim nodded. "What about the paper money."

"Take it to Alvord, but make sure no one sees you pass it to him, I'll see you back at the ranch."

Slim watched the big man retreat down the darkening street, then disappear into the gloom of the night. Looking down at the gold piece in his hand he turned back to the saloon. He doesn't look forward to riding into the Circle R and telling Raker that his wife will be in Medicine Mound in two days, it might not be to healthy. A week ago right in this street, he saw the rage in Raker and what the big rancher was capable of doing. Just today the younger man, Bowie Morgan had killed Frank Fisher deader than a doornail. Slim doesn't know for a fact if it was Morgan that did in Fisher, but who else could have done it. No one at the ranch knows why, but the tall rider from the Circle R has been prowling around the Lazy Bar range for several days. They also know Caldwell sent Fisher out hunting for him and apparently, Fisher found his man. Turning back to the saloon, Slim pocketed the coin and pushed through the door. A few drinks under his belt just might make things look better, but he doubted it.

Alvord looked over as Slim passed through the door, pushing back his chair he moved to the bar stopping beside the slender rider. Ordering a drink Slim nervously downed it then handed over the role of bills.

"You're kinda nervous." The words from Alvord where more of a statement than a question.

"Dang right I am, Caldwell wants me to ride out to the Circle R come morning and see Raker and his killer Morgan." Slims hand shook slightly.

The dark eyes of the gunman looked curiously at the Lazy Bar rider. "This Bowie Morgan, what do you know about him?"

"Nothing much, all I know is he brought Raker back from the war all shot up, and has been helping out on the Circle R." Slim took another drink. "I know he gunned Sandy and Fisher, and Brace said he killed Abner Hebbit up in the nations."

"Hebbit, he was a bad one for sure."

Slim nodded. "Brace said he never stood a chance against Morgan."

"How old would you say he is?"

"Maybe in his early twenties." Slim shrugged. "But, don't let that fool you mister, he's a hard customer."

"You've seen him in action?"

"I was there when he killed old Sandy." Slim downed his whiskey. "Never seen anything so cold, the man never batted an eye."

"Well, I reckon I'll find out how fast he is soon enough." Alvord started to turn. "One other thing, what does he look like just so I'll know?"

"Tall, dark eyed, broad through the shoulders." Slim studied the man before him, then shook his head. "You know Mister Alvord, no offense mind you, but y'all could be related, you kinda look alike."

"Well sir, we ain't." Alvord walked away, throwing over his shoulder. "I've never been to Texas before now."

The ringing of the axe sounded from behind the ranch house as Bowie split firewood and kindling into pieces small enough for the wood stove. A large pile of split oak lay strewn about as the double bladed axe sinks its sharp blade splitting another log. Stripped down to his bare chest, the muscles ripple across Bowie's chest and back as the axe raises and falls repeatedly. Looking up as Raker whistles from the house, Bowie gathers up an armful of wood and walked to the back door. Standing before the outside washbasin splashing water onto his face, he reached out blindly for the towel only to have it handed to him.

Opening his eyes, he finds Jackie smiling at him. "Thank you, ma'am." Bowie looked down at his bare torso, embarrassed. "I didn't know you were out here."

"Don't be silly." She laughed. "I've seen men bare-chested before."

"Yes ma'am, shall we have breakfast?" Bowie quickly put on his shirt.

"I thought we had a deal?"

Bowie smiled. "Shall we have breakfast Jackie?"

"That's better, and I'd love to." Her eyes smile softly up at him. "Very much."

Maria smiled from her place at the wood stove as the two young people come through the back door laughing. Jackie shook her head at the small woman then pointed her finger. Only the interruption by Talbert stops her forthcoming words.

"Where's the eggs?"

"I'm out of eggs; you'll have to settle for flapjacks and side meat this morning." The little Mexican woman looked about the room and dares anyone to grumble.

"Why don't you go into town and buy some hens Talbert? The old henhouse is still intact and we could sure use fresh eggs around here." Raker looked over his coffee cup. "We had some, but I reckon the coyotes got 'em when everyone abandoned the place."

"And what do I use for money?"

"We also need a milk cow to go with the hens." Raker looked over at Emma. "She needs milk."

"Maybe Señor Jacobs at the livery will know someone who has a cow for sale." Maria flipped a pancake over in the skillet. "Perhaps Señor Talbert can speak with him."

"Like I asked, what do we use for money? It's as scarce as hen's teeth around here."

"Well Talbert just ride in and have a talk with Mister Jacobs the liveryman, can't hurt anything."

"I'll do just that George, the poor child needs some good food and milk." Talbert winked at Emma and Carlos, who hover near the stove enjoying the fussing.

"You do that old man, in a day or two." Raker smiles as Emma and Carlos take their seats at the long table. "How does that sound to you, Emma?"

Nodding her blond curls, the girl giggled. "I like eggs and milk."

Raker smiled, his young daughter seems to be warming up to him. "Good, that settles that."

"Are you riding out today?" Raker looked over the six fat geldings standing around the troughs, their front teeth biting off kernels of corn from the cob, then grinding it between their powerful molars. In the last few days, he has spent many an evening sitting in this corral listening to the animals eating. It is a relaxing sound to listen to late in the evening after a hard day's work.

"I'm riding today, I found about four or five more of your cows south of here as I was riding in yesterday." Bowie nodded as Raker rolled himself a smoke. "Figured I would push them on in to the ranch today."

"If you'll wait a few days, I'll be able to ride."

"I believe I can handle five little old cows."

"Hey you fellers," Talbert hollered from the porch. "We got company."

Both men look toward the west as a lone rider comes down the sandy lane at a slow ground eating lope. Unsnapping his tie down, Bowie stepped out in front of Raker as he watched the rider rein his gelding to a walk.

Stopping less than twenty feet from where the two men waited near the corrals, Slim makes sure to keep his hands in sight atop the saddle horn. "Morning Mister Raker, now I'm not here looking for trouble."

"Then what are you here for?" Bowie's voice is hard. "You ain't lost."

"No sir, you know I'm not lost." Slim can see the cold look from the tall man's eyes. "I've got a message from Bacon Caldwell."

"What's the message?" Raker stepped forward. "Spit it out and be quick about it."

"Mister Caldwell sent me here to tell you that his wife will be in Medicine Mound tomorrow and she would like to see her daughter."

"She's coming into Medicine Mound." It wasn't a question, Bowie already knew the reason. "Caldwell's bringing her in?"

"I reckon, he just said she'd be in town."

"What about the Cord Alvord, the gunman that Caldwell imported?"

"I don't know anything about any Alvord." Slim looked inside the corral at the horses, avoiding Bowie's hard stare. Caught in a lie, he knows his face is turning red.

"You're a liar cowboy." Bowie took a step forward.

"I ain't lying to you, mister." Slim can smell death on the tall man. "I heard about Alvord, but I ain't ever met him and I don't know what his intentions are."

Bowie stepped sideways away from Raker. "You're lying."

"I ain't pulling against you Morgan." Slim grabbed the saddle horn with both hands. "We know you killed Frank Fisher yesterday and he was a lot faster than I am."

"Who said I killed Fisher?"

"The boss sent Fisher out on the range to find you and next thing we know his horse came home with him tied to the saddle like a dead hog." Slim shrugged. "We just figured he'd found you."

"I killed him alright, but at least he was a man and died like a man on his hind legs." Bowie looked straight into the man's eyes. "You ain't a man partner, you're just a coward licking Caldwell's boot heels and doing his bidding like a cur dog."

"I'm just carrying a message like I was told." Slim shrugged. "But I don't have to take this, there's no need for you to make small of me, mister."

"Okay you told us." Raker interrupted the heated words not wanting Bowie to kill the man. "Now ride."

"I'm just doing my job, Mister Raker."

Bowie pulled his pistol and rotated the cylinder. "I'll give you some advice boot licker, when you ride, you better keep riding clear out of the country because the next time I see you; I'll kill you where you stand."

Slim looked over at Raker; he knew the tall man wanted to kill him now. "You're a hard man Morgan."

"You're right about that, I haven't forgotten you were fixing to pull on me the day I killed your friend Sandy."

"And I thought Bacon Caldwell was cold." Slim turned his horse. "I'm riding."

"You do that, and keep riding."

Raker studied the face beside him and shook his head. He had fought alongside Bowie all through the war. He thought he knew the young man, but the face before him has changed it isn't like the one he knew and sided with on so many occasions.

"What is it Bowie, why have you grown so cold?"

"It's Louisiana all over again George." Looking over at Raker, the tall man shrugged. "I'm tired George, tired of the high-handed Caldwell's of the world with their bullying, killing, and most of all, their greed."

Raker looked up at the sun overhead and nodded. "Me too, reckon we'll ride into Medicine Mound and get Talbert his cow and some chickens."

"You taking the girl?"

"I don't know, what do you think?"

"Matt is still laid up; he won't be much help in case of a fight." Bowie toed the ground. "This could be a trick to pull us away from the ranch so Caldwell or his men can slip in here and grab her back."

"I never thought about that." Raker flipped his burned down smoke away. "We'll leave Miguel, Carlos, and the women here to tend to Matt; the rest of us will ride in."

"I figure it'll be safe enough to take her, Caldwell ain't about to get the girl hurt."

The big rancher stared out across the waving sea of grass and frowned. "You're figuring this Alvord is gonna brace me in town ain't you?"

"I've got it figured that way."

"And you don't think I can get the job done, ain't that right?"

"Alvord is a gunfighter and a killer George; he makes his living with a gun." Bowie nodded, avoiding the eyes staring across at him. "That's the way I've got it figured, alright."

"It's my town and my family." Raker shrugged. "I can't show yellow and lose face in front of them."

"It beats getting yourself killed in a no-win gunfight, don't it?"

"No it don't, I'd rather be dead than labeled a coward."

"Heard a man say one time; it's better to be a live coward than a dead hero."

Raker looked over at Bowie and scowled. "Tell me bucko, just who was that idiot?"

"Me." Bowie grinned, as a rare show of emotion came across his face.

"Yeah, you showed you were a coward back at Bull Run when you charged the Union line alone and captured their colors."

"Sun blind."

"What do you mean, sun blind?"

"I was temporarily blinded by the sun and just ran the wrong way." Bowie shrugged. "When I saw all the blue coats around me, I grabbed the flag and mixed in with them."

"Well, that's a whopper for the books."

"I swear, every word is the gospel."

"Jeb Stuart didn't give you that big medal for being sun blinded, I'll tell you that for sure."

"There was a real fighting general."

"Yes he was." Raker nodded. "We had good generals, lots of them, and we also had real fighting men, but just not enough of them."

Bowie looked off in the direction Slim had ridden. "Yes sir and we lost a lot of good men, the best of us I reckon."

"Ninety percent of our original company before the war was over."

Raker shook his head sadly. "At least that's what the colonel said one day."

"We lost a lot of good officers too, but none took lead in the back."

"No sir, they were a brave bunch alright, especially the ones from that school West Point."

"True enough, they must have fed those boys gunpowder while they were there."

"They were all fire and brimstone, that's a plain fact of life."

Bowie nodded slowly. "Wonder how Ham is doing back in Tennessee?"

"I figure he's lying somewhere on a creek bank fishing and having himself a high old time." Raker built himself another smoke. "Maybe someday he'll ride this way, sure would like to see the rascal again."

"Yeah, me too."

"Stick close today, rest up and maybe take Jackie for a long walk." Raker smiled. "We'll get an early start come morning."

"What are you saying George, why would I take Jackie for a walk?" Bowie blushed.

"Bowie Morgan, we sure ain't sun blind around here." Raker laughed and walked away. "No sir, we've all got real good eyes."

As usual the Circle R ranch house came awake early, already finished with their breakfast and morning coffee before the rising of the eastern sun. Anticipating what might happen in town, Raker hadn't slept much and he doubts anyone else has either. Emma doesn't know that she is going into town today to see her mother, but she knows something is amiss as she sits at the table. Everyone was quieter than usual during last night's supper and it is the same this morning. Nervous with anticipation, Talbert is over talkative as he helps the women clear the table.

Bowie with Carlos and Miguel following close behind him walked down to the barn to feed the animals and catch them up. Bowie studied the old wagon as he whistled for the saddle stock and waited for them to come in to the corral. At the time he stole the wagon from Grant's army, he would never have guessed the trouble they would have getting George Raker home, and now this.

"I think this will be a bad day señor." The young Mexican started pulling ears of corn from the corncrib and shucking them as Bowie moved back to the barn. "Very bad, I think."

Bowie nodded, Carlos is mature beyond his years the lad sees things other youngsters his age don't, and he is right, today could possibly be a very bad day. "You may be right Carlos, but let's hope you're wrong."

"Si señor, I do not wish bad things to happen, it's just that I feel this way."

"I know boy." Bowie listened as the powerful teeth of the horses grind the corn. "Let's go eat, and then we'll saddle up."

"Do I go with you and Señor Raker today?"

"No, I need you to stay here with your father to help protect your mother and help take care of Matt." Bowie closed the gate to keep the horses from escaping back to the pasture. "We're counting on you."

Carlos shook his head. "Señor Matt will not stay here; he will not be left behind."

"He cannot travel yet, he's still hurting too bad."

"He will go with you." Carlos grinned, his white teeth shining in the early morning sun. "Señor Matt will not stay behind with the women."

"Will Señor George be killed today?" Miguel spoke quietly.

Bowie looked at the small man curiously; he didn't think Miguel even knew of the upcoming fight. "How do you know of this?"

"Last night Señor Talbert and Señor Matt were talking after you went to bed, and I overheard." Miguel shrugged. "I will go with you today and fight for Señor Raker."

"And I will go also." Carlos insisted.

Bowie looked down the road leading to Medicine Mound. "No, he won't get hurt not if I can help it, but like I said before, I would like you both to stay here to guard the women and the ranch."

"Is the house more important than a life?" Miguel looked up at the house.

"The house is important Miguel, don't you want Señora Raker to have a home to come back to after we go get her from town."

"But, she is now the wife of Señor Caldwell."

"She is, but we're fixing to rectify that little problem."

"Do you really think bad men might come here and do us harm?" Miguel asked.

"Maybe, just be on your toes and keep the rifles handy."

"We will defend the rancho with our lives Señor Bowie." Carlos, in his youth and eagerness blustered.

"I know you will Carlos, you young man, are one of the bravest men I've ever known."

The young Mexican's chest expands as his face beams. Bowie has become a hero to him in the last few days, for one such as the tall one to say such a thing, makes him very proud.

Talbert waved one final time as he clucked to the team and started them down the sandy road. Smiling, he looked down at little Emma sitting between him and Matt and waving at Carlos and the others gathered on the front porch. For the first time he has seen a genuine smile on the little face as Emma found out she is going to see her mother. Raker and Bowie flank the wagon on both sides as the team kicked up dust and sand as the wagon passed through the gate leading away from the Circle R. It seemed such a long time ago since they passed through this same gate as they rode into the ranch for the first time, but actually it has been less than three weeks. Last night before turning in Bowie had told both Talbert and Matt about Alvord, the reason for their trip to Medicine Mound, and what might happen after they arrive. Hearing about what they might encounter in town Talbert only nodded, this way is best, maybe today will finish once and forever all the troubles with Caldwell. He hopes so he is tired of fighting, no longer a young man the four long years of war had taken its toll on him, making him feel old. Talbert's bones ache from so many years of marching, sleeping on the ground and fighting in freezing cold and rain, they tell him it is long past time for a rocking chair.

The day is warming up as Talbert keeps the team in a ground eating trot towards Medicine Mound. Meadowlarks, Dove, Quail, several different kinds of birds fly up in fright as they are disturbed by the passing riders. A meadowlark flies above the tall waving grass, and they hear the call of a dove from somewhere ahead. In the early morning coolness the soft wind with its clean air sends the fragrant smell of wild flowers floating on the breeze. Looking down at Emma; Talbert shook his head sadly, under any other circumstances they would be having a wonderful time traveling to town. There would be talking, singing, and occasional laughter, but not today, today death hung over them subduing their mood. The day's uncertainty is still too unknown for anyone to enjoy themselves, except for little Emma. Everyone knows in town Caldwell's hired gun could be waiting or there would be a happy reunion today, only time and the oncoming day will tell what awaits them.

Medicine Mound came into view almost at dinner as the wagon passed across the last small pasture bordering the town. As they pass the saloon, Bowie noticed several horses standing hipshot in front of the building, the Lazy Bar brand showing plainly on their hips. The streets and sidewalks are already full of people doing their shopping as Talbert pulled the wagon to a stop in front of the mercantile. It crosses his mind, are they here to shop, or have they heard about the impending trouble?

"Man there's a lot of people in town." Talbert looked over at Matt. "What day of the week is it?"

"Beat's me, old man."

"It's Saturday Talbert." Bowie spoke up from beside the wagon. "All day."

"Well thank you kindly, Bowie Morgan." Talbert spit. "That explains it then; most folks do their shopping on Saturday."

Matt shook his head. "Don't bet on it Talbert; I figure a lot have come to watch the fireworks."

"What fireworks Talbert?" The small face looked up.

"Nothing Emma." Talbert frowned at Matt. "Your Uncle Matt is just talking, that's all."

"I like fireworks."

"Me too honey, some fireworks that is."

"Are you my uncle too Talbert?"

"Why yes, I reckon I am Emma." Talbert smiled. "That is, if you want me for an uncle?"

"Yes I do."

"Well Uncle Talbert, let's get her inside." Bowie dismounted and is standing beside the wagon listening.

Chapter 14

Cord Alvord sat alone at the rear of the saloon shuffling cards to pass the time while several Lazy Bar hands stand at the bar or sit playing cards at another table. Neither Bacon Caldwell or Raker with his Circle R riders have put in an appearance yet in Medicine Mound. Slim has been sitting outside the saloon door for almost an hour watching off to the east and west, waiting to announce the arrival of either party. Suddenly, the Lazy Bar rider sits up straight as his eyes spot the wagon and outriders emerging in plain sight off to the east. Standing quickly and stretching, Slim enters the saloon and motioned behind him, grinning in expectation.

"You boys have been itching to see Raker and his gunfighter in person, well they're coming in big as life and bold as brass." Slim tossed down a whiskey. "Just like they're going to a Sunday picnic."

Another cowboy who was present at the Rock Creek shoot-out walked to the window then hurried back to where Alvord is playing solitaire. "Slim's right Mister Alvord, you been curious to know what Bowie Morgan looks like, well he's riding down the middle of town right now."

Tossing the deck of cards onto the table, Alvord walked to the door and focused his dark eyes on a tall man as he dismounted. "Is that him?"

"That's him alright." Slim's voice quivered a bit as he looked at Bowie. "He's rattlesnake mean, that one."

"You scared of him cowboy?"

"Yes sir and I ain't ashamed to admit it." Slim swallowed another shot of whiskey. "He scares the pants off me, promised to kill me if we should ever meet again this side of hades."

Alvord nodded then pushed the door open. "Well sir, at least you're man enough to admit it, most wouldn't."

"You going to open the ball before Mister Caldwell gets here?" Slim questioned as the tall, straight-backed gunman started toward the mercantile.

"Not yet, just satisfying my curiosity is all." Alvord stopped and looked back at Slim before stepping into the street. "You want to accompany me?"

"No thank you like I said, Morgan promised to kill me on sight the next time we meet."

"And you took him at his word?"

"Just like a banker's handshake." Slim nodded. "You wait until you look into his eyes, Mister Alvord. They're as cold as…"

"As what Slim?" Alvord stared at the worried rider's face then repeated himself. "As what?"

"As your eyes, Mister Alvord." Slim paled. "No disrespect meant."

"You don't think I can protect you?" Alvord seemed to smile with that peculiar way he has of dipping his head. "From only one man?"

Embarrassed and not wanting to offend the gunman, Slim looked away then answered hoarsely. "Against that man no sir, he'll do exactly what he said he'd do, shoot me dead on sight and no one man could stop him."

Nodding, Alvord strolled slowly across the street and stopped in front of the mercantile, just as Raker and his party were disappearing inside the store. Pushing the door open slowly, the gunman stepped inside, his eyes looking about the room stopping as they focus on Bowie. His entrance into the mercantile wasn't unnoticed as both Bowie and Matt had looked up as the doorbell jingled. Raker distracted with helping Emma pick out her favorite hard candy doesn't even bother to look up as the bell rings. Quickly Bowie steps forward blocking the gunman's path to Raker, while staring Alvord straight in the eyes. No introduction is needed, he knows before him stands Cord Alvord, the Kansas gunfighter Fisher had described down to the Concho hat.

"Can I help you with something Mister Alvord?" All noise inside the store ceases as the name is called out. "You looking for someone?"

Looking Bowie up and down, and without saying a word or even looking over at Raker; Alvord turned and walked slowly from the store. Talbert who had remained outside sitting in a chair enjoying his pipe studied the man as he passed by him and steps from the boardwalk. Following Alvord from the store Bowie stopped in the doorway and watched the man as he re-crossed the street and made his way back to the saloon.

"Is that him Bowie?"

"In the flesh, I believe."

"Did he say anything?" Talbert scratched his head as the gunman disappeared inside the saloon doors. "Did he introduce himself, what did he want?"

"Didn't say a word, just came in for a look is all."

"At George?"

"Not really, he didn't even look over at George."

"Who then?"

"Only me." Bowie stepped from the doorway as a buggy comes into sight out on the flats; there is no doubt who it is. In these hard times only one man is wealthy enough to have a matched pair of grays pulling a fringed surrey like the one that is approaching. Several outriders surround the man and woman as they approach at a fast clip toward Medicine Mound.

Ignoring the oncoming surrey, Talbert's eyes stay fixed on the doorway of the saloon where Alvord disappeared. Shaking his head he looked over as Bowie sat down slowly, then nodded at the oncoming buggy.

"Reckon that's Mister Bacon Caldwell and little Emma's Ma." Talbert eased himself a little on the straight-backed chair. "Nobody else in these parts would own a rig and matched pair of grays like those."

"S'pect so, they are a good-looking team alright."

"Yes they are." Talbert's eyes were fixed on the saloon. "Better than that old wagon."

Bowie followed the old man's eyes to the saloon, then elbowed Talbert. "What are you looking at, old man?"

Shrugging out of his thoughts, Talbert looked over at Bowie. "You get a good look at Mister Alvord?"

"All I wanted to I reckon, why?"

"See anything unusual about him?"

"Just that he's got the coldest eyes I ever seen on a live man's face." Bowie shook his head then watched as the surrey pulls to a stop in front of the hotel. "Guess I better tell George his wife is here."

"His ex-wife youngster."

"I know that Talbert, but I happen to still see Norma as George's wife." Bowie shook his head at Talbert, then retreats inside the store before leaning back out the door. "That makes her a Raker."

"See her any way you want young man, but she's still married legally to Bacon Caldwell." Talbert spit a stream of tobacco into the dusty street. "Maybe not for long if I don't miss my guess."

Raker looked out the store window, his heart skipping a beat as his eyes focused on Norma sitting alone in the rear seat of the surrey. Starting for the door, he stops as Bowie steps in front of him. "Let me go down and see how Caldwell wants to play this out George."

"It's my job Bowie, you stay clear of it."

"I will, but we don't want Emma or Norma caught in the middle." Bowie looked into the rancher's eyes. "Do we?"

Rubbing his chin, Raker took another look outside. "Alright Bowie you go talk, but you hear me, this is my fight and only mine."

"I'm just going to see what Caldwell has on his mind."

"Alright, go ahead."

Releasing the tie-downs from both pistols, Bowie checked the loads in the weapons before stepping from the store and crossing the sidewalk. Looking down to where Matt had joined Talbert on the sidewalk he winked as he started toward the saloon. The hotel is only a block away, but seems further as he approached the surrey and stopped momentarily to look up at the straight-backed woman sitting alone in front of the hotel. No emotion shows in her smooth complexion, not even a blink comes from her eyes as she stares down the street.

"You're Mister Morgan, aren't you?" The woman looked over at him. "The man who killed Sandy and Fisher."

"Yes ma'am." Bowie tipped his hat. "I'm Morgan, how did you know."

"It doesn't matter." Norma shook her head. "You did what you had to do; Bacon had paid them to kill you."

"Can I help you with anything, Miss Norma?"

"Yes, tell George to take Emma and go back home before they kill him."

"What about you, ma'am?"

"I'm a dead woman already, just waiting to be buried." She fought back a tear. "I don't matter anymore."

"You're wrong about that, because you are going home today Mrs. Raker." Bowie looked up at the woman; George hadn't lied, in spite of everything she is a pretty woman. "You have my word ma'am; you're going home to be with your family."

"That's impossible." Norma shook her head. "You know Bacon has hired the fastest gun in Kansas, and right now he's waiting over at the saloon."

"I've heard he's fast Mrs. Raker, but it'll be alright." Bowie smiled. "Where is Caldwell?"

"He's inside the saloon with his brother, and hired killers."

"He left you sitting out here alone in the heat?"

"Go home young man, and take my loved ones away from this place of death." Norma looked down into his upturned face. "Bacon has twenty riders from the Lazy Bar in town backing him, you don't stand a chance."

"Well ma'am, I can't do that." Bowie looked toward the saloon where a Lazy Bar rider is walking toward them. "It seems I have pressing business with Mister Caldwell."

"Tell George to take Emma home to the Circle R now." Norma pleaded.

"If you're Morgan, the boss wants to see you up the street at the saloon, right now." A short, heavyset rider orders then nodded arrogantly toward the saloon.

"I'll tell him ma'am." Bowie ignored the fat man. "But your husband is a mighty hardheaded man; I doubt he'll ride out without you."

"You hear me Morgan, get yourself down to the saloon, Mister Caldwell don't like to be kept waiting." The rider looked towards the saloon door. "Now!"

"You seem to be in a hurry fat man." Bowie turned his full attention on the rider.

"I ain't in no hurry at all, Mister Caldwell is."

"I ain't talking about Caldwell." Bowie squared off in front of the man. "I'm talking about you being in a hurry to die."

"I'm just delivering a message mister then I'm to see Mrs. Caldwell gets settled comfortably in the hotel." Backing quickly through the hotel door, the rider disappeared inside the hotel.

"You be ready ma'am, I promise George will be after you soon as this is over." Bowie tipped his hat to her then turned his attention to the saloon doors.

Her blue eyes study the broad back of the young man as he walked away. Nodding, she smiled nervously whispering to herself. "I believe you Bowie Morgan; I believe I am going home today."

The sun feels hot on his broad back as Bowie steps through the wide doors of the saloon where he finds at least twenty men strung out about the room, several standing behind Bacon Caldwell where he is sitting with Alvord. All eyes followed his movements to the bar, but not a word is spoken as the tall man calmly orders a beer from the nervous bartender.

Cord Alvord watched the proceedings curiously as the young man sips on his beer barely glancing Caldwell's way. Several minutes pass, the saloon has become completely silent as Bowie finally turned and focused his eyes on Alvord. The two men eye each other coldly for several seconds before Bowie finally sets his beer down on the oak bar. "Well Mister Caldwell you sent for me, I'm here you can speak your piece."

"So, I finally get to meet the man that has killed several of my men." Caldwell fingers a whiskey glass on the table. "You've got some nerve coming in here alone, Mister Morgan."

"I only killed men that were trying to kill me or harm the little girl." Bowie squared his body facing straight at the table, his hands relaxed ready to draw. "And it sure doesn't take nerve to face a fore flusher like you Caldwell; you could have met me earlier if you had the nerve to do your own fighting."

"You can't wave a white flag in here like you were still in the army." Brace grinned from where he sat, his one good eye no longer bandaged as it stared at Bowie. "You surely ain't expecting to leave here alive are you, Reb?"

"You must be Brace Caldwell, the one who had the Sharps blow up in his face."

"And what if I am?"

"Well then as long as I don't turn my back on you Caldwell, I'll be safe." Bowie smiled coldly. "You yellow back-shooting dog."

"Why you." Brace started to rise, but the powerful hand of Bacon Caldwell pushed him back down, holding him in his seat. "Shut up Brace, I'll handle this."

Alvord watched the cold demeanor of the tall young man and nodded, here stood a man all alone that held no fear for his own safety. "Where are you from, Mister Morgan isn't it?"

Bowie turned his attention back on Alvord. "My name's Morgan alright Mister Alvord, as for where I'm from, I believe that's my business."

"No offense intended sir; I was merely asking is all."

"You like to know where a man is from before you kill him, is that it?"

"Like I said Mister Morgan no offense intended, I was just wondering how you came to be here in North Texas."

Bowie studied the question for several seconds then nodded. "Louisiana."

"From the Bayou Country by any chance?"

"Yes."

"I use to know some people down around Baton Rouge, I believe it was Sera Leone, but I could be mistaken." Alvord smiled easily. "Would you be from around there?"

"I was, a long time ago."

"Their name was Trouilliard, you ever hear the name?"

Bowie looked sharply at Alvord as the name is pronounced, then shook his head. "No, I never heard the name before."

"This isn't a reunion Alvord." Caldwell slammed his glass down hard, glaring over at Bowie. "I'm here Morgan, to meet with your boss Raker."

"That should be no problem he's across the street at the mercantile." Bowie nodded toward the door. "Why don't you just walk over there and meet with him?"

"I want him to come over here."

"I expect you do, tell me Caldwell are you gonna meet with George Raker yourself, I believe you've already tried that once." Bowie smiled coldly at Caldwell. "Or is your hired gun Mister Alvord, gonna do your meeting for you?"

Caldwell ignored the question. "I've kept my word and brought Norma in to see her daughter."

"And after that?"

"After they have their talk Mister Morgan, then both you and Raker are on your own." Caldwell shook his head. "Then sir, I suggest you and Raker leave these parts quick as a fast horse can carry you."

"You're saying it might be healthier for us, is that it?"

"Exactly."

"Tough talk Caldwell." Bowie looked again at Alvord. "Are you planning to unleash your killer here on a defenseless rancher?"

"Defenseless?" Caldwell growled. "He dang near beat me to death."

"You deserved it as I remember, I should have let him." Bowie stared solemnly at Caldwell. "But, with a handgun George Raker is practically defenseless."

"Defenseless hah the man is a killer; he was in the army wasn't he?"

"Carrying a rifle in the army is far different than using a six-gun Caldwell." Bowie looked at Alvord. "You both know it."

"That's his problem, not mine." Caldwell frowned. "As I understand it, you're something of a gun hand yourself."

"I'm making it your problem mister." Bowie smiled across at the man. "And you're right, I am a gun hand if George Raker is called out, it will be me you'll be facing."

"Is Raker gonna let you do his fighting for him?" Brace Caldwell grinned. "I figured him to be a proud man, too proud to let you take his part in this."

"He is a proud man a better man than either of you Caldwell's, but this time I ain't giving him a choice." Bowie nodded again at Alvord. "You two sure ain't proud, or you'd be doing your own fighting."

"That's pretty tough talk for one man facing twenty."

"I'm not facing twenty men Caldwell, I'm just facing you let's get to it." Bowie's face turned hard as he looked at the Lazy Bar owner. "I'm through talking, stand up Caldwell or I'll shoot you where you sit."

"You'd be a dead man as soon as you draw that gun." Caldwell grinned smugly around the room. "I do believe you can see why."

Bowie nodded. "Probably, but wherever we're headed you'll get there first I'll guarantee it."

Caldwell seemed to pale then looked over at Alvord who hasn't moved or said anything. "I'm going to the hotel where my wife is freshening up."

"When you come out of that chair you better be ready to draw."

"I'm not pulling on you Morgan; I'm leaving here to check on my wife." Caldwell stood up slowly, his hands outstretched away from his pistol. "If you shoot me, it'll be in cold blood."

"It won't matter much cold blood or hot blood, you'll be just as dead either way." Bowie tensed as Bacon straightens. "But you go ahead and check on Mrs. Raker if you don't have the guts to fight."

"Then sir, I will send Norma to her daughter and to speak with George Raker for the last time." Caldwell started for the door. "You hear me youngster for the last time, get out of Medicine Mound."

"Just how long do you expect Mister Raker to wait over there?" Bowie nodded across at the mercantile store. "While you're checking on your wife?"

"Give us one hour." Bacon grinned smugly as he started for the door, relieved Bowie hadn't shot him. "We'll be there in one hour, the rest of you men just have a few drinks on me and stay in the saloon."

"Just remember what I said Caldwell." Bowie stepped away from the bar. "You or your hired killers come for Raker; you'll find yourself facing me."

"Well Mister Morgan." Bacon stopped at the front door. "You'll have to get past Mister Alvord there, but first I believe he's got business with Raker."

"Walk out of here Mister Morgan, while you can." Alvord interrupted the talk then looked around the room. "There's too many against you."

"Alright I'm walking out for now, if anyone of you touches a gun, I'll kill Caldwell before you get me."

Suddenly from behind the bar, Slim appeared his pistol pointed at Bowie's back. "Remember me Morgan; last time we met you promised to kill me."

"I remember you little man, and I do remember telling you the next time we met, I'd kill you." Bowie can see the Lazy Bar rider standing behind him with his pistol drawn, his image plain in the large mirror that runs the length of the oak bar. "You'll get off a shot, but your boss is a dead man when you pull that trigger."

Slim smiled, he knows he has the edge on Bowie and at this range, he can't miss. As with most cowards his courage quickly returns when everything is on his side. Stepping forward closer to Bowie's back, Slim started to pull the trigger when the roar of a pistol rattles the room. Bacon Caldwell standing at the door stared in disbelief as Slim crumbled slowly to the floor. Cord Alvord looked into Bowie's eyes then pulled a smoking pistol from under the table and laid it down softly.

"Can't stand a coward or a back shooter, won't tolerate one." Alvord looked over to Caldwell. "Anybody got a problem with that?"

No one says a word as Bowie backs slowly out the door and heads for the mercantile. He can't understand why Alvord, who is Caldwell's hired gun, would shoot the little rider. If he would have let Slim shoot him, Caldwell's road to killing Raker and taking control of the entire county would be accomplished. Passing the empty surrey he shook his head as Norma appeared in the window of the hotel lobby, a look of relief crossing her face. Perhaps Alvord had been afraid Bowie would get a bullet into Caldwell if Slim got off a shot.

Jackie stood waiting on the mercantile porch her hands clutched together tightly, her eyes glued on the saloon doors watching as Bowie had passed from her sight into the building. As the minutes passed she waits anxiously, fearing the gunshot that she afraid will come. Suddenly there it is the roar of the pistol, exactly what she fears most. Racing forward she started across the street when Talbert grabbed her from behind, then released the hysterical girl as Bowie appeared in the doorway of the saloon. Rushing into his arms as she reached him, she hugged him tightly causing him to look down at her in surprise.

Cord Alvord standing beside Bacon Caldwell at the window, watched the two young people hug then the dark eyes focused on the couple as they made their way back to the mercantile. "Who is she, his wife?"

Caldwell shook his head in surprise. "Her name's Jackie Harrison, her old pappy was killed in the late war and I picked up his ranch that I'm living on now for back taxes. No, she ain't his wife; I didn't even know they were sweet on each other."

"By the look of shock on Mister Morgan's face, he didn't know it either until just now." Alvord smiled. "She's a handsome young lady."

"Yes she is." Bacon looked over to where Brace is staring out another window at the couple. "My brother thinks so too."

"Is he sweet on her too?"

"I'm afraid so."

Brace Caldwell's knuckles had turned white from the grip he had on the window ledge as he watched Jackie hug the tall man, then walk away with him arm in arm. Brace cussed under his breath, swearing revenge as he turned from the window. First he lost the Circle R because of Bowie Morgan, now he lost the woman he intended for his wife. His hand's open and close in a jealous rage, if only he had the Sharps again, right now.

While Talbert played jacks with Emma on the wooden sidewalk outside the store everyone inside waits silently around the potbellied stove, anxious for the hour to pass. Caldwell said he would send Norma in one hour, now they all wait in anticipation. Jackie held onto Bowie tightly, refusing to turn him loose she knows the danger is far from over, she knows Caldwell and his hired killer are still to be reckoned with. Several times in the last week she has heard men from the Circle R speak of Cord Alvord, his reputation with a gun and his viciousness. For years after losing her father, the ranch and her home, she has had to take care of her frail mother, wondering how all this came about. Now for the first time, she has found something worth loving again, and she fears losing him.

Standing up as Emma suddenly leaped to her feet, Talbert watched as the girl raced across the street and throwed herself into her mother's arms. Pecking on the window Talbert beckoned Raker outside then watched as the rancher quickly crossed the street and grabbed up Norma and Emma in his huge arms. Everyone from both sides watch as they embrace then take a seat on the street between the store and saloon in plain sight of the town. They can tell as Norma sits with her hands in her lap, her head downcast and shaking she is talking to Raker, probably trying to convince him to leave town without trouble. Looking over at the saloon where she knows Caldwell would be watching, she stood and took Emma and George by the hand walking with them back to the mercantile.

On the sidewalk outside the store Norma pushed Emma inside with Mrs. Scott before turning to confront Raker and Bowie. "You're his friend Mister Morgan; tell him this gunman Bacon has hired will kill him if you're his friend get George away from here before it is too late."

"Beg your pardon ma'am, but I doubt George would be able to leave town now if he wanted to." Bowie looked over to where Alvord, Caldwell, and several riders have passed through the door of the saloon and stand watching from the sidewalk. "I believe it's already too late for that now."

"What will you do, George?" Norma turned her eyes up at Raker, pleading with him. "Bacon's land hungry and crazy, he'll kill all of you."

"He'll try." Raker took the frightened woman by the shoulders and turned her toward the mercantile's door. "I'm not running just to live, that wouldn't be living, now all of you stay inside until this is over."

Hugging him briefly, she tried to smile. "Come back to us George, we need you."

"I'll be back, now go inside."

Bowie opened the door and held it open while Norma and Jackie moved back inside the store. Only a brief hug passed between him and the pretty girl as she followed Norma inside. Talbert and Matt quickly fortify themselves behind several heavy barrels armed with rifles as the Lazy Bar riders spread out along the sidewalk, leaving only Alvord and Caldwell standing together in the street.

"You two, don't fire unless they shoot first." Bowie looked over at Talbert. "You hear me, old man?"

"I hear you; I've got ears you young sprout." Talbert spit a stream of tobacco into the street. "But, I'll guarantee that bunch over there is gonna start a shooting pretty quick now."

"Maybe, but we'll let them start it."

"Just like First Manassas, huh?"

"I like First Bull Run better." Bowie nodded.

"Well whatever it's called, I hope this little set-to turns out the same way." Talbert wiped his chin. "Us winning."

Bacon Caldwell moved along the sidewalk as Cord Alvord stepped into the dusty street and stood watching the four men in front of the mercantile store. Time seems to stand still as the gunman waits to see what the men will do.

"You can't beat him George; it'd be murder if you walk out there."

"I'll have my self-respect." Raker looked across at the tall gunman standing alone in the street. "A man can't live without respect."

"You step out there George and that's all you'll have." Bowie turned on Raker. "Think of Norma and your daughter can they live on respect?"

"I can't let you do my fighting." Raker started forward.

Suddenly, too fast for the eye to follow, the pistol flashed upward and slammed against the big man's head, knocking him senseless. Grabbing Raker as he slumped forward, Bowie eased him gently to the porch.

Talbert stepped from behind the barrels and shook his head. "What have you done, Bowie Morgan?"

"I just saved his life, old man." Bowie straightened up and looked behind him at the store's windows where Norma and Jackie had been watching from. "He'll be alright in a few minutes."

"And yourself?" Matt asked. "Now, it's all on your shoulders."

Holstering his weapon, Bowie stepped into the street. "Talbert if Alvord gets me, shoot him and Caldwell both."

"I will boy." Talbert spit again. "You can count on it."

"Good luck Bowie." Matt nodded.

Standing alone in the street Alvord had been watching the men at the mercantile, he saw Morgan knock the big rancher senseless on the sidewalk. Supposedly Raker's friend Morgan had still knocked the rancher out cold. Alvord knows why, the tall young man is trying to protect his friend from his own fierce pride and vanity the only way he could. Watching as Morgan walked slowly toward him then stopped in the middle of the street Alvord looked over at Caldwell and smiled. The young man has guts, he reminds him of another young man many years and a long time ago. With a wave of his hand, Alvord turned and walked slowly and deliberately across to his horse. Caldwell cannot believe his eyes; he watched in shock as the gunman he hired to do his fighting stepped onto the horse and turned straight down the middle of the street. Cord Alvord only stops momentarily to toss the money he was paid in advance at the feet of the frowning Caldwell, looking down into the man's face with disdain. Kicking the gelding he rode at a slow walk to where Bowie stood in the street, watching in curiosity.

"You take care of yourself, Bowie Trouilliard." Alvord nodded then turned slowly toward the east. "Someday our paths will cross again, hopefully in better times."

Bowie blinked, no one has ever used or known his real name, even Bowie himself hasn't used it for years. "How do you know my name is Trouilliard, not Morgan?"

Without stopping the gelding, Alvord spoke over his shoulder. "I knew your family many years ago; your father was Cord Trouilliard."

Bowie watched as Alvord rode to the east, passing out of sight as he turned on the road leading toward the Territory and on into Kansas. He wants to yell to the gunman to stop him; he wants to find out who the man is, how he knew his name. As the words form on his lips to call out to Alvord, he heard Caldwell shouting to his men to open fire.

"No, you Yankee scum." Talbert screamed as both sides start firing wildly about the street. "Fire Matt, give Bowie cover to get out of the street."

The roar of gunfire reverberates up and down the streets of Medicine Mound, echoing off the buildings as rifles from both sides spit fire and death. Bowie rolled sideways, firing as he runs across the street with bullets kicking up dirt all around him. He had fired his snap shots too quick, missing Caldwell by inches, but missing him. Diving behind a water trough, as bullets tear at his clothing and kick up dirt all around the trough, Bowie gets off several rounds dropping two Lazy Bar riders.

"Keep your head down Bowie you dang fool, we'll get you outta this mess." Talbert laughed as he placed another rifle slug into the saloon wall where most of the Lazy Bar men have taken refuge. "Just like Chancellorsville Matt; we've got them on the run."

"Yeah well, maybe you ought to tell them that they're on the run you old goat." Matt ducked as a bullet strikes the barrel in front of him. "I don't think they realize they're whipped."

"Smart aleck." Talbert swore. "They will, just you wait."

Matt shook his head. "Old man you're nuts, we're outnumbered twenty to three."

"Four." Raker touched his head gingerly then stood up from behind the barrels where Talbert had dragged him. "What happened, Talbert?"

"We'll George, I ain't exactly sure." The old man shook his head as he fired off another round. "All I know is Bowie conked you on the noggin, stepped into the street to face Alvord, then all kinds of hades broke out."

"Bowie, is he dead?"

"Nah, he's over there behind that water trough." Talbert grinned. "He's all wet as usual, but he's still in one piece I reckon."

"He kill Alvord?"

Talbert aimed his rifle. "That's the funny part; the gunfighter spoke a few words I couldn't tell what they were, but next thing I know the man got on his horse and hightailed it. He rode straight down the street and out of sight without looking back."

Raker looked across the street watching as bullets splinter the leaking water trough, then back toward the saloon. "We've got to give Bowie cover so he can run for it before they shoot that trough into kindling."

Bowie was trapped where he was; all he could do was lay low behind the trough firing blindly toward the saloon while trying to keep from getting hit. The water helped stop the penetrating power of the pistol and rifle fire, but the trough is losing water fast from all the bullet holes. Across the street three rifles open up sending a deluge of shots into the bullet-riddled saloon, causing the Lazy Bar riders to duck behind something more substantial than the thin board walls of the building. Rolling to his feet Bowie ran toward a doorway until a bullet caught him in the leg, forcing him back behind the riddled water trough.

"Where's the durn fool going?" Talbert swore as he fired again. "He ducked back behind that useless heap of boards."

"Let's go boys, charge."

"Charge!" Talbert swore. "Shucks George, we ain't in the army and there are only three of us."

"They don't know that Talbert, let's go." Raker checked his rifle and stood up. "Spread out now, so we'll be harder to hit."

Matt held up his hand. "Hold on George, it looks like the gunfighter Alvord is coming back this way at a dead run."

Drawing a dead bead on the racing man and horse, Talbert hesitated pulling the trigger as Alvord fired several shots into the saloon then dismounted beside the water trough where Bowie is lying. Shaking his head as he watched the gunman pull Bowie to his feet and help him to cover behind another building, Talbert spit a stream of tobacco.

"Well, I've seen it all now." The old man grinned. "Don't that beat all?"

"It looks like Bowie caught one." Raker shook his head. "I thought Alvord was on Caldwell's payroll, reckon I was wrong, he sure pulled Bowie's chestnuts out of the fire."

Yelling the confederate battle cry, Talbert charged across to the sidewalk in front of the hotel as bullets strike all about him. Hugging the building walls, he crouched as Bowie and Alvord fire point-blank into the saloon. Gun smoke filters across the wide street as rifles and pistols roar out hot lead from both sides. Talbert is just about to rush the saloon when a white flag sticks out from the shattered windows of the saloon.

"What you men want?" Raker yelled from where he hovers in a doorway. "You giving up?"

"Yeah, we're finished Raker, we've got several men down in here." A Lazy Bar rider yelled out from inside the saloon. "These walls are thin, they don't hold back flying lead."

"Then toss out your guns and walk out of there."

"You ain't gonna shoot?"

Raker peered around the doorsill and took a quick look at the saloon, the man isn't lying. The walls have been riddled, every window is out and the front door is barely hanging by a thread. "No we won't shoot."

Several pistols and rifles land on the sidewalk, then men that can still walk push slowly through the double doors. Raker and Talbert cover the Lazy Bar riders as Matt moved closer to check them for weapons. Alvord helps the limping Bowie across the street and sits him down on the sidewalk.

"You hurt bad Bowie?" Raker holds his gun on the beaten cowboys. "Talbert, go round up the good doctor."

"I've had worse, went through the fat of my leg." Bowie looked up at Alvord curious. "I reckon I owe you my life Mister Alvord, but I can't figure why you did it."

Cord Alvord removed a large bandanna from his pocket and worked to stem the flow of blood running down Bowie's leg and into his boot. No one thought to ask any of the Lazy Bar men where Bacon and Brace Caldwell are, or if they have been killed. Engrossed in helping Bowie and watching the other riders no one notice as the two brothers emerge quietly from the saloon. Sensing something behind him Alvord whirls with uncanny speed firing once killing Brace, but the full blast of the shotgun Bacon carries catches him in the side and back. Rolling sideways, Bowie pumps three shots into Caldwell then regained his feet. Rolling Alvord onto his back Bowie looks into the dark eyes.

"Why, why did you come back?"

The bloody fingers reach up touching the face hovering above him then he smiled slowly. "I never figured to see you again, Bowie."

"Who are you?" The damage from the buckshot has done its deadly work, the gunfighter is beyond help. He doesn't have long and Bowie needs to know who the man is.

"Lift me up I don't have long, I feel it." The pain-racked eyes looked up at Bowie. "It's time you know the truth."

Bowie raised the hurt man where he can talk without blood filling his air passage. "There, is that better?"

"Thank you, sir." The words come out barely audible. "The man you killed in Louisiana was a half-brother to Laseete Landeaux, but her name was really Trouilliard the same as your real name is."

"I don't understand."

"Senator Landeaux knew who you were, when you showed up at that dance, he knew his daughter was really your half-sister which is why he wanted you to leave. He knew it couldn't be and he also knew you two were sweet on each other after only one night of dancing."

"My half-sister?"

"I am Cord Trouilliard, you are my son." Alvord coughed up blood. "The girl Laseete is my daughter."

"My father, you?"

"After I killed a man in a duel over the Senator's wife, I was forced out of Louisiana, leaving you and your mother behind." Alvord shook his head. "I made mistakes Bowie, many mistakes I'm sorry, son."

"Laseete Landeaux is my sister?" Bowie shook his head.

Slowly the eyes close as the head rolls to the side with Alvord's last dying barely audible words. "She is."

Suddenly, two shots ring out as Matt fired two times, dropping a rider that had pulled a hidden weapon from his back. Raker raised his rifle and cocked it, covering the other riders just as Doctor Evans and Talbert run up.

"I believe there's been enough killing here today Mister Raker." Evans examined the men lying on the porch pronouncing them dead. "Caldwell's dead you've won, get your people and leave now."

Raker looked over at the Lazy Bar riders that are still able to walk and pointed his rifle. "You men get your horses and ride, don't let me see your faces around here again."

"We've got our trappings out at the Lazy Bar." One of the men argued.

"The only thing you'll get out there if you ride that way is a bullet through the head." Raker glared at the man. "Your boss is dead, you stick around here you'll probably join him faster than you think."

"When you men ride, go west and don't come back." Talbert slammed a rifle barrel into a Lazy Bar stomach. "Now, git your tails gone."

"The horses we're riding are Lazy Bar property."

"Keep 'em, but you better be on 'em and riding when I look up again." Talbert pointed his rifle.

Talbert watched the men ride away, then turned his attention to where Norma and Jackie are hurrying across the street to the saloon. Inside the saloon Evans is examining and tending to the worst of the wounded men where they lay across the poker tables. Talbert watched the street for danger then smiled as Jackie kneels beside Bowie.

"Man, that saloon looks worse than Shiloh." Shaking his head, the old man grinned. "Those boys weren't lying; the walls of the saloon wouldn't hold back a fast moving fly."

"Any dead men in there?" Raker held Norma tight, then looked over at Talbert.

"Nope, can't figure out why though, that place looks like a sieve." Talbert shook his head and laughed. "Several wounded, though."

Several minutes later Jackie held onto Bowie as Evans wrapped up his leg, then looked down at Alvord and shuddered. "Who was he, Bowie?"

"His name was Cord Trouilliard, he was my father."

"I knew that all along." Talbert spoke up. "I knew he was your pa."

"What?" Bowie looked over at the old soldier. "Did he tell you that before today?"

"Nope, he didn't have to." Talbert shook his head. "If you would've slowed up a minute to take notice yourself, you would have seen you two are as much alike as two peas in a pod."

"He's right Bowie." Jackie agreed. "I thought I seen a resemblance back at the store."

"I'd like to bury him under that big oak tree that stands in your dad's west pasture."

"For a man like him, that would be nice, he would be as free as the wind and could see forever in the distance." Jackie squeezed his arm and looked across at the church. "But first Mister Morgan, before we do that and go after my mother, I'd like to visit Reverend Avery."

"The name is Trouilliard." Bowie looked across at the church. "I thought the man is supposed to do the proposing?"

"Well Mister Trouilliard, I ain't proposing I'm ordering we're getting married."

Bowie pulled in the team stopping at the signpost that proclaimed the Lazy Bar Ranch and jerked the sign from the post. Looking up to where Jackie and her mother sit on the old wagon, he smiled.

"Peers like you ladies are home again."

"We are home, all of us." Jackie smiled happily. "Now that we've got the records to the ranch cleared up, and my dad's name is clean again. Seems his taxes were not behind and the ranch is ours free and clear."

"Caldwell was slick."

"He wasn't too slick; he started a fight with you and Señor Raker." Carlos spoke up from where he perched atop Bowie's saddle horse. "But, he was one bad hombre."

"You're right Carlos; he shouldn't have crossed George Raker." Bowie nodded softly. "We'll ride over in a few days and check on everyone at the Circle R."

"And I'll see my folks," Carlos whooped. "But, if it is okay, I will return here to this ranch and work for you and Señorita Jackie."

"That'll be fine, providing it's okay with your folks."

Jackie patted the wagon seat. "I don't know how Talbert rode this thing all the way from Virginia."

"I reckon he was in a hurry to get far away from the war." Bowie watched as she tried to ease herself. "You're almost home, then you'll be off it."

Jackie looked toward the ranch house, appearing just across the grass covered pasture. "Yes my husband, we are all almost home."

The End